A Dog Lover's Mystery
Sire and Damn

Susan Conant

This book is a work of fiction. The characters and events
in this novel are the products of the author's imagination
or are used fictitiously.

Cover Designer: Terry Albert
Editor: Jim Thomsen
Interior Designer: Jovana Shirley, Unforeseen Editing,
www.unforeseenediting.com

ISBN-13: 978-1512053784
ISBN-10: 1512053783

In loving memory of my darling Mandy (1997-2013)

"Oh what a tangled web we weave,
When first we practice to deceive!"

Sir Walter Scott

acknowledgments

Many thanks to Elaine Jordan for answering my many questions about psychiatric service dogs and, in particular, about her beautiful Belgian sheepdog, Cibola's Destry Rides Again, CGC, TT, SD (2004-2013), who was an admirable ambassador for service dogs and, indeed, for all dogs. Thanks, too, to Russ Livingston, MD, for talking with me about prescription-drug samples. For help with the manuscript, I am grateful to Jean Berman, Tanja Gube, Roseann Mandell, Lillian Sober-Ain, Geoff Stern, Anya Wittenborg, Carter Umbarger, and Corinne Zipps. Special thanks to my friend and editor, Jim Thomsen, and to my delightful proofreader, Christina Tinling.

chapter one

"**S**top comparing me to a dog!" Rita demanded.

The comparison was inevitable. On that hot Monday morning in August, my dear friend Rita looked and sounded as sick as one. I'd have made the comparison, anyway. Drawing parallels between people and dogs is an occupational hazard: I'm a dog trainer. Holly Winter? Maybe we've met at shows or trials. I'm the one with the malamutes. Or maybe you've seen my column in *Dog's Life?* Or read my blog or one of my books? You see, I'm also a dog writer.

The term *dog writer* should be self-explanatory, shouldn't it? Since you can tell to look at me that I'm not a dog who writes, I must therefore be a woman who writes about dogs, which is to say, a dog writer. But around here? In Cambridge, Massachusetts? Yes, Cambridge, where your neighbors can explain a Green's function approach to quantum many-body systems in fluent Pali or discuss the hagiographical tradition in relation to the growth of density fluctuations, but you get blank looks when you say that you're a dog writer. These are people who sprinkle metaethics on their granola. They make jokes about igneous petrology and Chaucer's self-canonization. *Ulysses* is their idea of a beach read.

And when I say that I'm a dog writer, I have to add, "I write about dogs," or they don't know what I'm talking about. And then when I've explicated, what do I hear? I'll tell you what: a snooty little laugh followed by a response reflective of almost unfathomable ignorance, namely, "Dogs? What is there to write about dogs?"

Everything, that's what. Why? Because if it exists, it exists in dogs. Take morning sickness.

"Morning sickness is actually quite uncommon in dogs," I told Rita. "That golden retriever bitch I told you about was an exception, and she didn't get really sick. She'd just eat her breakfast and then get a funny smile and—"

"I do not want to hear the details!" Rita croaked. "I always thought that morning sickness was psychological."

"You always think that everything is psychological." Another occupational hazard: Rita is a clinical psychologist. "But you really are under a lot of stress. Transitions are stressful. Good transitions and bad transitions. Or that's what I read in a magazine in the dentist's waiting room. Anyway, you're pregnant, you and Quinn have just bought this house, and you're about to get married."

Rita was only two months pregnant, so except for the greenish tinge to her complexion, she looked the same as ever: attractive and stylish in a distinctively New York way, as if she were about to be photographed by Bill Cunningham for *The New York Times*. What could be more New York than being dressed for Cunningham's "On the Street" when you're in your own backyard? She wore a white outfit of linen pants and a sleeveless top. On her pedicured feet were espadrille sandals with platform soles, wedge heels, and thin leather straps. The polish on her fingernails and toenails matched her pale-rose lipstick. Her hair formed its usual neat little brown cap, but I wondered whether the chemically blonded streaks were doomed. She was obsessed with protecting her unborn baby—my godchild-to-be—from toxins.

"Human pregnancy is so damned long," I added sympathetically. "Nine months! Dogs are incredibly efficient. It takes them only sixty-three days to accomplish—"

"Please! Enough!"

"I wasn't comparing you to a dog," I said. "I was just pointing out that if you *were* a dog, you'd be whelping a whole litter right about now instead of wasting seven more months to produce one human baby."

"Dear God," Rita said to herself. "And don't say '*Dog* spelled backward'!" She shook her head and added inexplicably, "I'll never get used to it."

If Rita meant my interest in dogs, she'd had plenty of time to get used to it. Until a few weeks earlier, she'd lived in the apartment on the top floor of my house, which is the three-story barn-red one at the corner of Appleton and Concord. *My* house. Pardon me. My husband hates that *my*. *Our* house, as it truly is, Steve's and mine. Before we got married, *our* house was *my* house, and Steve lived above his vet clinic. Steve Delaney, DVM: first my vet, then my lover, then my husband, and now all three at once. I'd always dreaded . . . Pardon me. We, Steve and I, had hated the thought that Rita would ever move, but it hadn't occurred to us that she'd move a half block down the street from us and that we wouldn't lose her after all.

Our end of Appleton Street, the Concord Avenue end, started life as a working-class neighborhood, but Harvard's thirty-one-odd-billion-dollar endowment has trickled down on us, pooled beneath our property values, and buoyed them up on waves of gentrification. Rita and Quinn's new house rode at the top of a crest, while Steve's and mine floated in a trough, albeit a spacious and attractive trough. When I bought the house, I lived in the ground-floor apartment and rented out the other two. Then when Steve and I got married, we extended our living space to include the second floor, mainly because merging our canine households meant that we needed room for three Alaskan malamutes, a German shepherd, and a pointer.

The improvements I've made and we've made over the years have been piecemeal: our kitchen now has a tile floor instead of the original linoleum, and the second-floor kitchen has become a bedroom. By far the best kitchen and bathroom are in the third-floor apartment, in Rita's old apartment, which got redone when she moved from the second floor to the third. Rita and Quinn's house, in contrast, had been totally renovated about ten years earlier, and only five years ago, the kitchen had been all redone in cherry and glass and granite and stainless steel.

But the enviable feature of Rita and Quinn's new house was the fenced yard, where we were sitting on that hot Monday morning in August. In Cambridge, Steve and I are lucky to have a yard at all, and our fence is perfectly adequate, but we don't have the space that Rita now does to train our dogs for advanced obedience and agility and rally. In our yard, I could set up one jump, or two crammed close together, or a tunnel or some other piece of agility equipment, but Rita's new yard was at least three times the size of ours, long enough to let the dogs run full tilt and big enough to set up a smallish rally-obedience or agility course.

Also, its potential as a dog-training area wasn't ruined by flower beds, sundials, decorative pools, or other obstructions. Since the vegetation consisted of a rather rough lawn and a variety of shrubs in mulched borders along the fence, there was almost nothing for dogs to ruin. Not that the yard was barren. Far from it. Next to the glass doors to the kitchen, over the bluestone patio where we were sitting, rose an iron structure covered with grapevines, and Rita and Quinn had already furnished the shady area with a wrought-iron dining table and chairs, two teak recliners with flower-patterned cushions, and a variety of small wrought-iron chairs, side tables, and coffee tables.

Begonias and impatiens bloomed in pots and planters, and the pale-yellow of the house added warm color.

A temporary feature of the patio was one of my malamutes, Rowdy—my first malamute, first among equals, eighty-five pounds of beauty, brawn, and brains in a dark-gray-and-white standoff coat. He was as sweet as he was strong, and thus, in my opinion and that of many esteemed American Kennel Club judges, the Alaskan malamute standard incarnate, archetype of gorgeous Arctic dog, and quintessence of canine perfection. Do I exaggerate? Certainly not. And at the moment, the handsome boy wasn't even at his best: In spite of being asleep, as he was now, he had a hint of resentment on his face. So profound was Rowdy's loathing of hot weather that even in deepest slumber, he detested the heat.

"You're discombobulated," I said to Rita. "A lot is happening all at once. Maybe too much."

We were seated across from each other at the dining table. Because the smell of coffee exacerbated Rita's nausea, I was drinking tea, and she was taking small sips of the raspberry tea I'd given her as a present. As every old-time breeder knows, raspberry leaves are a traditional panacea for pregnancy-related complaints, but I hadn't said so to Rita. As I've already suggested, Rita clung to the irrational, unscientific view that human and canine pregnancies were utterly dissimilar, and that my wealth of knowledge about the care and feeding of pregnant bitches was inapplicable to her present circumstance.

She took another sip of the raspberry tea and said, "Well, I'm beginning to feel a little better now."

I was, of course, tempted to say, "So there! Cured by a dog remedy," but if I had, she'd have stopped drinking the tea.

"Could I just whine a little?" she asked with a smile. "Can you stand a litany of complaints? It sometimes helps to verbalize."

"What are friends for?" I said, without adding anything about the raspberry remedy.

"Okay." She held out her left hand and tapped her left thumb with her right index finger. "I can't stop throwing up." Tapping her left index finger, she added, "Hostility personified, my aunt Vicky, is getting here today." Left middle finger: "Quinn just had to pick this time to move his office, on top of everything else, and instead of shifting all his office junk to his new office, he's moved everything here, supposedly to sort it out, which is what he hasn't done." Smacking her left ring finger, she said, "All of the relatives who are about to arrive are fighting with one another or are going to." Left little finger: "Instead of ordering from the bridal registries, Quinn's relatives in Montana are sending zebra-patterned towels and leopard-patterned sheets."

I interrupted. "Steve and I can always use extra dog towels, and the sheets will do for crate pads. Give them to me."

"Consider it done. Once Quinn's parents go home." Raising her right hand and bending the thumb, she said, "Sixth, on that subject, Quinn still hasn't told his parents about the baby."

"They'll guess. They're bound to notice that you're throwing up all the time."

"I don't do it in their presence. By the way, bless your father and Gabrielle for inviting them to Maine. I can tolerate only so many houseguests at a time."

Gabrielle: my dear stepmother, whom my father married because he fell in love with her and not because she owned a big house right on the ocean on Mount Desert Island—which is to say, practically in Acadia National Park.

"Rita, we have plenty of room, including your apartment. You're welcome to shift everyone up the street to our house."

"Thanks, but Uncle Oscar is no trouble—he sleeps a lot, and he's a sweetheart—and you're going to have my cousin John and my parents, and as of tonight, you'll have Zara and Izzy. John is going to bore you talking about his horrible ex-wife—she really was ghastly—but since he's a pathological liar in a minor way, it's hard to know what to believe, but he's basically a nice guy. And my parents are"—she shrugged and eyed the heavens—"my parents."

Rita's cousin John was due to arrive in Cambridge the next day, Tuesday; and Rita's parents were getting here two days after that, on Thursday. My father, my stepmother, and my cousin Leah would arrive on Friday, the day before the wedding. The last to get here would be Rita's Uncle Dave, who was Zara's father and Vicky's husband; he was flying in on Saturday morning, just barely in time for the wedding. As for Rita's brother and his family, they weren't even bothering to return home from Italy in time for the wedding.

"I'd love to get rid of Aunt Vicky," Rita continued, "but I won't inflict her on you, and besides, you're taking Zara, and we can't ask Zara to stay in the same place as her mother. Vicky is at her worst with Zara, and she's just impossible about Izzy."

Vicky was Rita's maternal aunt. Zara, Vicky's daughter, was . . . well, let's skip the family tree for now. What I want to say is that Zara was my favorite member of Rita's family, unless you count Izzy, a charming black Labrador retriever who was Zara's psychiatric service dog. I, of course, certainly do count Izzy. In describing Izzy as a *psychiatric* service dog, I am, by the way, saying exactly what Zara herself said, and, according to Zara, precisely what Vicky hated hearing her daughter say.

Rita contemplated her right hand. "Where were we?"

"Seven, I think, but it doesn't matter."

"Seven or whatever it is, there's Willie."

Rita's Scottish terrier, Willie, had been hospitalized for a puzzling case of acute gastritis and consequent dehydration. He'd seemed like a dog with a foreign object lodged in his intestines—a toy, a corncob, a chunk of plastic, a bone, a rock—but thorough diagnostic investigations had revealed no such object and, in fact, no actual obstruction. Having cost Rita a tremendous amount of money by spending time at the Angell Animal Medical Center, he'd made an excellent, if mysterious, recovery.

"He's coming home today," I said.

Rita contemplated her right hand. "Are my fingers puffy? Eight. Nine? Zara has put my wedding all over Facebook, and my patients are going to see everything about my private life."

"There are privacy settings, as you'd know if you'd get *on* Facebook."

"I *am* on Facebook. Zara put me there."

"If you'd use it, Rita, you'd like it, and all Zara has done is post on her own Facebook page."

"I don't want anything to do with social media. Look what's happened! It's only because of Zara and that Facebook page or whatever it is that John is here. This is supposed to be a small wedding for family and friends, and he is not someone I'm close to, but when he invited himself, I couldn't say no, could I?"

Before I could reply, Rowdy rose to his feet and uttered a peal of *woo-woo-woo*s. The gate to the yard burst open, and in flew Zara, who announced, "Rita! Holly! Something terrible happened! Someone tried to steal Izzy!"

chapter two

A few minutes before the arrival of Zara and Izzy, Rowdy presses his belly to the cool bluestone. Through almost-black almond-shaped eyes, he regards the glass doors to the frigidly air-conditioned kitchen. In contrast to Rita, he has only one complaint, and it's so simple that it can be stated in a single word: *heat*. He does not say or think the word *heat*, of course, but feels a hideous, pervasive sensation of sultry, feverish toxicity. Heat? He loathes it with all his Arctic heart. Even here on the bluestone in the shade of the grapevine, the temperature is at least twenty degrees too hot for Alaskan malamute comfort and fifty degrees short of frozen bliss. As for the melting ice cubes in the nearby metal bowl, are they some kind of joke? Ice cubes are nothing, nothing, nothing! Rowdy doesn't want piddling little *ice cubes*, damn it! What Rowdy wants is an entire glacier.

Alternatively, he'd like something to eat. Delicious scents of bacon, eggs, and toast leak through the narrow spaces between the glass doors and their frames. Traces of yogurt, granola, and milk linger in the air. High up in the house, the ancient man plods across a floor. No one but Rowdy hears the footfalls. Rowdy not only hears them but also attends to them, as he attends to everything the ancient man does. As Rowdy knows, the ancient man has a secret habit of slipping food to dogs. Therefore, he is a revered personage.

But wait! A big car pulls up nearby, and—*wham!*—here's the bang of the gate, and here's an excited shriek, and here's that black Lab bitch. Yes, she's spayed, but sex isn't everything. If anything is everything, it's food. Cold weather is another strong candidate. So is fun. And the bitch is fun.

chapter three

Zara was immediately recognizable as a blood relative of Rita's. They had the same pretty facial features and the same slim build, though Zara was in her mid-twenties, younger than Rita, and she had the height that Rita achieved only by wearing high heels. They also shared the distinctive look of New York City. Zara's hair was lighter and longer than Rita's and cut in the kind of sleek style you see on models in fashion magazines.

If Zara were a dog, I'd know the proper term for her haircut, and I'd be able to guess the techniques that the groomer had used to create smooth lines and artful angles. Maybe fashionable women, like poodles, get continental clips? Like Rita, Zara wore white, but her pants were loose and flowing, and on her feet were the practical running shoes of someone who's been exercising a big dog.

I'd met Zara only five days earlier, but her resemblance to Rita made me feel that I knew her better than I really did; some of my immediate liking for her stemmed from my affection for Rita. In fact, Zara benefited from a double halo effect: she shone in the twin lights of Rita and of Izzy, her simply marvelous dog.

For his own reasons, Rowdy shared my opinion of both Zara and Izzy—this despite Zara's tendency to mistake Rowdy for his son, Sammy, and to mistake Sammy for Rowdy.

After making her dramatic announcement, Zara responded to Rowdy's greeting by laughing melodiously. "Oh, Sammy," she told him, "you say that to all the girls!"

"This is Rowdy," I told her.

"Sorry! Rowdy, I am so sorry!" Both she and Izzy went up to my handsome boy and jostled with each other to get right in his face. For all that Rowdy is eighty-five pounds of show dog, multi-titled obedience dog, gentle therapy dog, and beloved soul mate, he can be a shameless showoff. His showoff show-dog mode is fine when his object is an AKC judge, but far from reserving it for the show ring, he glories in strutting his stuff for anyone who happens to glance at him. When Zara crouched in front of him, he scoured her face with his tongue. Then Izzy joined in, and the three shared a three-way kiss.

"Zara," said Rita, "you can't just make an announcement like that and then not tell us anything."

"Everything's okay now." Zara removed Izzy's service-dog vest and rose to her feet. "Izzy is fine. We're both just hot. She drank all of our water"—Zara pulled a flattened fabric water bowl from a pocket in Izzy's vest—"but she's still thirsty. Me, too."

"You can use the hose to fill that metal dog bowl," Rita said.

Zara made a face. "Izzy doesn't drink hose water," she said with an apologetic laugh. To me, she said, "New converts are always the most devout, huh? Oh, thanks for the OmniThrive. Izzy loves it."

"It's great stuff," I said. "It's the best supplement going. Just don't mention it to Steve! I have to sneak it to Rowdy and Sammy and Kimi when he's not around."

Izzy was Zara's first dog. To my surprise, Zara had told me that she'd adopted Izzy from a shelter. My experience in malamute rescue had taught me that show-quality dogs sometimes ended up in rescue; some of the most beautiful rescue malamutes I'd seen had been found wandering. Like those malamutes, Izzy would have looked more at home in the show ring than in an animal shelter. To a large extent, the Alaskan malamute is a unified breed: some breeders place a heavy emphasis on preserving the malamute's original ability to work in harness, but the breed as a whole isn't split into what would be, in effect, two sub-breeds or varieties, working malamutes and show malamutes.

In contrast, there are two somewhat separate lines of Labrador retrievers. What are known as American, field, or working Labs tend to be tall, lean, and active. In contrast, English, show, or conformation Labs are shorter in the leg and broader in the head and body than working Labs. Overall, show Labs are comparatively stocky and blocky, as Izzy was, and her calm temperament was typical of those lines.

When Zara adopted Izzy, she knew nothing about Labs, nothing about service dogs, and, in fact, almost nothing about dogs. While Zara was growing up, her mother had refused to let her have so much as a goldfish, never mind a dog, but Zara had always been attracted to the dogs she'd seen in Central Park. Two years earlier, when she got Izzy, she was simply looking for a pet. Although she hadn't told me the details of her psychiatric problems, she'd said that she'd had a lot of difficulty in leaving her condo, which was in the West Sixties, just off Central Park West. She worked as a freelance book editor and copy editor, so she never had to leave home to go to work, and when she was unable to go out, she had groceries, meals, and everything else delivered.

Oh, and by the way, no, Zara didn't pay for the ritzy address and all the rest on her income from editing. Her paternal grandfather, an investment banker, had left all of his money to Zara's father, Dave, who was an only child, and to Dave's only child, Zara.

Before adopting Izzy, Zara made plans to hire a dog walker if she found herself unable to take Izzy out. She soon discovered, however, that she enjoyed taking Izzy to

Central Park. No longer just an observer of the dogs there, Zara was part of a group. Until then, her social networks had been mainly online; now she belonged to a real-world group. She'd intended to hire a private dog trainer, but with the help of her dog group, she found an obedience class that she and Izzy enjoyed.

Soon after that, Izzy showed some behaviors that initially disconcerted Zara. One day, Zara's mother called and kept her on the phone for thirty minutes. "My mother has an irritating voice," Zara had told me, "and at first, I thought that Izzy just didn't like the sound, but what happened was that Izzy leaned up against me and then started barking and barking. So, I got off the phone. And said thanks! I didn't want Izzy to make a habit of barking when I was on the phone, of course, and she didn't.

"But the next time my mother called, Izzy did the same thing. And I had the weirdest sense that it wasn't my mother's voice that was bothering her. I had the freakish sense that Izzy knew I was upset and was trying to help me.

"And not too long after that, I made a big mistake. I was doing great, okay? Taking Izzy out, going places, feeling good, so I decided not to take my meds. I take a mood stabilizer and some other stuff, and they have side effects I don't necessarily like. So I decided I didn't need them. And what happened was that I ended up lying in bed. For hours. All day. I'd get Izzy out first thing, but then I'd go back to bed. And after maybe three days of that, Izzy dragged the blankets off the bed, and then she tried to drag me off.

"She was very determined. She knew something was wrong. And she sort of woke me up—in more ways than one. Among other things, I saw what I was doing to myself. And to Izzy. So, I took my meds and took a shower and took Izzy out, and she was happy and so was I. Well, not exactly happy. But I was myself again."

Zara's psychiatrist had heard of psychiatric service dogs and put Zara in touch with people who knew about them. Zara did research online, too. Before long, Zara and Izzy were getting individual instruction that prepared them for certification and also taught them specific tasks. Especially difficult, Zara said, was the multi-part public-access test designed to make sure that Izzy really could go everywhere with Zara and could not only behave herself but also create a good impression. Among other things, they were tested on Izzy's ability to accompany Zara on the New York subway, a test I might have flunked myself.

Where was I? Oh, yes, talking about dogs. Surprise! Specifically, Zara had refused to let Izzy drink water out of the hose and had said that new converts were always the most devout, by which she meant that in converting to the cult of dog worship, she'd become fanatical about taking perfect care of her dog, not that taking perfect care of dogs is a sign of suspect extremism. I strive for the same thing myself. In any case, once Zara had supplied Rowdy and Izzy with fresh kitchen water, as opposed to hose water, and had settled at the table with a big glass of lemonade, she finally told us what had happened.

"We were going to go running, but it was too hot. I didn't even feel like walking all the way around the little lake."

"Fresh Pond," I supplied. Cambridge has its own reservoir, Fresh Pond. Yes, indeed. Cambridge eccentricity! Is there something in the water? Anyway, Fresh Pond is surrounded by trees, fields, and a golf course, and a trail runs around the pond itself. Runners and bikers complain about the rough paving on the trail, but some of them use it anyway, as do walkers, birders, and especially dog walkers. Dogs with Cambridge licenses are allowed off leash there—provided that they are under, and I quote, "voice control," by which the City of Cambridge must mean the control of God's voice, since

I've never seen a single one of these off-leash dogs obey a human being.

Unfortunately, while the owners are issuing futile orders ("Fang, here! Come! Come here, Fang! Good boy. That's it! Yes, come to Mommy!"), God apparently remains silent. I've quit going to Fresh Pond. I got sick of fighting off aggressive dogs who tried to attack my dogs— the only dogs there who truly were under voice control and who were, of course, safely on leash.

"And you scared me off, Holly," Zara continued. "I got worried that Izzy would get attacked. So we walked a little, and we got to a sort of park, near a couple of busy streets, and then we picked up the trail again. And all of a sudden, a young guy jumped out of nowhere and grabbed Izzy's leash. I was watching for loose dogs. He caught me totally off guard. And he ripped her leash right out my hands."

"Good lord," said Rita.

"I screamed. And then I started calling Izzy, and she tried to come back to me, but then some guy saved us. A runner. He'd seen what had happened, and he was fast! He flew after the guy, and meanwhile, other people were yelling, and the runner got his hands on Izzy's leash, and the dog thief ran off."

"Did you get a good look at the thief? What did he look like?" I asked.

Zara's face lit up. "Hot!" She laughed.

"Like the rest of us," Rita said. "Including the dogs."

Black dogs like Izzy are solar collectors. Izzy had flopped down on the bluestone. She and Rowdy lay sprawled near the water bowl.

"Not that kind of hot, Rita. Cute. Great body. Tan. Tallish. Curly brown hair. Hot!"

"We get the point," I said. "What was he wearing?"

"Jeans. A white T-shirt. Running shoes. Nothing distinctive."

"That's what I'm wearing," I said. "And a million other people. Tattoos? Scars? I guess that would be too much to hope for."

"The only distinctive thing about him was his looks. He wasn't just ordinary cute. Seriously, he was gorgeous."

"Zara," I said, "I think maybe we should call the police. Unless you already have?" Besides the phone that she was never without, she probably had another device or two—or ten or twelve—in the pockets of Izzy's vest.

"No, I haven't." Zara rose from her seat.

Rita caught my eye and, while Zara was bending over to pick up Izzy's vest, gently shook her head and made a cool-it gesture with her right hand.

"I'm taking a shower," Zara said. "Izzy!"

"Please don't take her in the bathtub," Rita said. "I really don't want dog hair in it. Or in the drain."

"Rita, there are limits," Zara said. "Really, I promise. No dogs in the tub."

When Izzy got up, Rowdy did, too. He shook himself all over and started to follow Izzy, but at my request, Zara let herself and Izzy into the kitchen and closed the door without admitting Rowdy. My own kitchen is moderately malamute-proof, but if Rowdy had been loose in Rita's, he'd have surfed the counters and raided the trash before checking the cabinets for edibles.

"Sorry, big boy," I said. "The only reason I don't trust you is that you're not trustworthy. So, Rita, what was that about?" I mimicked her hand gesture.

Rita blew out a puff of air. "Let's keep the police out of it. Zara doesn't have a thought disorder—at least I've never known her to have one—but she's capable of dramatizing things."

"She made it up? Or she was imagining things?"

"No. Not exactly. Something happened, I'd say. But whatever it was, it doesn't warrant calling the police. Could you just let it drop?"

"Of course," I said.

chapter four

When I returned to Rita's in the midafternoon, her husband-to-be, Quinn Youngman, was unloading boxes from the back of Zara's car, which looked like a gigantic black cube on wheels. For someone who lives in Manhattan, the sensible vehicle is a bus, a subway car, or a taxi, but Zara had told me that she'd bought the gargantuan SUV during what she'd called a "little up episode" shortly after she'd adopted Izzy and that she now kept it at a friend's house in Westchester County.

"I wanted a way to get Izzy out of the city," she'd told me. "And I wanted the safest car I could find. Also, after being afraid to go anywhere, before Izzy, I was psyched at the idea that all of a sudden, we could just jump in the car and take off. I was a little too psyched. But I'm not sorry I bought it. We do use it now and then."

Zara spoke of her life before and after Izzy as people typically speak of monumental milestones that divide their lives in two. In many cases, the milestones are traumatic: *before the war, after I lost my leg.* Is there such a thing as positive trauma? Maybe. When Zara said *before Izzy* and *after Izzy,* she referred to a cataclysmic disruption for the good.

After greeting me, Quinn said, "Zara's Benz really came in handy. I don't know how I accumulated all this stuff, but with my Lexus, it would've taken me three trips to move it from my old office."

Damn! If dogs could talk, they'd call cars *cars*, whereas Quinn always referred to his as *my Lexus*; and as for that *Benz*, well, *Mercedes* can squeak by as an abbreviation, but *Benz* is an outright affectation.

As a dog trainer, I'm a convert to positive methods. Furthermore, as Zara had recently mentioned, converts are often the most devout. My pockets are so reliably filled with goodies that my dogs view me as a human treat-dispensing machine. Because dogs respond to human expectations by acting as expected, I cultivate happy visions of perfect canine behavior. I wear a pleasant expression. I ooze cheerful pheromones. I am optimistic to the point of nauseating Pollyannaishness.

So thoroughly am I the spiritual disciple of B. F. Skinner, the patron saint of operant conditioning with positive reinforcement, that I sometimes sneak Rowdy into Mount Auburn Cemetery to visit Skinner's grave, where I murmur prayers of thanks while doling out liver biscotti to my well-trained dog. Quinn, however, frequently inspires in me the urge to reach into my pockets and then pelt him with microwaved hot-dog slices and bits of desiccated liver brownies.

But in the upbeat spirit of positive methods and positive thinking, let me say that if sized up as a sperm donor, Quinn had almost everything to recommend him. He was older than I'd have liked, but he was tall, healthy, and not bad-looking, and he was intelligent enough to have graduated from medical school. The previous May, he'd done a lot to win me over by helping to save the life of one of my dogs. When my Kimi had been in danger of bleeding to death, his medical training had kicked in. He'd applied pressure to her wound, and he'd remained calm.

While saving Kimi, he'd made the discovery, self-evident to me but new to him, that dogs have souls. At the same time, during a period of personal crisis, he'd opened himself to his love for Rita and to hers for him. He was admittedly a lot older than Rita, but the age difference didn't bother her, and they had interests in common. In her clinical practice, she did talk therapy, and he was a psychopharmacologist, but they both worked in mental health.

They both read *The New York Times* and the *New York Review of Books*; Rita because her interest was genuine, Quinn because he liked to be seen consuming highbrow publications, at least in his mind's eye, or so I suspected. Their shared taste in movies ran to those depressing foreign art films in which almost nothing happens. The characters mope around muttering about life's meaninglessness. They have symbol-infested dreams and occasionally rouse themselves from their torpor to have languid sex and commit suicide.

I picked up a box and trailed after Quinn, who was carrying an open carton of drug samples.

"Some of this stuff is so old that I almost don't remember what it is," he said. "Most of it's expired. I need to sort it out and dispose of it in some responsible way. Public water supplies are filled with traces of prescription drugs as it is. I don't want to add to the problem."

He put the carton down and opened the side door to the house. Even before I entered, a blast of cold hit me. I am half malamute. Central air: bliss.

"I'm putting everything in the playroom," he said. "Just temporarily. Some of my old files can get stored in the cellar, and most of the books can get donated, but I have to decide which ones."

This driveway-side entrance gave access to a little mudroom that led to the kitchen. Straight ahead, on the far side of the kitchen, was a family room that Rita and Quinn intended to use as a ground-floor nursery and, later, as a repository for toddler furniture and toys, hence the term *playroom*. Like the living room, dining room, and kitchen, and like all of the bedrooms and bathrooms, the playroom complied with the City of Cambridge code that forbids all persons holding advanced academic degrees from using any color of paint except white. Both the kitchen and the playroom had floors of shiny Mexican tile. At the moment, the playroom held only two pieces of furniture, a long table and a chair, but it was crowded with wedding presents, many still in boxes and shipping cartons.

On the table sat an old notebook computer that Zara used to keep track of who'd sent what. Also on the table were silver serving pieces and place settings, and on the floor were open boxes of china and crystal. Sealed boxes displayed pictures of the usual wedding-present kitchen appliances, including the inevitable duplicates. Because the living room had a fireplace, fireplace implements must have seemed like the perfect gift: two doomed-for-return sets were of wrought iron; the keeper was a gorgeous brass-and-copper toolset that I'd admired at the nearby Adams Fireplace Shop but hadn't been able to afford.

Quinn put his box of drug samples on the table and had me put the box of books in a corner of the room. Then we made more trips to and from Zara's car. When we'd finished transferring everything from the car to the playroom, Quinn thanked me, and then Rita appeared and said, "Holly, thank you. I was watching from the bedroom window. You are amazingly strong. Look at your arms! You're going to look wonderful in your dress."

My matron-of-honor gown was a silk number in a deep shade of peach chosen to echo the color of Rita's palest-possible-peach silk wedding dress. I was going to look like a piece of peeled fruit—but with strong arms.

"We have to go," Rita said. "Willie's crate is in my car." They were due to spring Willie from Angell—that is, the Angell Animal Medical Center. "Holly, could I ask you a favor? Uncle Oscar should be down in a minute. Could you make him a cup of coffee?"

"Of course. What kind of coffee?"

"Dark. He's Italian!"

Because Rita had always described Uncle Oscar as Italian, I'd expected him to have an Italian accent, but he didn't. The occasion for him to speak seldom arose because he was often asleep in his room, dozing in a recliner outdoors, or napping in a chair in the living room. He was Rita and Zara's great uncle—their mother's uncle—and the only obviously Italian thing about him was his last name, Carino. Zara had picked him up at his assisted-living apartment in Connecticut. They'd arrived five days earlier so that Zara could help her morning-sick cousin with the move to the new house and with the wedding. Zara was also going to house-sit and dog-sit while Rita and Quinn were in Norway on their honeymoon.

As an aside, let me mention that a potentially mal-de-mer-inducing cruise of the fjords was entirely inappropriate for someone who already had morning sickness, but Quinn had always wanted to visit the fjords, and Rita had failed to stand up for herself.

"Or you can let Uncle Oscar decide," Rita added. "He likes picking out his own K-cups, but the Keurig confuses him."

When Rita and Quinn had left, as I was turning on the coffee machine, Uncle Oscar entered the kitchen. He was short and wide, with none of the visible frailty that sometimes occurs in great old age. His short white hair was remarkably thick. In other respects, too, he defied the stereotype of a nonagenarian. His blue-and-white-striped shirt would've been appropriate for a man of any age, and he hadn't covered it with a moth-eaten cardigan; his loose chinos were belted at his waist, not three inches above it; and on his feet were well-polished penny loafers rather than battered bedroom slippers. His face, however, was a mass of shar-pei wrinkles. So thick and deep were the lines and folds on his cheeks and chin that I found it hard to imagine how he shaved as closely as he did. He must have used an electric razor and used it carefully. Otherwise, he'd have been covered with scabs and scars.

"Holly Winter," he said with a smile. "Holly Winter and no dog? That's a first." He gave me a smile and big hug.

"A strictly temporary situation," I said. Then I offered to make coffee.

As Rita had predicted, Uncle Oscar took obvious pleasure in examining the K-cups in the little rack on the counter. Having made his decision, he handed me one. As I was inserting it in the machine, I noticed to my surprise that he was slyly pocketing two of the others. Why? I didn't ask.

When I'd settled Uncle Oscar at the kitchen table with his cup of coffee, Zara bounced in and gave him a big hug, and Izzy wiggled all over and nuzzled him.

"Moving day!" Zara announced. "Must make room here for Mommie Dearest. Uncle Oscar, there's a new wedding present. It's a set of demitasse spoons. They're in there"—she pointed toward the playroom—"on the table." To me, she said, "Uncle Oscar loves presents."

"Even when they're someone else's," he said.

Although Zara and Izzy were to stay with us only until the wedding and then move back to Rita and Quinn's, Zara wanted to have none of her belongings in the guestroom that her mother, Vicky, would be using. Zara voiced no such objection about her father, Dave, probably because he wouldn't arrive in Cambridge until just before the wedding and would leave almost immediately after it. I helped her carry down suitcases, leather tote bags, and briefcases as well as Izzy's gigantic dog bed. When we'd loaded everything into her car, she said, "Now we just need Izzy. And I want to check on Uncle Oscar."

We found him in the playroom, where he was happily sorting through Quinn's drug samples. The capsules and pills weren't loose; rather, they were attractively packaged in colorful little boxes. Uncle Oscar looked like a child having fun with blocks or Legos. For Uncle Oscar, the playroom was just that.

chapter five

The plan for the evening was that we'd all gather for drinks at Rita and Quinn's before walking to a nearby restaurant, Vertex, where we had a seven-thirty reservation. Once Zara had transferred her belongings to Rita's old apartment on the third floor, she stayed there, supposedly to work on a book she was editing. In fact, she spent some of the time on Facebook, as I know because when I was supposedly working on my new book, a light-hearted memoir of my dog-rich childhood, I checked Facebook, too. Before Facebook, we self-employed people had no office water cooler. Now we're hyperhydrated with status updates.

Earlier in the day, Zara had, of course, reported about the attempted stealing of Izzy. Her most recent status update was this: *Izzy and I have moved to Holly and Steve's lovely third-floor apartment, where we'll be until Rita and Quinn's wedding. Tonight, drinks with Rita and Quinn and family, then dinner at Vertex, a neighborhood restaurant. Whoops! Sounds like a greasy-spoon pizza joint. Amend that. Dinner at trendy restaurant in the neighborhood.*

My cousin Leah, who was about to begin veterinary school at Tufts, had posted an update on my wall: *Hey, Holly, great news! Kimi's late application to vet school has been accepted, so she'll be spending the next four years here with me.* Leah was, of course, joking. Kimi was strictly a visitor. Leah, who was sharing a little house with five other veterinary students, had actually tried to talk me into letting her keep Kimi there, but I'd refused.

I posted: *Sorry, but Kimi won't settle for anything less than a full professorship. I miss you both!*

Of our three Alaskan malamutes, Rowdy was the only one who belonged exclusively to me. Leah had finished Kimi, as it's said—handled her to her breed championship—and had put Kimi's obedience and performance titles on her, too, so I'd given Leah a co-ownership. Steve and I co-owned Rowdy's handsome young son, Sammy. Lady, our timid pointer, and India, our GSD—German shepherd dog—had been Steve's before we were married. Lady's neediness made her attach herself to all sources of strength, so she was now mine as well as Steve's. India was like a planet: she accepted me as part of our solar system, but she revolved around Steve.

As I was scanning my e-mail, Lady, India, and the center of India's universe entered the kitchen from our fenced yard. In part because our foul-tempered cat, Tracker, occupies my office, I work mainly in the kitchen, where I can enjoy the inspiring presence of Rowdy and Kimi, who can't be trusted with Tracker. At the moment, I was seated at the kitchen table with Rowdy and Sammy at my feet.

Although I missed my fiery Kimi, her temporary absence had the benefit of simplifying our dog-dominated lives during the hectic week before the wedding. In particular, I didn't have to monitor Kimi in case she decided to lift her lip at India, and I wouldn't have to worry about how she behaved with Izzy. Because Rowdy and Sammy were intact male malamutes, I always kept an eye on them, but they'd never had a fight, and they did fine with India and Lady. As to Izzy, who liked other dogs, neither India nor Lady had much interest in her; Sammy saw her as a lively playmate; and, for some unknown reason, Rowdy had an oddly worshipful attitude toward her. If Zara heeded my warnings about malamutes and food, all would be well.

The warnings? Malamutes are obsessed with food. They'll steal it, and they'll fight over it. Worse, they have a highly inclusive definition of what constitutes food: food itself, of course, but also pizza cartons, paper towels, tubes of toothpaste, the bark on firewood, clothing with traces of treats in the pockets, mulch, compost, and outright garbage. For obvious reasons, we feed our malamutes in their crates.

"Rowdy, crate!" I said. "Sammy, crate! Good dogs!" I latched the doors. We always have a crate or two in the kitchen and just about everywhere else. When dinner is about to arrive, malamutes are true believers who respond to the last trumpet by trying to drown it out. Since it was impossible to make myself heard over the screaming of the malamutes, I greeted Steve only with a smile; and to preserve the hearing I have left, fed all four dogs as quickly as possible. In the twinkling of an eye, Rowdy and Sammy had emptied their bowls and were casting eager glances at India and Lady, who were munching their kibble in civilized fashion.

"It takes a brave woman to tame wild beasts." Steve swept me into a bear hug.

Could I love Steve if he looked like a toad? The question doesn't arise. If he had an ugly face, warts, and short little arms and legs, the chemistry would have been missing to begin with, and I'd never have had the chance to find out whether I loved him or not. Happily, he's princely rather than amphibian. He's tall and lean, with wavy brown hair and blue-green eyes, but what's special about him is his combination of passion and authenticity, and also a kind of magnetism, I guess, that draws creatures to him, all creatures. Even my scratchy, hissing cat, Tracker, loves and trusts Steve. So do I.

But Steve does have a few shortcomings. In particular, when our landline phone rings, instead of checking caller

ID, he has an annoying habit of answering immediately. Worse, if the call is for me and if it's from someone I don't want to talk to, he can't seem to understand my nonverbal demands to say that I'm unavailable. In this case, I had good reason to suspect that the caller was Tabitha Treen, and I just didn't have time to talk to her. Consequently, when Steve answered, I shook my head, mouthed the word *no*, and pointed to the clock, all to no avail. Looking mystified, he handed the phone to me.

"Tabitha Treen," he said.

Speaking so that Tabitha could hear me, I said, "Steve, we have to get ready to go to Rita's. I need to take a shower and get dressed. Hi, Tabitha! Sorry, but we're going out."

"I won't take any time. I just need to vent. I am so upset! Did you see my post?"

I almost asked which one, but it didn't matter. She'd posted the same lament all over Facebook, and this was far from the first time that she'd posted exactly the same thing.

"Yes," I said. "I'm so sorry that you lost track of that puppy, but it does happen, you know. You've done your best, but even the most responsible breeders sometimes lose track of puppies."

If it's possible for a breeder to be responsible to a fault, that's what Tabitha was. She was a conscientious person who cared deeply about her dogs and her puppies. Also, as the author of two excellent books about her breed, the Labrador retriever, and as the author of dozens of articles about all aspects of breeding, she wanted to serve as a model for other breeders and consequently set exceptionally high standards for herself.

Okay. I'm making excuses for her. She drove everyone crazy. Or maybe I'm just jealous. Both of her books were incredibly successful. One was a long, detailed, gorgeously illustrated volume about the history of the breed, the foundation stock, famous kennels, Labs in movies, health problems of the breed, and so forth. The other was a succinct and inexpensive book for pet owners. The market for both books was gigantic because the Labrador retriever is the most popular breed in the United States, Canada, the UK, Australia, Israel, New Zealand, and possibly the world.

Still, Tabitha irritated everyone by insisting that we help her to locate the missing puppy and that we offer her endless emotional support during her search. Tabitha acted more or less as if the puppy had been stolen, when, in fact, a few years earlier, she'd sold the puppy to some people who'd promised to stay in touch with her and who'd vanished. As I'd reminded her, it happens.

"Well, Holly," she said, "it may happen, but it doesn't happen to me, and what I'm really, really upset about is some of the private messages I've had. What's wrong with these people! These are dog writers! They're supposed to know better. Cheyenne was *my* beautiful puppy, and I'm just supposed to forget the whole thing? Let it go? That's what two people told me. Let it go! Well, my beautiful puppy was not a *thing*. "

She went on to say that her puppies came into the world in her hands and that this puppy was *somewhere*, and so were those liars who'd bought the puppy. Then she got to the point of her call, which was to blame me: "You know, the only reason I ever sold my puppy to those people was that *you* referred them."

"Tabitha, I know how frustrated you are, and I'm really sorry, but I've told you before that I have no recollection of sending them to you. They weren't friends of mine. They weren't people I knew. It's possible that I gave someone a list of names of reputable Lab breeders, but I just don't remember. I'm sorry. And about the private messages? Ignore them. Just—"

Once in a while, God rewards my devotion to the Sacred Animal. At that moment, sirens sounded on Concord Avenue, and two of my own Sacred Animals,

Rowdy and Sammy, bless them, took up the call, and their howling put a swift end to Tabitha's. It's often brothers who excel at close harmony: the Louvin Brothers, the Everly Brothers. So do my sire-and-son duo. Come to think of it, it's exactly what I want in my entire household, in the relationships among my dogs, in my relationship with each of them, and in my relationship with Steve: close harmony. That's how I like all of us to sing.

chapter six

"**N**ow, Steve," I began as he and Zara and I were walking down the street to Rita's. Izzy was with us, too: where Zara was, there was Izzy.

"Now, Steve," he mimicked in a voice pitched a good two octaves above his normal bass, "don't tell Quinn's parents about the baby!"

"Well, don't!" I said.

"His parents are from Montana. They're not time travelers."

"What's that supposed to mean?"

"That they live in the same century that we do. They'd probably be happy to hear they're going to be grandparents."

"They're ultraconservative," I said. "Family values. Besides, Rita and Quinn don't want them to know yet, and it's Rita and Quinn's decision, not ours."

Zara spoke up. "Aren't babies family values? But aren't they going to notice that Rita isn't drinking?"

Quinn's parents, Monty and MaryJo, who had driven from Montana, had arrived in Cambridge ten days earlier. After four days here, they'd gone to Maine, so Zara hadn't met them yet.

"No," I said. "They had dinner at our house before they went to Maine. They don't drink at all, so they just think it's normal. They probably approve. Zara, watch your heel on this brick!"

The high-heeled gene ran in Zara and Rita's family, or maybe it was the style gene. They were the kinds of women who have handbags and shoes that coordinate with different outfits. Zara's handbags were oversized, presumably to make room for all of the electronic devices that she carried everywhere. Tonight, she wore a white-dotted black sleeveless dress with wide lapels. Her high-heeled black sandals were hazardous on the rough sidewalk, but they looked great, and she carried a black satchel that was almost as big as a tote. When I admired it, she paused to open it.

"It has room for everything," she said. In addition to a wallet and a cosmetics bag, it held two phones, a headset, a tablet, and a high-end Nikon digital camera that I couldn't help envying.

Izzy had service-dog vests for all occasions. At the moment, she wore a black one with white trim. Zara didn't go so far as to paint Izzy's nails, but she did keep them short, and she trimmed the hair on Izzy's feet. Rita had picked out my new white sundress, so I didn't look too shabby myself in spite of my flat-heeled sandals. I wish that avoiding high heels were a political statement, but the truth is that I just hate pain.

When we got to Rita's, we found her sitting rather stiffly in the living room with Monty and MaryJo Youngman. When I'd first met them, before they'd left for Maine, I'd been irrationally surprised at how old they looked and had wondered whether it was safe for them to drive long distances, especially at night. Quinn had inherited his height from his father, and when I studied Monty closely, I could see a family resemblance, but Monty was fleshy, especially around the middle, and had pouches under his eyes that looked like shucked oysters. To his credit, I guess, he was exceptionally clean. He took showers all the time and was forever brushing his teeth.

Furthermore, he made ample use of minty aftershave and matching breath drops. Consequently, I thought of him as Minty Monty.

MaryJo, his wife, was a jumpy little bird of a woman with scrawny arms and legs, a bony nose, exceptionally round blue eyes, and white hair swept back from her forehead in stiff wings. As I happen to know from a wildlife special that Steve and I once watched, there's an African bird called the oxpecker that subsists on ticks, flies, and maggots that it pecks off the backs of cattle, rhinos, and other large mammals. Disgusting though the comparison may be, whenever I saw the birdlike MaryJo and the big, fleshy Monty, I was reminded of an oxpecker and a rhino, particularly because MaryJo had a habit of plucking invisible bits of lint from his clothing.

Let me add that unlike the oxpecker, MaryJo didn't eat her gleanings.

Asleep in an armchair, Uncle Oscar was physically present but mentally absent. I was reminded of Ogden Nash's "Reflections on Ice-Breaking": liquor would have been quicker, but couldn't Rita at least have offered candy? Everything about the scene was barren and cold. New furniture had been ordered but not yet delivered, and Rita's leather couch and cherry coffee table were still in her old apartment, so the room was sparsely furnished. The walls were still bare, and like the window shades, they were white. The temperature was frigid. I felt as if we were entering a walk-in refrigerator.

Ah, but Ogden Nash ignored the quickest and dandiest ice-breaker of all: a big, friendly dog. In no time, Izzy had awakened Uncle Oscar by poking at his pockets, she'd offered her paw to MaryJo Youngman, and she'd even managed to get the reluctant Monty Youngman to shake her proffered paw. As a service dog, she performed specific tasks for Zara, I'd been told, but as I watched her play the little crowd, it occurred to me that her great gift was her infectious happiness.

In almost no time, the atmosphere was warm, and if we'd had tails, they'd have been wagging to the beat of Izzy's. All of a sudden, everyone was talking at once. En masse, we moved to the kitchen, where Rita belatedly served drinks and put out cheese and crackers. The Youngmans asked for ginger ale. To make Rita's abstemiousness seem normal, I joined her in drinking orange juice, as did Zara, but Steve had single-malt scotch. Quinn, Rita told me, was on his way back from the airport with Zara's mother. Quinn, I thought, would also have scotch, and from everything I'd heard about Vicky, she'd seek alcoholic beverages as assiduously as the Youngmans avoided them.

When we arrived, Willie had been in his crate in what I reminded myself not to call the *playroom*. Although Rita was very protective of him, once all of us were in the kitchen, she agreed to let him out, and the whole group moved to the not-playroom. MaryJo and Monty were clearly more interested in the wedding presents than they were in Willie. As Rita opened the door of his wire crate, Steve, Zara, and I hovered, but the Youngmans examined some silver spoons and other presents that lay on the table. As I'd observed for myself when the Youngmans had first arrived from Montana, before they'd left for Maine, they weren't dog people, and my father had complained about their lack of interest in dogs, but when it comes to dogs, I'm definitely my father's daughter: by *interested* in dogs, we mean *totally obsessed*.

"Zara," Rita said, "could you keep Izzy away? She won't hurt him, but I don't want him roughhousing."

At a signal from Zara, Izzy dropped to the floor.

Willie was a subdued version of his usual fiery self. The shaved patches on his forepaws gave him a wounded look, and although his handsome dark eyes shone, they didn't sizzle. Instead of bursting out his crate and barking at everyone, he emerged quietly and almost reluctantly. In fact, I felt worried until Steve knelt next to him and said softly, "Still under the weather, buddy?" At the sound of Steve's voice, Willie perked up and wagged his tail.

"Steve, is this normal?" Rita asked.

"Low-key is the way to go. It's an adaptive response."

"He won't make eye contact," Rita said. "He thinks it was my fault he was in the hospital."

Almost tripping over one another's words, Zara, Steve, and I told her that Willie thought no such thing and that, in any case, he'd belonged in the hospital.

"That's not how dogs think," Zara said.

In an effort to speak Rita's language, I said, "Willie is mildly traumatized. He's been in the hospital with strange people and strange dogs and scary smells. He's been hooked up to IVs. Besides, a lot of dogs are standoffish when they've just been boarded for a few days."

"Willie, I am so sorry," Rita said.

Steve put his arm around her and murmured softly. Anyone observing them from a distance would've assumed that he was whispering sweet nothings. In fact, he asked, "Would you like me to check him over?" Ah, veterinary love!

She burst into tears. "Yes!"

Throughout this minor drama, Izzy held her solid down-stay. I reminded myself to urge Zara to train Izzy for formal obedience competition. Like every other true competitor, I hate to see flawless behavior wasted in real life when it could be put to good use scoring points and earning titles and awards in totally artificial situations.

Kneeling down, Steve stroked Willie and muttered inaudible but sympathetic-sounding questions in his basso profundo rumble. The thought crossed my mind that if someone talked to me like that, I'd happily roll over for him. Then I realized that I already had. Often.

Soon after Steve had palpated Willie's abdomen and informed Rita that everything felt fine, the back door banged open and from the kitchen, a woman shrieked, "Rita! Your house has such possibilities! Such a darling little fixer-upper! I can hardly wait to see what you're going to do with it."

Zara's immediate response to her mother's arrival was to use one of her phones to take a picture of Willie and Steve. Covering her ears, Rita murmured under her breath, "Fixer-upper! God grant me patience." Aloud, she said, "Hi, Aunt Vicky!"

Vicky's age? She was a generation ahead of me and a generation behind the Youngmans, which is to say that she was about Quinn's age, but her look of calculated sophistication made her seem older than Quinn. Vicky was so New York that by comparison, Rita and Zara were provincial. Her long hair, artfully tinted in dozens of shades of blonde, was swept dramatically back from a face in debt to dermatology and cosmetology. She had no wrinkles, no pouches, no laugh lines, and, as a result, no expression at all.

In makeup, she did not favor the natural look. The contrast between the pale background color and the variously shiny, matte, whitish, creamy, and peach zones suggested the application of products intended exclusively for the forehead, the eyelids, the under-eye areas, the cheekbones, and the hollows beneath them. Her lips were oddly puffy and bright metallic pink. She wore a short, tight jersey dress with black-and-white horizontal stripes and white sandals with three-inch heels. Her perfume was so powerful that I pitied Willie and Izzy; for once, I didn't envy canines their preternaturally acute sense of smell. Everyone, I thought, would have been happy to breathe through a mask.

But Vicky's looks and scent were the least of it. The most was her voice, which was so high in pitch and volume that she could have been imitating an annoying child. "Quinn, a martini, please! Sapphire Bombay, and simply open the vermouth in its vicinity. Uncle Oscar!" She threw her bony arms around him. "My favorite uncle!

Zara, does that animal have to be here? I hope you've given up all thought of taking it to the wedding."

"We're a dog-friendly household," Quinn said lightly. He reached down and rested a hand on Willie.

"Oh, god, another one. What's wrong with it? It looks sick."

"Willie is recovering, but he's been in the hospital," Rita explained.

"I can imagine what that cost," Vicky said. "Wouldn't it have been better to start over with a puppy?"

As Quinn supplied Vicky with the martini and himself with a small glass of scotch, Rita said, "Let's introduce you to everyone. This is—"

Vicky interrupted her. "No, let me guess! Pointing at me, she said, "This is the dog lady."

I made the inevitable reply: "Woof."

"Holly Winter," Quinn said. "And—"

Again interrupting, she jabbed a finger at MaryJo and Monty. "And you're Quinn's grandparents! All the way from Idaho."

"Montana," said MaryJo. "We're Quinn's *parents*."

"MaryJo and Monty," Rita said. "And this is Steve Delaney, Holly's husband."

Holding out his hand, Steve said, "How do you do."

Instead of returning the routine greeting, she grasped his hand, clung to it, and bounced up to give him a peck right on the lips. "Whoo! A special pleasure to meet you, Steve."

I cringed. If I'd had Vicky for a mother, I'd have needed a hundred psychiatric service dogs. As it was, Zara's dog did the work of a thousand. Sitting at Zara's left side, Izzy leaned into Zara and trained loving eyes on Zara's face. I've had emotional transfusions from dogs, too. I knew what I was seeing.

As if by unspoken agreement, Steve, Rita, Quinn, Zara, and I divided up the task of managing Vicky. Sharing my sense that MaryJo and Monty deserved protection from her, Steve asked them about their trip to Maine and effectively drew them out. From what I overheard, I gathered that my father, as their guide, had, as usual, applied a principle derived from life with dogs—namely, that a tired dog is a good dog. In other words, he'd force-marched them all over Acadia National Park. Still, they'd enjoyed themselves, and in telling Steve about their adventures as well as about lobster dinners, they were engaged with him and isolated from Vicky.

Rita and Quinn concentrated on removing Vicky, Quinn by picking up her two suitcases and offering to show her to her room, and Rita by asking her whether she wanted to freshen up before we left for the restaurant.

"Now?" Vicky demanded.

"We have a seven-thirty reservation," Rita said. "The restaurant is just around the corner, but we need to get going soon."

Grumbling about the early dinner hour, Vicky turned to Uncle Oscar. "You're not dressed to go out," she told him. "You can't go like that. Can't you at least wear a sport coat?"

"Vertex isn't that kind of restaurant," Rita said quietly. "It's informal, but it's right nearby, it's open on Mondays, and the food is good. But Uncle Oscar prefers to stay home, don't you, Uncle Oscar? You've already eaten, but if you get hungry, there's ice cream in the freezer, and I've left a bowl on the counter."

"Vortex? What kind of name is that?" Vicky demanded. "It's very unappetizing. And this business about leaving Uncle Oscar all by himself is ridiculous." In a stage whisper, she added, "He's not safe alone!"

Quinn and Rita moved in on her. Rita went so far as to take her by the arm and propel her after Quinn, who was heading toward the stairs. "We'll show you to your room," Rita said firmly.

Once Vicky had left the kitchen, Uncle Oscar said that he was going to his room to watch television. As he passed by me, he said, "Al got off easy when he married Erica instead of that one. Erica's a nice girl."

I wondered whether Rita knew that her father, Al, had even thought about marrying Vicky. Had Al dated one sister first and then the other? First Vicky and then Erica. Had Rita's mother stolen Vicky's boyfriend?

"Rita got off easy, too," Zara murmured. "I didn't."

chapter seven

B ecause of subsequent events, I wish that I'd paid close attention to the precise times when everything happened during the next few hours, but I had no reason to clock-watch and I didn't. When Vicky and Quinn came back downstairs, Rita was crating Willie. Vicky, I remember, complained that it was cruel to lock an animal in a cage, and I noticed MaryJo and Monty nodding in agreement. As Zara and I were putting the drinking glasses in the dishwasher and tidying the kitchen, Vicky reverted to the topic of Uncle Oscar's safety.

Why had he been given a room all the way up on the third floor? And shouldn't someone make sure that he was all right before we left? When she volunteered, Quinn insisted that he'd do it. Quinn, I felt sure, was seizing the chance to get a break from Vicky, whom he'd had to endure throughout the ride from the airport.

To the best of my recollection, all of us except Quinn left for Vertex at about twenty minutes after seven. The walk was uneventful. MaryJo, I remember, clutched her big black purse to her middle and kept looking around anxiously. Vicky devoted herself to chastising Zara for taking Izzy along and for planning to take Izzy to the wedding.

"A dog at a wedding is totally unacceptable," she said. "And if you're hell-bent on having it with you tonight, you could at least get rid of that damned coat it's wearing. It's not as if it's a Seeing Eye dog, Zara, and there's no use pretending it is."

By the time we arrived at Vertex, I'd resolved to serve as a buffer between Zara and Vicky, but Vicky foiled me by moving from her original seat and insisting that Zara sit there next to her. To my relief, Vicky initially withheld negative comments about Vertex, possibly because it was a charming little bistro with French lace panels across its big windows and lots of crisp white linen and fresh flowers on the tables. Because of Vicky's maneuvering, Zara was next to me, with Izzy under the table between us, and Vicky on Zara's other side. Steve, however, nobly took a seat next to Vicky, so it seemed to me that he and I were decently positioned to protect Zara. Monty sat across from me, with Rita on his right and MaryJo on hers.

The chair at the end of the table, between MaryJo and Steve, was temporarily empty because Quinn hadn't yet arrived. As if to reserve the chair for her son, MaryJo placed her big black patent-leather purse on it.

Zara, a dedicated user of location apps, pulled out a phone and checked in to Vertex. Vicky shook her head and made a playful bat at the phone, but she said nothing. A server appeared to take orders for drinks. When Rita ordered two large bottles of San Pellegrino for the table, MaryJo said, "That's water. We aren't used to buying water!" She paused. "But it's very nice."

Predictably, Vicky was put out to discover that Vertex served wine and beer but no hard liquor. After studying the wine list, she took it upon herself to order a bottle of sauvignon blanc and another of Brunello di Montalcino. "Two should be enough to start with," she said. "Except, of course, Rita—"

I cut in. "Those sound lovely." I paused. "Don't they, Steve?"

As we ordered appetizers, Monty and MaryJo shifted the topic of conversation to the menu, and everyone pitched in to translate. I said that ramps were wild onions. Looking up from her phone, or one of her phones, Zara said that aioli was garlic mayonnaise.

When Steve explained that calamari were squid, Monty said, "Octopus?" In reply, Steve gave an unnecessarily detailed and biological explanation of the relationship between the squid and the octopus.

When Quinn finally showed up at about quarter of eight, he said that he'd been checking on both Uncle Oscar and Willie.

"All this fuss over a dog!" Vicky exclaimed. To Steve of all people, she said, "I think it's ridiculous, don't you?"

He had the grace just to smile.

Vicky wiggled all over. To me, she said, "He's gorgeous! How did *you* manage to catch him?"

"I'm the fisherman," Steve said. "I caught her."

Welcome distractions followed. Zara used a phone to take pictures of all of us for Facebook and three or four other social-media sites. The bottles of water and wine appeared and, soon thereafter, our appetizers. We ordered main courses. Because Vicky had been grabbing the attention that belonged to the bride and groom, I was happy when Steve set a precedent by proposing a toast to Rita and Quinn. Others followed Steve's lead.

"To my dearest cousin and my newest cousin," Zara said.

I said something about losing one tenant but gaining two wonderful neighbors.

"Wishing health and joy to the new family!" Vicky exclaimed.

"To our son and our new daughter," Monty said, and MaryJo added, "And to everyone who's welcomed us here."

Rita made a toast to Quinn, and he replied with a long toast to her that strung together quotations from Bob Dylan about chaos, death, and eternal youth.

After Quinn had finished but before the arrival of our main courses, at maybe eight o'clock, Izzy, who was on my left, got quietly to her feet and gently but repeatedly pawed at Zara's leg. In what I took to be a response, Zara made a show of fishing through her oversized purse.

"My camera," she said. "I thought I had my Nikon, but I don't. I want a good picture of everyone. I'll run and get it."

The Nikon had been in Zara's bag when she, Steve, and I had been walking to Rita and Quinn's; when Zara had shown me how capacious the bag was, I'd noticed the camera. She'd subsequently used a phone to take a picture of Steve and Willie. I didn't remember seeing her use the Nikon. I assumed that she was inventing an excuse to leave. As she'd explained to me, one of Izzy's most important tasks was to monitor Zara's state and to alert her to leave a situation, to take medication, or both. Izzy's pawing? The alert.

Steve got to his feet and offered to go with Zara, and although I doubted that anyone had actually tried to steal Izzy, I offered, too. Still, darkness was falling, and Cambridge *is* a city.

She refused: "No, thanks. Really, we'll be back in no time."

Vicky said, "Preferably, *you* will be. By yourself."

Soon after Zara and Izzy's departure, Monty asked Steve an inaudible question, excused himself, and headed for the back of the restaurant, presumably in search of the restroom. During what proved to be Monty's rather prolonged absence and Zara's near disappearance, the atmosphere at the table improved. The main courses not only tasted good but also gave the diverse group a shared topic of conversation.

When Monty returned, Vicky referred to him as Marty, and she called his wife Mary Ellen, but in Zara's absence, we were spared having to listen to her take cracks at her daughter. She cross-questioned Rita and Quinn about the wedding.

As she'd have known if she'd read the invitation, the wedding was to take place at Harvard's Appleton Chapel, and the reception at the nearby Harvard Faculty Club. So many of Rita's and Quinn's friends were on vacation in August that they'd decided on the chapel instead the Memorial Church sanctuary; it was to be a small wedding for family and close friends. Rita was to wear a Vera Wang gown. Her "something new," as she called it, was a gift from Quinn, a pair of diamond stud earrings.

"From Tiffany," added Quinn, the fan of brand names. Yes, there would be champagne. "Dom Pérignon," Quinn specified.

When Zara and Izzy finally returned, Vicky demanded to know whether she'd checked on Uncle Oscar.

"We didn't go there," Zara said. "We went to Holly and Steve's."

"Someone needs to make sure he's all right," Vicky said. "I will."

Everyone told Vicky that Uncle Oscar would be fine. We pointed out that she hadn't finished her meal and that her food would get cold. She refused to listen. Monty, who had a key to the front door, gave it to her. She must have left shortly before eight thirty. When the restaurant's weather-stripped door closed behind her, I briefly mistook the sighing sound for a collective expression of relief. I almost hoped that she'd find Uncle Oscar in some trivial but time-consuming crisis that would detain her throughout the rest of our dinner.

For a moment, everyone savored the silence. Then all of us talked at once. The Nikon evidently forgotten, Zara satisfied MaryJo's curiosity about smartphones by showing her photos and demonstrating how location apps worked. Steve and Monty talked about fishing. The topic somehow led Monty to remark that my father, Buck, held solid views on the Second Amendment and was a man who knew his

Bible. It's true that Buck believes in guns, but when he quotes the Bible, it's invariably in some self-serving way connected to dogs. For instance, Ecclesiastes justified every breeding that Buck thought was a good idea and my mother didn't: "To every thing there is a season."

But the content of our dinner-table talk didn't matter; the conviviality did. It was so delightful to have Vicky gone that no one wondered aloud about what she was doing or whether she was all right. When she finally showed up looking flustered and red in the face, she belatedly began to eat her dinner and had the nerve to complain that her food was cold. Even so, she dragged out the simple business of chewing and swallowing lobster ravioli for a good twenty minutes.

Finally, at five or ten minutes after nine o'clock, we began to order dessert. Monty said that if no one minded, he'd skip it and head on home; he'd had a long day and was worn out. When Vicky had returned the front-door key that she'd borrowed from him, he thanked Rita and Quinn and left. Although my chocolate hazelnut tart was delicious, I could hardly wait to have the dinner end, as it did at sometime after nine thirty. We said our goodnights on the sidewalk outside Vertex. Rita, Quinn, Vicky, and MaryJo went in one direction, Steve and I in another. Zara wanted to take Izzy for a little walk but said that she'd join us soon.

"We'll be outdoors," I said. "Just knock on the gate."

When Steve and I got home, we let the dogs loose in the yard and settled ourselves right next to each other at the picnic table with wine glasses and a bottle of sauvignon blanc. Since I know nothing about wine, I choose on the basis of low price, a canine theme, a funny name, or a cute label. We'd recently had wines called Tasty Bitch, Sweet Bitch, Bitch Bubbly, and Lab. Tonight's was Dog Point. The label displayed a tree, chosen, I guess, as an attractive alternative to a fire hydrant.

I leaned against Steve, clinked my glass against his, and said, "In dogs we trust." I took a sip. "I wish to God that they'd just gone to city hall and mailed announcements to the family."

"The Youngmans are all right. Oscar. Zara. It's that woman. What's she doing here so far ahead of time? It's five days until the wedding."

"She invited herself. Rita couldn't stop her. Poor Zara! It's so stereotyped to blame the mother. I feel guilty. Feminist guilt. Post-feminist guilt. It's ridiculous, but I feel angry at feminism. Wasn't feminism supposed to do something about women like that? Liberate them. Transform them."

"Poison them."

I laughed. "Seriously, I'm struggling. You know, one of Rita's clinical specialties is dealing with unlikeable patients, people who have no friends, people whose own families can't stand them. What Rita says is that she somehow always finds something about those people that she genuinely can like. 'They all have their stories, too.' That's what she says. I'm trying to remember that, and—" I broke off. Zara could arrive any second. I didn't want her to overhear.

"Steve, we are so lucky. Your uncles who came for our wedding are sweethearts, and Gabrielle is the best stepmother on earth, and when we got married, my father wasn't even too bad, at least for him. Oh, but, Steve, damn it! Never mind the relatives. Why can't Rita stay here and have the baby by herself? She's more than capable of supporting a child, and he's—"

"He's not such a bad guy. And Rita wants to get married."

"But to *him*?"

As if issuing a mournful reply, Rowdy planted his rear end of the ground, raised his head to the sky, and let forth a prolonged, melodious howl. The beautiful boy has a voice to match his looks. If grand opera offered parts suitable for Alaskan malamutes, he'd be on the stage at the Met. Sammy, Rowdy's son, looks remarkably like his sire and sounds like him, too, but it's always Rowdy who conducts the performance and howls the lead, and Sammy who takes his cue from Rowdy, as he did now. The inspiration for the malamute musicale was, as it often is, the wail of sirens. Our house is on the corner of a quiet side street, Appleton, and a busy thoroughfare, Concord Avenue. Noisy vehicles are so common that I notice them only when the malamutes answer back. Once I'd silenced Rowdy and Sammy, however, I could hear that the vehicular howling was coming from Appleton Street, and I could also hear frantic knocking on our gate and Zara's voice hollering, "Steve! Holly! Open the gate! Open the gate!"

Before I had a chance to comply, one of Zara's phones rang. She answered almost immediately and, seconds later, called out, "It's Rita. Their house has been robbed. Meet me there! Willie's gone."

chapter eight

As soon as we'd put the dogs in the house, we hurried to Rita and Quinn's. One cruiser was parked on the street. Another blocked the driveway. If the house had belonged to strangers, I'd have assumed that they were throwing a big party and that the police were there to control traffic and crowds. Every indoor and outdoor light was on. The gate at the end of the driveway stood open, and from the yard came the sound of voices.

When Rita caught sight of us, she ran up, hugged both of us, and said, "Willie's not here. We've been robbed, but I don't care. There's blood all over. Why does Kevin have to be away *now?*"

Kevin Dennehy lives with his mother in the house next to mine of Appleton Street. A Cambridge police lieutenant, Kevin has a proprietorial and protective attitude toward the entire city and especially to this neighborhood. As Rita knew, he was away now because he and his girlfriend were taking advantage of low summer rates to spend a week in Bermuda.

Sounding uncharacteristically childish, Rita added, "Kevin never goes anywhere. Why did he have to pick this week? These people won't let us back inside. They even dragged Uncle Oscar out of bed."

Glancing behind Rita, I saw Uncle Oscar stretched out on one of the teak recliners. MaryJo, Monty, and Vicky were seated in wrought-iron chairs. Zara, with Izzy at her side, was peering in through the window to the playroom.

Quinn moved quietly to Rita's side. "The police didn't do that, Rita," he said gently. "Aunt Vicky did. But the reason we're all out here is that they want to do a thorough search. That's reasonable. Rita, for all we know, Willie's in the house somewhere. Maybe they'll find him."

"Or his body!" Rita started sobbing. "I want Willie! I want my dog back!"

Quinn, I have to admit, was wonderful. "I do, too, love. We'll find him. The wedding presents don't matter. All that matters is Willie. We'll find him."

"For God's sake, Rita, do you have to have hysterics about a dog?" The speaker—the shrieker—was Vicky. "Uncle Oscar could've been murdered in his bed."

"Vicky, hold your tongue," Oscar said.

"You could've been! It's no joke."

When I joined Zara and Izzy, Zara turned away from the window.

"What exactly happened?" I asked softly.

"The burglar broke the window on the far side of the house and got in that way."

"Good choice. There's nothing there, really but the neighbors' fence. No gate to the yard. No one ever goes there. What's this about blood?"

I peered through the window. A uniformed officer stood in the entrance to the kitchen, presumably to prevent her fellow officers from entering and contaminating the scene. Quinn's boxes of books were still stacked in one corner, and the laptop was still on the table, but almost everything else had been disarranged. The appliances and other large presents had been moved, I thought, and the boxes that had held Quinn's drug samples had been knocked off the table. The sets of fireplace implements were no longer upright. A brass poker lay on the tile floor, which was splotched with dark liquid. Willie's crate held nothing except the crate pad.

"You can see the blood there, near the poker," Zara said. "And on it. There's more in the kitchen. The burglar seems to have left through the kitchen door, the door to the driveway. What's missing is mostly small stuff, like the spoons that were on the table. Flatware. Serving pieces. The big things, like the boxes of crystal and china, are still here. And the drug samples are gone. Obviously."

MaryJo joined us and said, to my surprise, "Monty and I think that someone cased the joint. Isn't that what it's called? It is in old movies. We think that some crook saw all the wedding presents being delivered and decided to help himself."

"You're probably right," Zara told her.

Looking away from Zara and MaryJo, I saw Rita and Quinn near the gate, where they were conferring with two men in suits. Quinn continued talking to them, but Rita came to me and said, "Detectives. Willie's not in the house. The crime-scene people are here. We're allowed to go inside, but just to the living room and the little bathroom."

I was careful to say nothing about the poker and the blood. "The burglar could just have let Willie loose. He could be right here in the neighborhood. I'm going to look for him. Steve will, too."

"I left his leash on top of his crate," Rita said. "It's gone."

"We'll look for him anyway."

Steve and I made a quick trip home for flashlights and, in my case, Rowdy. To maximize the area we covered, Steve and I had agreed to divide the task of searching for Willie, and I had no intention of wandering around Cambridge alone at night. Besides, Rowdy was more likely to detect Willie's presence than I was. By comparison with dogs, human beings are hard of hearing and have no sense of smell. Rowdy knew Willie. My main task, I told myself, was to read my dog.

Rowdy and I began our search at home, which had been Willie's home until recently and might be the home to which he'd return. Calling Willie's name, I made my way around the perimeter of our property and checked under the cars in the driveway.

"Damn Rita for not teaching Willie a reliable recall," I told Rowdy as we turned onto Concord Avenue. Steve and I had agreed that he'd check Huron Avenue and the streets north of Appleton and that I'd cover Concord Avenue and the area immediately to our south. "Willie, come! Willie, here!" I have a dog trainer's voice, which is to say, a voice that conveys the genuine expectation of attention and cooperation. The key word is *genuine*. "Willie, come!"

Even to my own ears, my calls sounded phony. I didn't expect Willie to come running me; I expected to find his body lying in the street. I was tempted to put my hands on Rowdy, to cling to him, but I wanted his attention on his surroundings and not on me. We crossed Concord, made our way to the intersection with Huron, crossed the street again, walked by Imperial Cleaners and the Hi-Rise bakery, and turned onto Royal Avenue, which runs parallel to our block of Appleton. All the while, Rowdy strutted steadily along, pausing in his usual fashion to sniff tires and to lift his leg on utility poles. Although I know the handsome boy so well that I can practically see him in the dark, I played the flashlight on him. He neither sped up nor slowed down. His ears remained erect. His plumy white tail sailed over his back. "Not a thing, huh?" I said to him. "Nothing at all." We were then about halfway down Royal, and as I spoke to Rowdy, I heard the despair in my voice and realized that our search for Willie was a waste of time except to the extent that it boosted Rita's morale. Willie could be lying wounded or dead in any of the dark yards we were passing.

I was pointing my flashlight under a parked car when my cell rang.

"Holly," Steve said, "meet me at Rita's. Willie's been found."

"Alive?"

"Yes. Some woman found him and called Rita."

I waited for him to continue. He didn't. "And?"

"He's in Watertown."

"What?"

"Near the Waltham line."

"That's, I don't know, five miles from here? Is he all right?"

"The woman told Rita that he was timid, so that's got her worried, but it sounds like he's okay. I said that you and I would go get him. Rita wants me to take a look at him, and she's supposed to stay here and talk to the police."

"Willie's not bleeding?"

"No."

"Then whose blood is it? Whose blood is all over the floor?"

chapter nine

"**M**y own little doggie-wog crossed the Rainbow Bridge on Memorial Day," said Enid Garabedian, "so when this darling little Scottie dog showed up, I thought, Well, God has sent him to me, or maybe my very own Edgar Pooh has sent him to me, so after I gave the little Scottie dog a drinkie of water, I said a prayer, and you know what?" Enid's face fell. There was a lot of it to fall: she was at least two hundred pounds overweight.

"What?" I asked.

"God said that the little Scottie dog was somebody else's pet and that I had no business saying thanks for something that wasn't a gift and wasn't mine at all."

God, I thought, had shown great common sense.

Steve and I were seated on chintz-covered chairs in the tchotchke-packed living room of Enid Garabedian's house, a single-family ranch a few blocks from Pleasant Street in Watertown. Enid lived on the memorably named Pecker Drive, where I'd never been before, but I knew the area well. Just over the line into Waltham was a gigantic deep-discount big-box store where I periodically bargain-hunted for whole tenderloins, paper products sold by the multidozen, restaurant-sized jugs of olive oil, and near-lifetime supplies of everything from aspirin to Zyrtec. After stocking up on household goods, I always crossed back into Watertown to stop at Pignola's, a sort of farm stand on steroids that offered hundreds, if not thousands, of varieties of familiar and exotic fruits and vegetables, domestic and imported cheeses, fresh and dry pasta, baked goods, houseplants and seedlings, and, since Watertown, Massachusetts is the American capital of Armenia, utterly delectable Armenian specialty foods. When the weather was cool enough to take dogs along, I then drove along Pleasant Street to Watertown Square, parked in the lot for the Charles River Reservation, and walked a dog or two along a section of the paved trail that begins at Boston Harbor and follows the Charles River for more than twenty miles.

Enid Garabedian probably shopped at Pignola's, too. Steve and I had a hard time persuading her that we'd just eaten and couldn't manage the hummus, baba ghanoush, Syrian bread, and melted kasseri that she generously offered. No baklava, either, thanks. Not even a taste? No, really. Thank you. Although Enid lived in walking distance of Pignola's, she couldn't possibly have gone there on foot, but as the cliché about obese women would have it, such a pretty face! She had springy white curls, too, and beautiful violet-blue eyes. Her caftan was blue, and she filled a blue armchair that was meant to be oversized but wasn't. I liked her a lot.

Willie obviously did, too. The barking we'd heard when we'd rung Enid's doorbell wasn't up to Willie's typically robust standard, but he'd felt at home enough to bark; and to my relief, he looked astonishingly well for a dog who'd evidently been dognapped and then lost and then found, all the while recovering from a hospital stay.

Once we'd introduced ourselves to Enid, Steve had immediately examined Willie and found no cause for concern. In particular, Willie had no injuries that could account for the blood on Rita and Quinn's floor. The normally sparkling Willie was, however, weak and subdued. He lay at Steve's feet with his eyes on Enid.

"Thank you so much for calling," I said. "Willie really is someone's beloved dog. Aren't you, Willie? His owner was frantic."

"I knew when I saw his pretty little collar with the Scottie dogs on it and the tag with three phone numbers. And his poor little shaved legs. I said to myself, Somebody loves this sweet little boy. Somebody paid a big vet bill. Somebody bought him his pretty collar and bothered to put all those phone numbers on his tag. It just wouldn't have been right to keep him."

"I'm curious," I said. "How did you happen to find Willie?"

Enid blinked. "Why, he just showed up on my doorstep. That's why I thought he was a gift, you see. He was right at the door, like he'd been delivered by UPS."

"He wasn't wearing a leash?"

She shook her head.

Steve asked, "Has he had anything to eat? Have you fed him?"

"No. After my Edgar Pooh passed on, I gave all his little cans of dinner away. I didn't want to have to keep seeing them. That's his picture over there."

Every surface in the room was crammed with framed photos, ceramic kittens, figurines of medieval ladies, heavily decorated china plates, and geegaws and knickknacks of all sorts. The table to which she directed our attention held a lamp encrusted with gilded ivy, a framed snapshot of two little blond boys at a beach, and a large professional photo of a Yorkshire terrier with a long silky coat. The dog had a violet bow on his head. I picked up the photo and examined it.

"He was beautiful," I said. "Most pet owners trim their Yorkies. They don't want to bother taking care of a coat like this."

"I didn't mind."

Returning the picture to the table, I said, "What handsome little boys!"

"My babies," Enid said.

As practical as ever, Steve asked, "So, you didn't feed Willie anything?"

"Not a thing." To Willie, she said, "We didn't want to upset our tum-tum with table scraps, did we?"

"You did the right thing," Steve told her.

After we'd again refused Enid's offer of food and again thanked her, I put Willie on the slip lead I'd brought with me, and we left for Cambridge. Just in case Willie needed vet care, we'd taken Steve's van, which he keeps well stocked with supplies for veterinary first aid and emergencies. Glancing at the odometer as he started the engine, Steve said, "Five point two miles."

"Willie didn't travel on foot," I said. "What happened? The burglar stole him, and then Willie roused himself and went for the burglar's ankles? Or Willie was let out on Appleton Street, and someone picked him up and then let him go in Watertown? Or the burglar stole him, but he escaped?"

"We'll probably never know," Steve said.

Steve is seldom wrong. This time, he was.

chapter ten

"Holly, our burglar is dead!" Rita announced.

She called while Steve and I were having breakfast and simultaneously checking our e-mail and Facebook.

She added, "I can't talk now, but I couldn't wait to tell you. He was fished out of the river. A runner saw the body and called the police."

"How do you know it's your burglar?" I asked.

Steve murmured, "And not someone else's?"

I clarified. "How did—"

Rita helped me out. "He has a head wound, and they found one of Quinn's drug samples in his pocket. Provigil. I'll be okay in an hour or two. I'll tell you all about it."

"He died from the head injury?"

"Presumably. I did warn you that my family was crazy, didn't I? Someone whacked the burglar over the head and killed him and won't admit it." She excused herself. I promised to visit later in the morning.

"A runner found the body," I told Steve. "In the river, she said. The Charles, I guess. There's a head wound, and there was a drug sample in his pocket. One of Quinn's. That must be how the police made the connection."

"Did Rita say who the burglar is? Was?" Steve asked.

"No. She couldn't talk. I'm sure she has morning sickness. She thinks that someone in her family hit him with the poker, and then, I guess, he had a delayed reaction and died."

Having once had a head injury, I know a little about them. I didn't die. Obviously. I got off easy. Anyway, something I've learned is that after head trauma, you can seem to be just fine and then develop symptoms, maybe a headache, and then have a fatal reaction. I was incredibly lucky.

"Rowdy," I said, "it is not your morning for the skillet. It's Sammy's. It's your morning for the plates. And the skillet is still too hot, and we're still eating."

My sensible words didn't stop the saliva from dripping out of Rowdy's mouth and onto the floor, and they didn't diminish the almost irresistible cuteness of his expression. He just loves scouring the skillet we use for scrambled eggs, and Sammy and Kimi do, too. In fact, the main reason we have scrambled eggs for breakfast is to provide the dogs with the joy of serving as canine Brillo. Steve and I eat so many eggs that we'll probably die of heart attacks, but if the dogs are happy, so what? Story of my life.

"There was a lot of coming and going last night," Steve said. "Somebody could've interrupted the burglar. Vicky was gone for a while."

"Quinn took a while to get to Vertex. Monty went out, and then he left before the rest of us. And Uncle Oscar was at the house the whole time." Zara had left Vertex, too. I didn't say so. "Well, we'll know more later. Oh, not again! Tabitha has sent me that same damned blurry picture of the people she sold that puppy to. Breeder responsibility is one thing, but it doesn't mean that you have to plague people who can't help you."

"Leah says that her roommates want Kimi to stay."

"She e-mailed you?"

"Facebook."

Steve is on Facebook, but I'm the one who's active. Checking my cousin Leah's Facebook page, I saw the status update about the roommates' supposed eagerness to add a malamute to the household. "Hah! But the pictures are cute."

I typed a comment: *Dearest Kimi, raid the refrigerator! I want you home.*

Steve said, "Zara chronicles every minute of her life. She's posted on my wall to thank us for having her here."

"Mine, too. She gets little carried away."

"She's already thanked us, and she's two floors up from us right now."

I refilled my coffee cup. "If it hasn't been said online, it hasn't been said."

"Does she know that privacy settings exist?"

"Does Mark Zuckerberg?"

"Presumably."

"Well," I said, "Zara presumably does too, but she believes in accepting practically every friend request she gets."

"You do the same thing. Who are all those people? You don't know them."

"Most of them have malamutes. Or Siberians. Or dogs, at least. Even if they post in Russian or Polish or Japanese or some language I can't even identify, I like seeing the photos, and I can always get a translation. I like the international feel. Paws across the water."

"Holly, the burglar wasn't some dog owner in Russia or Poland or wherever. Anyone could've known when we left for Vertex. Look at this. She posted when she and Izzy got here. Then she posted pictures from Rita and Quinn's, and then she checked in at Vertex with Foursquare. And she posted pictures from Vertex. That's my dinner!" He sounded as if Zara had stolen the food off his plate. "And last night, she couldn't wait to tell everyone about the burglary."

"She uses Twitter, too. And some other sites and apps."

Steve peered at his screen while I was crating Sammy with the skillet and putting my plate on the floor for Rowdy.

"Anyone could've known ahead of time," I said. "The burglar probably knew that we were going to Vertex and what time we'd get there. Scroll down on Zara's page. There's a link to the Vertex website somewhere and something about when we were going. So the burglar is—was—a Facebook creeper. There are plenty of them. They never post anything. They just get information from the people who do, and especially from people like Zara."

"Holly, no wonder Rita's upset. Zara's already got three albums about the wedding and one status update after another."

"With more to come. Actually, all the photos and stuff on Facebook are a compromise. Zara wanted to do a wedding website, but Rita talked her out of it. I think that she doesn't know quite how much Zara has put on Facebook. Rita hates Facebook. She doesn't understand it."

Steve laughed.

"Well, she doesn't. She thinks that everyone uses it the way Zara does. Anyway, after she absolutely refused to let Zara do a website, she let all the rest go because she didn't want to sound like Vicky."

"You could talk to Zara."

"Me? I don't want to sound like her mother, either. Did you notice what Izzy did at Vertex? She alerted when Vicky was stressing Zara. What if Izzy started alerting to me? I don't exactly see myself as the kind of person that a service dog has to warn her handler about."

"Just have a little talk about privacy settings. And common sense."

"She'd tell me that she gets a lot of clients through Facebook. And she does. She does a lot of freelance editing for people who are self-publishing, and she stays in touch with other freelance editors."

"And ten thousand other people."

"You're exaggerating. Besides, Steve, Zara will work it out for herself. She'll know how the burglar found out when we'd be at Vertex. No one will have to tell her."

"She'll know that the burglary was her fault."

"It wasn't! And I hope that she doesn't see things that way. If she does, she'll end up blaming herself for the death of the damned burglar, and that's the last thing she needs to do. And what if Vicky turns out to be the person who hit him with the poker? Where would that leave Zara? Feeling responsible for making her mother kill someone. Please! She's had enough problems in her life."

"No one made anyone kill the burglar."

"True. But someone did kill him. Someone did."

chapter eleven

"He was a small-time crook named Frankie Sorensen." Rita sipped her mint tea. She was so protective of her unborn child that she was afraid to consume large quantities of anything, including raspberry tea and the ginger tea that I'd also recommended. "Little Frankie. That's what the police called him. No one came right out and said that it was good riddance, but that's the distinct feeling I got, and I can't say that I like that attitude. Holly, he was just a young man! Twenty-four. I asked. Not that I'm happy that he robbed our house and stole my dog, but that young man is *dead*."

Unless you count Uncle Oscar, who was asleep on a recliner, Rita, Willie, and I were alone on the patio in her backyard. Probably because no one knew what had caused Willie's gastroenteritis, Rita was almost as protective of him as she was of her baby-to-be. Among other things, she insisted on limiting Willie to short on-leash walks. At the moment, Willie was on a six-foot leash that Rita had hitched to a table. He'd barked at me when I'd arrived and had even eyed my ankles. He was dozing now, but I was delighted to see that he was regaining his spirit.

In deference to Rita's canine invalid, I'd left Rowdy and Sammy at home, and India and Lady were at the clinic with Steve. Quinn, who'd been on the phone with the insurance company, was on his way to Lexington and

Concord to visit the Revolutionary War sites with his parents. Zara had stayed home to work on an editing project.

"And," Rita continued, "I take that young man's death seriously."

"Of course."

"Well, the police evidently don't. At least that's my impression. Not that this Little Frankie sounds like an altogether admirable individual. He was a drug user with a criminal record. He'd served a prison sentence."

"For what?"

"He sent someone to the hospital. It sounds thoroughly sordid. He and his brother teamed up in a fight in some sleazy bar. The police seem to think that the brother did the major damage, but the one who went to jail was Frankie. They'd both been in jail before for drug possession. I had to *pry* this information out of the police. Do you think that I'd be justified in calling Kevin?"

"No! Kevin almost never takes a vacation. Besides, he'll be back on Friday. It isn't as if he could do anything."

"He could tell me what's going on. I feel the need to know who this young man was."

"We could look online. If I can't find anything, Zara probably can. Speaking of Zara, where's Vicky?"

"Madame is taking her bath. She had the nerve to complain about the towels."

"If Vicky's washing off her venom, you'd better watch out. It'll run down the drain and corrode the pipes."

Rita laughed. "I wish that *she'd* run down the drain. She's been unspeakably horrible about Willie."

"Willie's looking great."

Rita beamed. "He is, isn't he. His adventure doesn't seem to have done him any harm. I've sent a cookie basket to the woman who found him. Enid."

I'd have advised flowers or fruit, but I didn't say so. Besides, what business of mine was Enid Garabedian's weight? None. "She was tempted to keep Willie. She had a

Yorkie who died recently, and when Willie showed up on her doorstep, she thought he was a gift from God. Or maybe from her Yorkie."

"Then it was especially noble of her to call me."

"So, what else did you learn about your burglar?"

"*My* burglar." Rita was pensive. "Frankie Sorensen. What I learned was not much. He had a head wound compatible with being hit with the poker. The sample of Provigil was how the police made the connection. The packaging is distinctive."

"What kind of drug is it?"

"Actually, Quinn says that it's been somewhat displaced by something called Nuvigil. The patent was running out, so the company started pushing the new drug. Those samples were old. Anyway, it's a stimulant. It keeps people awake. Quinn says it's used for narcolepsy. And it's given to people with sleep apnea to keep them from falling asleep in the daytime. Shift workers take it."

"Why was Quinn prescribing it?"

"He wasn't. Not very much. That's why he had so many samples left. So, what else about Frankie? Not too bright. Good-looking. Grew up in Waltham. He still lived there. He was in trouble from the time he was a kid. Stealing cars, breaking into cars, a little drug dealing."

"Breaking and entering?"

"Oddly enough, no. I asked."

"Anything to do with dogs?" My eternal question.

Rita said, "I have no idea. But it's curious that Frankie came from Waltham and Willie ended up near the Waltham line. And Frankie's body was downriver from there, somewhere above the Watertown dam. Of course, who knows where he went in. And how."

"He stole Willie and then what? Willie got loose when Frankie died?"

"Maybe."

"Rita, did anyone see or hear anything? Uncle Oscar was here all the time."

At the sound of his name, Uncle Oscar stirred and opened his eyes. "Holly Winter," he said. "Where's Rowdy?"

"A lot of people just ask for Rowdy, Uncle Oscar. They don't even bother about me."

"Just the way you like it," Uncle Oscar said.

I laughed. "Exactly."

"Uncle Oscar," Rita said, "have you given any more thought to last night? Maybe you've remembered something."

Uncle Oscar looked miffed.

"People forget things. Everyone does," Rita said. "While we were at the restaurant, you got up and had some ice cream."

Oscar looked uncomfortable.

"Rita doesn't begrudge you the ice cream," I said.

"Of course not," Rita agreed. "It was chocolate. Your favorite. The bowl was in the sink. Did you see anyone? Hear anyone? Uncle Oscar, did you hear Willie bark?"

With maddening vagueness, he said, "Once or twice."

"Did you see anyone? Or hear anyone in the house?"

"Vicky. She stuck her head in my room. Barged right in. I let her think I was asleep. That's a very nervy woman. Your father's a lot better off with your mother. Erica's a nice girl. It's a good thing Al married her. I hope he comes to his senses." Uncle Oscar had made a similar remark to me. I wondered whether this was the first time Rita had heard him allude to a relationship between her father and Vicky.

Her response suggested that she dismissed it as a figment of Oscar's imagination. She caught my eye, shook her head gently, and changed the subject. "Uncle Oscar, would you like some coffee?"

"Thank you, my dear, no." He yawned. "If you'll excuse me, I'll head up to my room."

When he'd left, I said, "He certainly does sleep a lot."

"He gets up in the night," Rita said. "He doesn't have sleep apnea. He's been tested. It's just his age. Sleeping a lot is one thing, but it bothers me when he seems so vague. You just heard him. He can't seem to remember that last night, sometime after we left, he fixed himself a bowl of ice cream."

"It's pretty unlikely that the burglar, Frankie, helped himself to a snack."

"It was Uncle Oscar. He left the bowl where he always does, in the sink, filled with water, and the spoon in the bowl. It was there when we got home, so he got up either before or after the robbery, but he can't seem to remember."

"Maybe he was half asleep."

"That's exactly what's worrying me, that maybe he drifts into states where he's half asleep. Fugue states. Sleep walking. Something like that. Holly, you don't think—"

"That Uncle Oscar grabbed the poker? And—"

"He is not a violent person," Rita said. "But he's very devoted to me, and if he was in a dissociated state and saw this Frankie stealing my wedding presents? I guess it's remotely possible."

"Speaking of the presents, has anything turned up? The police must have Frankie's address. They must have looked there."

"I don't know. Maybe they haven't yet. They're not very communicative. But if they'd found any of our possessions, I think they'd have said so. Oh, Holly? You know what else is missing? My earrings. Quinn's special present."

"Damn! Oh, Rita, I'm sorry. What were they doing in the playroom?"

"They weren't there. They were in our bedroom, in the top drawer of my dresser. They were still in the Tiffany box. We think maybe that's why Frankie took them, why he knew they were worth stealing."

"Are you missing any other jewelry?"

"No, but I don't own anything else like those earrings. Most of what I have is strictly costume jewelry or from local silversmiths. Goldsmiths. Artisans."

"Don't you own a pearl necklace?"

"Yes, but a kid from Waltham wouldn't necessarily realize that the pearls are real. We're hoping to get the earrings back, of course. And everything else. We made a list last night. Thank God for Zara's database of presents! What's missing is silver. Flatware. Some Christofle serving pieces. Vicky's idea of being helpful was to tell us that they should've been in a safe deposit box."

"So, Frankie was in the house long enough to go upstairs to your bedroom and find your earrings, before or after he took the silver. Presumably before, since he was in the playroom when he got hit with the poker. Or maybe he returned to the playroom to get Willie. It's weird. With all that sterling, I wonder why he bothered to go upstairs."

"Looking for a present for his girlfriend? I don't know. Burglars usually want to get in and get out fast. Kevin told me about it once. I don't remember why. Anyway, Kevin said that the average burglar is in the house for less than ten minutes. The burglar breaks in, makes sure he has a second way out, grabs what he wants, and bolts."

"I wish that Uncle Oscar could remember *when* Willie barked," I said. "And when he had his ice cream. It would help if we knew what happened when."

"How would it help? I don't see how."

"Rita, if we knew that Uncle Oscar came downstairs for his ice cream at, let's say, seven thirty, and we knew that Frankie broke in at eight o'clock, then you could stop worrying that—"

"—that Uncle Oscar killed someone and has totally forgotten the little incident."

"No one intended to kill Frankie."

"If you bash someone on the head with a poker, exactly what *do* you intend?"

Without answering Rita's question, I said, "Since Frankie walked out of here, whoever hit him didn't realize—"

"Holly, please! Enough rationalization. And excuses. As of this morning, everyone knows that Frankie's dead, and no one has stepped forward to say, 'Sorry. I caught him in the act of stealing your wedding presents, and I acted on impulse.' Furthermore, for all we know, Frankie passed out, and whichever one of my relatives hit him may very well have thought he was dead."

"If he blacked out, maybe he was in the house for quite a while. Longer than ten minutes. Damn! It's so confusing. Rita, I think that if we made a chart of who was where when, it would help. That's what Steve would do. He'd make a timeline."

"A timeline. Isn't that another one of those Facebook things? I am so sick of hearing about Facebook!"

As if conjured up by the mention of social media, Zara appeared—but not silently. She slammed the gate open, paused to close it, and ran to us with Izzy at her side. "Look at this!" She held out a phone. "Pictures of the guy stealing Izzy! You remember? I told you that someone took pictures. He finally sent them." Her cheeks were pink with excitement, her eyes flashed, and she talked so fast that it was difficult to understand her. "You didn't believe me. I know you didn't. Neither of you believed me, and neither did anyone else. But it's okay. Really, it's okay. Holly, look!"

Feeling guilty, I took the phone and examined the photos, which were sharper than I expected.

"He Photoshopped them," Zara said.

"Zara, sit down," Rita told her. "Take a deep breath. You're upsetting Izzy."

To me, Izzy looked happy but relaxed, and I know a lot more about dogs than Rita does. Izzy's tail-wagging was enthusiastic rather than anxious, and she wasn't leaning against Zara, pawing at her, or regarding her with concern.

As far as I could tell, she was sharing Zara's excitement. Fluent as I am in the language of dogs, I'll translate: *Something good has happened! Isn't that great!*

In contrast, the furrows on Rita's forehead and her locked jaw radiated psychotherapeutic suspicion. Of what? At a guess, Zara's rapid speech and elevated mood led Rita to worry about the onset of a hypomanic episode. I happen to know what such an episode is because I'd once had an encounter with Steve's horrible ex-wife when she'd been having one, and Rita had subsequently explained it to me. That time, the trigger had been prescription drugs. This time, in what I assume to be Rita's view, hypomania could signal the resurgence of the bipolar disorder that I'd been told Zara had.

So, Izzy said one thing, and Rita said another. Whose assessment did I believe? If you ever have to choose between the judgment of a psychotherapist and the judgment of a dog, trust the dog. Even the best shrinks can misread and misinterpret. But dogs? Dogs are never wrong.

Ignoring Rita, I said, "Zara, you were right. He's hot! He's really hot."

The first of the four pictures showed the dog thief stealing Izzy: He had her leash in his hand. He was moving away from the camera but had turned his head to look back. The second picture, which must have been taken after Izzy's rescue, was a rearview shot of the would-be thief running off. The other two photos, cropped from the first two, were close-ups: one of his face, the other of the back of his head. As Zara had reported, he was tan and had curly brown hair. She'd said that he was tall. Was he? It was hard to tell. In the first photo, the one with Izzy, he seemed to be of at least medium height. Just as Zara had reported, he wore a white T-shirt and jeans. His shoulders and arms were muscular, and he'd been born—*born*—to wear jeans. The close-up of the back of his head showed that his ears didn't stick out; it was otherwise uninformative. But the blown-up picture of his face? Geez! Even with that startled expression, even when Zara must have been shouting at him, even when he'd discovered that he'd been caught on camera, he was gorgeous. Whew!

Where was I?

"Does he look familiar?" Zara asked. "Have you seen him around?"

"No. I'd remember."

Rita took a look, too. "I've never seen him, either."

Vicky's voice rang out from the kitchen. "Rita? These croissants are stale."

"Back to work," Zara said. "Editing calls."

"I'd better get going, too," I said. "I need to get food for tonight. Hi, Vicky! Have to run. See you tonight!"

chapter twelve

An hour later, when Zara and I set off for Watertown, I understood why people succumb to the temptation to pass off their pets as service dogs. Izzy was with us because she'd be allowed in Pignola's, but my poor dogs were stuck at home because they'd be banned from the store and because it was too hot to leave them in the car. I also understood why people rob banks, run Ponzi schemes, and otherwise acquire quick fortunes: we were in Zara's Mercedes (I sound like Quinn), which was so luxurious that merely sitting in the passenger seat made me feel like a pampered billionaire.

As Zara and I had walked home, which is to say, as we'd been running away from her mother, I'd told her that I really did have to shop for food; I hadn't just been making an excuse. She, Rita, Quinn, Vicky, Uncle Oscar, MaryJo, and Monty were all coming to our house for dinner, as was Zara and Rita's cousin John Wilson, who was going to stay at our house. I'd accepted Zara's offer to help me shop and get ready. I'd also started to tell her about Frankie Sorensen, but she'd already talked to Quinn and had been about to check Frankie out online when the photos of the would-be dog thief had arrived.

Zara and I were not headed to Pignola's because we intended to pop in for a quick visit with Enid Garabedian or because we felt drawn to the place where Frankie

Sorensen's presumably unappetizing corpse had been dragged out of the Charles River; rather, we were going to Pignola's because it's where I often shop when people are coming for dinner. As the author of a slim volume titled *101 Ways to Cook Liver*, I'm an acknowledged authority on making homemade dog treats, but my expertise in the kitchen—and everywhere else, come to think of it—begins and ends with catering to dogs. When I cook for members of my own species, that is, my *other* species, I stick to fresh, simple, or foolproof food, which is what Pignola's supplied in abundance. Tonight's menu included the same appetizers that Enid had offered us—hummus, baba ghanoush, and melted kasseri with pita; a big Greek salad; hot and sweet Italian sausages made by a little local company; and fresh fruit salad with ice cream.

Zara's car was so splendid that even the male voice on the GPS spoke in aristocratic tones, but since I knew the way to Pignola's, I persuaded her to make Lord GPS quit interrupting us by silencing him altogether.

"If it only it were this easy to turn off my mother," Zara said. "Or if she were an app, it would take seconds to remove her. Life should come with a drag-and-drop feature for moving impossible relatives to the trash."

I said, "Operant conditioning is slower than drag-and-drop, but I've used it to shape my father's behavior when he's being especially irritating. The problem is that he finds *any* attention reinforcing, and he's hard to ignore when he annoys me."

"My mother, too." In an apparent change of subject, she said, "My mother is very devoted to Uncle Oscar. She irritates him just as much as she does everyone else, but she'd do anything for him."

"And?"

"He never left the house last night, and he went downstairs and had ice cream. You know how slowly he moves. He must've been there for a while. He could've been the one who killed the burglar. Sorensen. If my mother knew that he did or thought that he did, she'd cover up for him. You know, she was gone from the restaurant for a long time."

"Take a left here," I said.

"Of course, so was I, but I was getting away from my mother. Or obeying Izzy!"

"I thought she was alerting."

"She was." Zara glanced in the rearview mirror and projected her voice. "Weren't you, good girl!"

The dog's tail beat a happy rhythm against the sides of the crate.

I said, "It was a happy day for both of you when Izzy ended up in that shelter. You want to turn right here, and then bear left at the fork."

"Was it ever my lucky day! Before, I used to dread leaving my apartment. I'd go for weeks without leaving home. Izzy won't let me stay in bed, you know. It's one of the things she's trained to do—grab onto me and drag me out of bed if I'm depressed. But she doesn't have to do that now. I *want* to get up and take her out and do things. It feels like a miracle that I can go places. Anywhere! And love it. Well, it *is* a miracle. The miracle is Izzy."

When we were passing through Watertown Square, Zara took a moment to check in with a couple of location apps, and she did the same thing when we arrived at Pignola's. Because she had no visible need for a service dog, I was a little worried that someone would challenge us about Izzy's presence or even outright refuse to let Izzy in, but no one did. As I was filling my cart, a couple of people admired Izzy and got permission to pat her. When it comes to stealing food, Labrador retrievers are almost as bad as malamutes, so I was impressed, as I'd been at Vertex, by Izzy's self-control.

Watching Izzy, I realized that if I'd slapped service-dog vests on Rowdy and Sammy, they'd have chomped their way through Pignola's. I could just see Rowdy rising up on his hind feet and shoving his face in the display of cheeses. Meanwhile, as I was trying to stop him from devouring thousands of dollars' worth of triple crème and Parmigiano-Reggiano, Sammy would've taken advantage of my preoccupation by dashing to the meat cooler and gorging himself sick on steak, sausages, and chicken. Once my beautiful boys had revealed themselves as naughty dogs rather than service dogs, I'd have been forced to pay for the cheese and meat, kicked out of the store, and subjected to well-deserved public humiliation. As it was, Izzy was a credit to all service dogs, as the social-media world got to see in the six or eight photos that Zara took and immediately posted.

When we'd finished loading the bags of food into the back of the car, Zara said, "I have a surprise for you."

"I hate waiting. Tell me."

"The burglar?"

"Frank Sorensen."

"I found his address. Or *an* address, maybe an old one. Peach Street. We're doing a drive-by."

"It better be a quick one. Most of the food is perishable."

"It's right near here." She entered an address in the GPS.

As we pulled out of the parking lot and turned left onto Pleasant Street, I said, "I was going to look online, but I got interrupted. What else did you find out?"

"Not a lot, but Waltham has police logs online, and they give people's ages and addresses. About a year ago, Frank and Gil Sorensen got arrested at a bar in Waltham. They had the same home address, the one we're going to. Frank was twenty-three. Gil was twenty-six. So, add a year. They both got charged with disorderly conduct and disturbing the peace, but Frank also got charged with assault and battery, and something about a dangerous weapon and bodily harm. He punched a guy in the head. And drug possession. Class B and Class E, whatever that means. I'll find out, and I'll look more later. I had to get back to a client. I just thought that since we were out here, we'd take a look. I'm curious to see where they lived."

Directed by the aristocratic GPS, we followed Pleasant Street into Waltham, where it changed its name to River Street. After a few turns, we arrived at a narrow side street lined with two-family and three-family houses. If my own block of Appleton Street had gone down in the world instead of up, it would've looked a lot like the block where the Sorensens lived, or had lived a year earlier. The shabby wooden houses were set close together. The paint that remained on them had faded from the original lime greens, whites, and browns to a uniformly colorless gray. Worn little aluminum awnings dangled precariously over front doors. Nourished by the summer rain, burdock, chickweed, purslane, dandelions, and crabgrass grew from cracks in the asphalt driveways, and weedy vines clambered up rusty chain-link fencing. In little patches of what had once been tiny lawns, tropical-looking vegetation reached almost alarming heights.

Peach Street, as it was called, had a strikingly inappropriate name. Peachy it was not.

"No wonder Frank turned to crime," Zara said. "The address is fifty-five."

"It's this one on the right. With the green awning. There are three mailboxes. Do you want me to get out and—"

"No!" She put her foot on the gas.

"You're right. This car is pretty distinctive. There's no reason to draw attention to ourselves. And what would we have learned? That Frank still lived there or that he didn't. Either way, so what?"

"I was just curious," Zara said.

"I wasn't being critical, Zara."

"I know."

"I was curious, too."

chapter thirteen

"Most people are going to have to eat with their plates in their laps," I told Steve. "I hope that no one minds."

"Vicky will."

We both laughed. We were in the kitchen getting ready for the arrival of our dinner guests. We'd already fed the dogs, let them out, and then cleaned and hosed down the yard, put out extra chairs, set up the grill, and otherwise converted the yard from dog space to human space.

"There's room at the picnic table for her," I said. "The food and the serving stuff can all go on the folding table. I put out real plates, not paper, and we're using real glasses, not plastic, and the wine is decent."

"Bitch?"

I laughed. "Steve, how unlike you! No, the wine isn't Bitch, but if Vicky is horrible enough, I'll open a bottle of it and present it to her as a subtle little hint."

"She was gone from Vertex longer than anyone else, wasn't she?"

"I'm not sure. I told Rita that we should make a timeline. I said that that's what you'd do. But we never got around to it. Zara showed up with the pictures of the guy trying to steal Izzy."

"A timeline's not a bad idea."

"We can't do one now. We have eight people coming for dinner."

"While they're here, we can ask them about who was where when. Who saw what. They might lie, but we can ask."

"They're our guests! We can't interrogate them or cross-examine them. And the liar in the family is supposed to be John, anyway."

"Who told you that?"

"Rita. She says that John is a harmless pathological liar. But we can leave him off your timeline. He wasn't even here."

"Or so he says."

"What do you—" I gave a belated laugh.

"Gotcha." He smiled. "Seriously, Holly, we'll do a timeline after everyone leaves. No one wants to think about it, but Oscar could have some organic condition. And Vicky could be worse than hostile. Monty—"

"Steve, we'd better stop talking about people who are going to get here any minute. We don't want to be overheard."

"Just pay attention. If anyone says anything about leaving Vertex, getting back there, whatever, just listen. And remember."

"With luck, we'll have better things to talk about," I said. "Like the wedding." Then I remembered something. Dropping my voice to a whisper, I said, "But in case someone mentions Quinn's drug samples, watch what you say about drug companies. John Wilson is a pharmaceutical company rep. A drug salesman."

"Does he sell veterinary drugs? Maybe he'll shower us with presents and take us out to dinner."

"That's just what you're not to say. And he sells human drugs, anyway. He works for one of the big companies. I forget which one."

"The perfect job for a pathological liar."

"Excellent," I said. "You know *exactly* what we can't say."

Although we'd been talking softly, I put a finger to my lips when I heard Zara and Izzy dancing down the back stairs from Rita's old apartment. When I opened the kitchen door and let them in, Zara flung her arms in the air and announced, "Editing catch of the day! Vocal *c-h-o-r-d-s* are now vocal *c-o-r-d-s*. And that's not to mention *Jell-O*, which now has a hyphen and a capital *O*."

"That's certainly cause for celebration," I said. "If you'll open that bottle of wine, we'll drink to your triumphs. Izzy, hello, good girl."

I somehow took it as a compliment that Izzy's only clothing, so to speak, was a heavily embroidered flat collar; the absence of her service-dog vest meant that Zara felt at home with us. Zara's designer jeans had the look of new denim, and her teal T-shirt had pretty scalloping and tucks, but by her standards, she, too, was dressed for home. I knelt on the floor to say another hello to Izzy, who smelled of clean dog. Her nails were short, and either Zara or a groomer had done a tiny bit of trimming to neaten her feet. As I stroked Izzy's throat, I couldn't see her teeth, but I didn't need to: I already knew that Zara brushed them every day. I suppressed the shameful thought that such meticulous grooming was wasted on a dog not destined for the show ring.

When I stood up, I saw that Zara had opened the bottle of wine but hadn't helped herself to a glass of it. Of course! She'd told me that she wasn't supposed to mix her medications with alcohol. Instead of making matters worse by apologizing, I asked, "Ginger ale? Lemonade?"

"Lemonade would be great. But I really came down here to help. Put me to work!"

The three of us spent the next five minutes ferrying appetizers and drinks to the yard. While Steve was out there starting the grill, I put the salad together, and Zara kept me company.

"Any luck finding out more about Frank Sorensen?" I asked.

"Not really. He's not on Facebook, at least not under his real name. Gil Sorensen isn't, either. Quinn gave me a list of the things that were stolen. I looked on eBay and Craigslist, but I couldn't find anything."

The back doorbell rang, but Izzy made the bell unnecessary. She started barking, bouncing, and working herself into a state of high excitement. Calm, demure Izzy?

"That'll be John," Zara shouted. "Izzy, cool it! Holly, I'll let him in."

John Wilson proved to be yet one more good-looking member of Rita and Zara's family and one more carefully groomed one, too. He was maybe five ten, with even features, short sandy hair, dark brown eyes, and a deep, even tan. He wore a starched white shirt, a yellow tie, and a lightweight suit exactly the color of his skin. As he reached out to Izzy, who had the nerve to jump on him, I noticed that his hands matched her front paws in the sense that man and dog had manicured nails. His smile showed teeth so even and white that I wondered whether they'd been capped. I reminded myself that his job as a drug-company rep probably required a polished appearance. To his credit, instead of trying to protect his light-colored suit from Izzy's paws, he grinned, put his face right in hers, and accepted her gleeful licking.

"Izzy, off!" Zara finally said. "Enough! Holly, this is John Wilson, my cousin. John, Holly Winter. You're staying here. We both are. We're all eating dinner here. Outdoors. You better change clothes. Where's your suitcase?"

With Izzy's paws back on the floor, John shook my hand and thanked me for letting him stay with us. "Just got off the plane." He went on say that he'd rented a car at Logan.

I had him move the car from the street to our driveway, and when he got back in with a rather large suitcase, I showed him to a guest room on the second floor. By the time I got back downstairs, Rita, Quinn, MaryJo, Monty, Vicky, and, somewhat to my surprise, Uncle Oscar had arrived and were all out in the yard. For the next twenty minutes or so, I was busy supplying drinks, passing around hummus and the other appetizers, and making everyone welcome.

Vicky complained that the first chair she chose was uncomfortable, and when she moved to another chair, she shifted back and forth while making a sour face. "Zara, does that dog have to be here?" she demanded. "It's not very sanitary to have a dog around while we're eating. We could all catch something."

Instead of informing her that our five big dogs played in this yard all the time, I said, "Another martini, Aunt Vicky?" *Maybe you'll get dead drunk and pass out.*

"Not quite yet, Holly, thank you. And the next time, a hint less vermouth, if you would."

Fortunately, John Wilson appeared, and the whole family, even Vicky, greeted him warmly. Izzy, instead of jumping on John, flung herself malamute fashion at his feet, and he obliged by rubbing her tummy. When John offered his congratulations to Quinn, whom he was meeting for the first time, I hoped that we'd have a happy discussion of the wedding, but as soon as John had shaken hands with MaryJo and Monty, Vicky launched into an account of the burglary and of Frank Sorensen's subsequent death.

Looking annoyed, Quinn got up and joined Steve at the grill, which was at the far end of the yard, and I went indoors for more appetizers. Returning, I noticed that Rita was pale with exhaustion, her skin white beneath her careful makeup. I wanted to do anything to make her feel better, but by then, John was asking questions about the burglary, and Vicky, MaryJo, Monty, and Zara were answering him.

"How'd he know that the house would be empty?" John asked. "Or maybe he didn't care."

With unusual energy, Uncle Oscar said, "It wasn't empty. I was there the whole time. I was upstairs in my room except when I went to the kitchen for some ice cream."

Did Uncle Oscar remember getting the ice cream? Or was he saying what he'd been told? I couldn't tell.

"To answer your question, John," Rita said, "we think that he looked on that damned Facebook."

"Blame Facebook!" Zara said. "Blame me!"

I watched Izzy, who kept her eyes on Zara but took no action.

"No one is blaming you," MaryJo said.

"I did post that we were all going to Vertex," Zara admitted. "And when we got there. And I posted some pictures. Rita, if it was my fault, I'm sorry."

"Of course it wasn't your fault," Rita said. "How were you to know?"

"Common sense," Vicky said.

"Aunt Vicky, let up," John told her. "Zara, I saw on Facebook that someone tried to steal Izzy. Could that have been the same guy?"

It was a relief to hear the idea spoken aloud. Even so, I said, "But in that case, why take Willie? Who'd mistake a Scottie for a Lab? And if it was Frank Sorensen who tried to steal Izzy, he'd already seen Izzy. He'd've known that Willie wasn't Izzy."

"The damned things all look alike to me," Vicky said.

To my annoyance, the conversation then degenerated into pointless questions and guesses about the burglary. Hadn't the neighbors seen or heard anything? Had we noticed any strangers lurking in the neighborhood? Steve said that he'd seen a woman who looked like the young Elizabeth Taylor but that she hadn't been lurking. Rita and Quinn added that since it was August, some neighbors were away on vacation. New people in our area could be house sitters and pet sitters. Also, since rentals turned over at this time of year, some strangers were bound to be new neighbors.

Dinner initially had the same happy effect on our guests as it does on our dogs, not that the dogs harp on a burglary when they're supposed to be celebrating a forthcoming wedding. But they enjoy eating, and so did our guests. John displayed what I thought was a salesperson's slickness in drawing out MaryJo and Monty, but at least he made them comfortable and got them talking about Cadillac Mountain, Otter Cliffs, and other famous spots in Acadia National Park that he said he'd loved too. With visible enthusiasm, he heard about their visit to Lexington and Concord. Steve, who was determined to like Quinn, asked him all about his new office, and I had considerable success in doling out positive reinforcement to Vicky when she exhibited target behaviors or approximations thereof, which is to say that I smiled at her, refilled her wine glass, or nodded in agreement when she addressed pleasant or neutral remarks to Zara—or even had a friendly expression when she looked at Zara.

Vicky, however, outfoxed me by redirecting her hostility elsewhere: She got in a dig at Steve and me by commenting on the informality of the meal ("How rustic!"), and she went after John Wilson about the failure of his marriage. "John had the most beautiful wife you've ever seen," she told me. "Cathy was a gorgeous, gorgeous girl. I'll never forget their wedding. There'll never be a bride more beautiful than she was."

Take that, Rita.

"And," Vicky added, "John let her get away. Didn't you, John?"

Zara, who was seated next to me, whispered in my ear. "Cathy was a drug addict and a thief. Otherwise, she was the perfect wife."

When the time came to serve dessert, I was delighted. I'd had more than enough of Vicky, who made me long to have the dogs freed from their temporary confinement. Yes, dogs sometimes raise their hackles, bare their teeth, snarl, and even fight, but they never sneak in painful gibes, and they never go out of their way to make people squirm or feel small. Given a choice between an honest growl and a devious verbal dig, I'll take the growl any day. And my dogs almost never growl.

chapter fourteen

The outside sensor for our new wireless weather station was on the picnic table when everyone except Vicky pitched in to carry the remains of dinner inside and to ferry the fruit salad, ice cream, coffee, and such outside. The weather station was a hostess gift from Zara, a present to thank Steve and me for our hospitality. She'd given it to us the previous day. Steve, who loves gadgets, had set it up and made sure that the indoor unit was reading the signals from the outdoor sensor, but we hadn't yet mounted the sensor on a wall. Instead, we'd placed it on the picnic table, which was, I suppose, a silly place to leave it, but it was definitely there when I spooned fruit salad and scooped ice cream into our bowls.

Since there was no reason to keep a close eye on the little plastic unit, I didn't, and in any case, I was soon diverted by Uncle Oscar, who amazed me by standing up and announcing, "I don't want to let the evening end without thanking Holly and Steve and without paying a tribute to my grandniece and my new grandnephew." He cleared his throat, smiled, and began to sing the romantic old song about a bicycle built for two. This from a man who'd spent most of his time in Cambridge asleep!

Anyway, with Uncle Oscar's encouragement, our whole group joined in, and so successful was the bicycle built for two that with Uncle Oscar leading us in his on-key tenor, we sang along with him for four or five other songs, including "Oh! Susanna" and "Yankee Doodle." MaryJo and Zara turned out to have lovely voices and a shared gift for singing harmony.

When Uncle Oscar launched into "Goodnight, Irene," Rita drew me aside and murmured, "Holly, I'm fading, but I don't want to spoil Uncle Oscar's show."

"He's wonderful," I said.

"He's an Italian-American Pete Seeger, isn't he? This is what he used to be like. I'm glad you're getting to see him at his best. Anyway, I'll just slip out through the kitchen. Thank you. I really appreciate everything you and Steve are doing."

She quietly made her way up the stairs to the house. When the song ended, conversation resumed, but the sense remained of the individuals having become a group. In particular, MaryJo and Zara, bonded by harmony, had an animated chat during the course of which MaryJo remarked on Zara's unusual name.

"I'm named for my mother's college roommate," Zara told her. "Is Quinn a family name? Your maiden name?"

MaryJo laughed a little nervously. "Oh, we didn't name him that. I don't know where he got it."

I did: Bob Dylan's "The Mighty Quinn."

"He was christened Ishmael," MaryJo said.

An innocent statement, huh? To say that Quinn overreacted to his mother's revelation would be a whopping understatement. Rising to his feet, he took a couple of paces and then raised his right arm, bellowed, and drove his fist into the nearest object, which happened to be the wooden fence that separates our yard from the driveway.

Because of my friendship with Rita, I understand quite a lot about the value systems of psychotherapists—less than I understand about the value systems of various dog breeds, but more than a shrink-naive person grasps, possibly because shrinks' values are weird and seemingly senseless. Dogs, I might mention, have practical and rational values. Border collies, for instance, believe in hard work and intelligence as effective means for imposing order on the universe. In the Alaskan malamute value hierarchy, food is right at the top, followed by companionship, entertainment, and frigid temperatures.

Psychotherapists, in contrast, place a high value on the expression of emotion and are never happier than when people are either crying hard or putting their feelings into words. As a general rule, smashing fists into fences is frowned upon, especially if the feeling-venter breaks his knuckles, as Quinn seemed to have done, but as Rita had explained to me, Quinn was in, I quote, "expressive psychotherapy" and was doing what she called "deep work," and he'd certainly expressed his anger clearly and unambiguously. Besides, he'd probably earned shrink value points by smashing his fist into our fence instead of into his mother's face.

Because we'd been keeping bottled water, soft drinks, and the white wine chilled, there was plenty of ice handy, and when Quinn had finished leaping around and groaning and clutching his hand to his stomach, Steve borrowed a clean white handkerchief from Uncle Oscar and fashioned an ice pack that he applied to Quinn's hand.

"I wasn't supposed to say that," MaryJo told me.

"It was a simple enough request, MaryJo," Monty said. "I don't know why you couldn't keep your trap shut."

Addressing me, MaryJo said, "I really don't understand my son at all. You won't tell Rita, will you?"

"Of course not," I said. "And there's nothing wrong with the name Ishmael." Ishmael was Abraham's son by his wife's maid, wasn't he? And once Abraham's wife, Sarah, produced a son, Isaac, trouble ensued. So, Quinn might've preferred the name Isaac to Ishmael, but not to the extent, I thought, of slamming his fist into other people's fences.

Zara said, "*Moby-Dick*."

Evidently misinterpreting the word *Dick*, MaryJo looked shocked.

"'Call me Ishmael,'" I hastened to quote. "It's the opening sentence of Herman Melville's *Moby-Dick*." Sufficient? "The book," I added. "The novel."

This little interchange took place out of Quinn's—Ishmael's?—hearing. Steve had rather forcefully led him indoors to examine the injured hand in bright light.

"We won't say anything to Rita," Zara assured MaryJo. "It should be Quinn's decision. If he doesn't want to tell Rita, we won't. Mom? John? Uncle Oscar? Promise?"

Uncle Oscar nodded.

"Of course," John said.

"Ludicrous," said Vicky. "But if that's what he wants."

"Steve won't say anything," I said, "and neither will I."

This ridiculous episode of Quinn's real name and his injured hand brought the evening to an end. Steve and Quinn decided that Quinn had bruised his knuckles but probably hadn't broken any bones and didn't need to go to an emergency room. Still, suffering more from embarrassment than from physical pain, Quinn decided to go home, and his parents, Uncle Oscar, and Vicky left with him. John and Zara wanted to help us clean up, but we let them carry only a few things from the yard to the kitchen before insisting that we'd do the rest ourselves. We said the usual things that gracious hosts say in this situation: No, no, you're our guests, it won't take us any time, and we know where everything goes, by which we meant that we could hardly wait to be rid of them so we could be alone with each other and our dogs.

To my relief, instead of hanging around, John and Zara decided to walk Izzy to Harvard Square, where they'd have a drink and maybe listen to some live music. I wondered whether Zara wanted to go to the Square to enjoy herself by being there or to acquire pictures and status updates for Facebook, but then I realized that from her viewpoint, being there and being there on Facebook were one and the same.

It was after they'd left, when Steve had moved the grill to the driveway to keep it away from the dogs and when we'd put away the food, loaded the dishwasher, and cleaned up the kitchen, that I checked the new weather station, which sat on the windowsill above the sink. "Steve? The weather station isn't showing the outdoor temperature. Damn it! If it had to break, couldn't it have waited until Zara was back in New York? Now she'll see that her present has quit working."

Steve never minds when electronic devices malfunction; he welcomes the chance to fix them. In this case, he said that the weather station probably needed to be reset, and when we went to yard with the dogs and some wine, the first thing he did was to look for the outdoor sensor.

"It was right here on the picnic table no time ago," I told him. "I noticed it when I was serving dessert."

"Well, it's not here now."

Our first thought was that John or Zara had carried it inside, but Steve insisted on looking in the kitchen even though we'd have seen the sensor when were cleaning up.

"Steve, if the sensor were in the kitchen, the indoor unit would still show a supposedly outdoor temperature, wouldn't it?"

"It should," he said. "But the indoor unit could've lost the signal. There could be a problem with either of the units."

There followed a fruitless search for the missing device. Although our outside lights provide good illumination, we used a flashlight to check under the tables and chairs, and we looked everywhere else, including in Sammy's and Rowdy's mouths. After going through the trash, Steve brought the indoor unit outside, reset it, and made it look for the signals of its missing half.

"The dogs couldn't have swallowed it," I said. "Besides, India and Lady wouldn't, and Rowdy and Sammy are too interested in the food smells to bother with a plastic box. It's what? Two inches by three inches? It wouldn't have gone down smoothly. We'd have noticed if one of them had been chewing on it. We'd have heard. It's just not here."

"Someone took it," he said. "Someone walked off with it by mistake."

"Presumably by mistake," I said. "But what could anyone mistake it for?"

We sat in silence for a few moments.

Reluctantly, I said, "Rita warned us that John was a pathological liar. You don't suppose that he's also—"

"A kleptomaniac? But we don't know that he—"

"We don't know that anyone took it. If we have to, we'll order a new one. We have better things to think about. Or worse things." Lowering my voice, I said, "Quinn. For a start, do you think that their marriage license is valid?"

"He could've gone to court to change his name."

"Maybe he did. Or maybe the license is valid even if he didn't. He wasn't pretending to be someone else. Steve, what about his medical license?"

"Holly, that's beside the point. The point is, what kind of guy gives himself a new name and keeps the old one secret from the woman he's marrying? And slams his fist into a fence when his mother lets the old name slip out? It's not normal. It's crazy."

"He's a poseur. We've known that. The affectations. Always calling his car a Lexus instead a car. Rita has to notice how pretentious he is. I know that she does. But she wants to marry him anyway. She loves him, and I think that he loves her, at least to the extent that he can. Besides, he saved Kimi's life. Without him, she could have bled to death. Steve, I think that his feeling for Rita and for the baby is genuine. God, I hope so."

Steve refilled our wine glasses. For a few minutes, we watched the dogs. Rowdy and Sammy ran figure eights around the yard before running up to me for neck massages and gentle thumps on the flanks. Imitating the Sphinx, India lay on the ground with her eyes on Steve, and love-hungry Lady nuzzled him and begged for pats even when he was petting her.

Eventually, Steve said, "You know, Holly, Quinn took an awful long time to get to Vertex. Those were his wedding presents, his and Rita's, and it's their house."

"And his drug samples. Rowdy, Sammy is my beloved dog, too, so please don't shove him away. He could've felt guilty about leaving the samples just lying around. And if Quinn picked up a poker and smashed someone over the head with it—"

"It would be just like him not to admit it. But Quinn was alone there—except for Uncle Oscar—just after we left, when it wasn't all that dark out. Wouldn't a burglar wait until later? But maybe not. There *are* daytime burglaries."

Steve excused himself and returned with a notebook computer.

"The dreaded timeline," I said.

"I'm a systematic guy." He gave me that smile of his.

"You have the cutest smile."

Ignoring me, he entered information in his timeline. "Seven twenty. All of us except Quinn and Oscar left. We got to Vertex at maybe seven thirty. Quinn must've walked faster than our whole group did, so he left the house at seven forty."

"So Quinn was alone there, except for Uncle Oscar, from seven twenty to seven forty. What was he doing for twenty minutes?"

"Vicky'd been nagging everyone about checking on Oscar, and Quinn said he'd do it."

"I remember," I said. "Yes. When Quinn volunteered to check on Oscar, I remember thinking that he'd been stuck with Vicky on the way home from airport and that he wanted an excuse to get a break from her. Who could blame him?"

"Not me," Steve said. "Okay, so at seven forty-five, we were all at Vertex. Who left first? Zara?"

"Yes. Vicky was being worse than ever, so Izzy alerted. And then Zara left."

"To come here and get her Nikon."

Instead of saying that I'd seen the Nikon in her purse when we'd been walking to Rita and Quinn's, I said, "And right after that, immediately, I think, Monty got up."

"To go to the men's room," Steve said. "He asked me where it was."

"Where is it? The ladies' is in the cellar."

"In the back. It's down a corridor, near the kitchen."

"He was gone a long time," I said. "Fifteen minutes? About that. Just about long enough to go to Rita and Quinn's, discover the burglar, attack him, and get back to Vertex."

"That would be cutting it close. And why would Monty have gone back there at all?"

"I have no idea. Why else was he gone for so long?"

Steve shrugged. After keyboarding for a few seconds, he said, "So, Monty got back to our table at eight fifteen. Zara wasn't there for another fifteen minutes. She left at eight and didn't get back until eight thirty. Now *that's* a long time."

"Not for someone who's escaping a mother like Vicky. And maybe she left to get medication of some kind and waited for it to kick in."

"She'd have had it with her," Steve said, "and it wouldn't work that fast."

"If Zara had done it, she'd have taken pictures and posted them on Facebook." I shifted his focus. "Vicky left as soon as Zara got back. Remember? She said that someone had to check on Uncle Oscar. And she was gone maybe twenty minutes."

Staring at the computer screen and typing, he said, "Vicky returns at eight forty-five."

"Or later," I said. "She had enough time. Well, if she hurried. And then Monty left Vertex for good at about nine fifteen, and the rest of us had dessert and left maybe fifteen minutes later. No, more than that. We had dessert, and Quinn paid the bill. And then Zara walked Izzy, and you and I went home. It would've taken Rita and Quinn and Vicky and MaryJo maybe ten minutes to walk home. So Monty had plenty of time to grab the poker and hit the burglar."

"And then he stood there and watched the burglar walk out or stagger out with everything that got stolen?"

"Well, if you put it that way—"

"What other way is there to put it?"

"Steve, this timeline is a waste of time. It's a waste-of-timeline. All it really shows is what we knew all along, and that's that the person who was in the house all along was—"

"Oscar."

"Uncle Oscar," I said.

chapter fifteen

When I took out the trash the next morning, I caught sight of Elizabeth McNamara, who lives in the house next to Rita and Quinn's. Instead of just waving hello, Elizabeth hailed me, and when I'd made my way to her driveway, she said, "Holly, could you do me a favor?"

"Of course," I said. "Do you need help getting something to your car?"

Elizabeth was a pure Cambridge type of the old school, even to the extent of driving a venerable Volvo station wagon. The Volvo's tailgate was open, and the interior was packed with two medium-size Vari Kennels, a couple of suitcases, a variety of cardboard boxes, and a big Styrofoam cooler. Elizabeth had her two pulis on leash. Well, the Hungarian plural is *pulik*, but since my entire Hungarian vocabulary consists of the names of dog breeds—kuvasz, komondor, vizsla—it's a bit affected to burst into apparently fluent Hungarian when all I'm doing is referring to my neighbor's dogs. In fact, it's exactly the sort of thing Quinn would do.

Anyway, pulis, aka pulik, are medium-size herding dogs of Hungarian origin notable for their long corded coats, and Elizabeth's adult puli, Persimmon, had a splendidly corded black coat, whereas the darling little black male was too young to have grown the dreadlocks he'd eventually sport. Elizabeth herself, a petite woman, had a lovely human version of a coat, namely, beautiful curly white hair. On this drizzly morning, her hair looked even fuller and curlier than usual, and the dampness made her pale skin dewy. On her feet were fair-trade flats hand-embroidered by artisan women in Mexico, as I happened to know because I'd seen the same shoes on Facebook. Most of Elizabeth's clothing and accessories, including her bright blue scarf and silver earrings, had been handcrafted in Third World countries, but her yellow rain slicker was from good old L.L. Bean.

"Thank you, Holly," she said. "Everything's in the car except Persimmon and The Baby." The puppy presumably had another name, but I'd never heard it. "I'm going to Vermont for a week, and I wondered whether you and Steve could just be aware that I'm gone. I've set the alarm, and someone's dealing with the mail, but could you keep your eyes open? With a burglary right next door—"

Persimmon nuzzled my hand, and I petted her. She and I were friends.

"Of course. I walk the dogs by here all the time, and I'm at Rita's a lot."

Elizabeth collected quilts, and she and her late husband, Isaac, had amassed a big and undoubtedly valuable collection of folk art. It occurred to me that her house would've been a more lucrative target for a burglar than Rita and Quinn's had been.

"I'm a little unnerved," Elizabeth said. "I was home when the burglar was there. The dogs and I were in and out of the yard."

"Did you hear anything?"

"I didn't pay much attention. There are people staying with Rita, so I just assumed that anyone there was one of her guests."

"You know that Willie was stolen? Or let loose? He ended up in Watertown. It's not clear how."

"Rita told me. And the burglar is dead, poor thing. Rita is such a dear person, isn't she! She's upset that he died."

"She is a dear person," I agreed. "Elizabeth, did you happen to hear Willie bark that night?"

"A couple of times. I noticed because when he's healthy, he's a good watchdog, and I thought to myself, 'Well, Willie's feeling like himself again!'"

"Do remember what time?"

"Eightish, I think. Then a couple of times right after that."

"And later? Eight thirty? Nine?"

"Not that I remember. But I might not have noticed. I'm used to a little barking." She smiled at Persimmon and The Baby. "It doesn't bother me. Not the way bad language does." She lowered her voice. "I'm not blaming Rita and Quinn. We can't choose our relatives, and a wedding is a wedding. Sometimes they have to be invited, like it or not."

"Yes," I agreed. "But I haven't heard them swearing."

"Well, you won't hear me repeat what I overheard. And that woman! The one with the high-pitched voice." Elizabeth shook head. "The way it carries!"

I nodded. "Did you hear her that night? Two nights ago?"

To my surprise, Elizabeth said, "Talking to her boyfriend. At her age! I was disgusted. I won't repeat what she said, either."

"Elizabeth, she's married. She's been married for a long time."

"Is her husband's name Al?"

"It's Dave," I said.

"Well," said Elizabeth, "there you go."

chapter sixteen

If the people in question hadn't been Rita's father and her aunt, Rita would have been the first person I'd have told about Elizabeth's revelation. As it was, I had to settle for Steve, who is useless for what he dismisses as girl talk. There is, however, no one more useful than Steve when it comes to cutting dogs' nails. When I got home, he and Rowdy were sitting companionably on the kitchen tile, and as I told Steve all about my conversation with Elizabeth, he casually clipped every one of Rowdy's nails—Rowdy's *black* nails—without using treats and without quicking even one nail. Damn! I like to imagine that I'm the dog maven in the family, but Steve is the one with X-ray vision, the one who sees the invisible vein in a black nail and never cuts into it. I can trim nails, but I can't do it effortlessly. Still, despite his nail-trimming gift, he was a captive audience.

"Vicky and Al!" I exclaimed. "You want some coffee?" I put on the kettle. "No? Vicky and Al! Steve, that horrible woman is having an affair with Rita's father. And you know what?" I didn't wait for an answer. "And Uncle Oscar knows. I'm sure he does. I thought that he was confused, but he isn't. Steve, what I heard from Uncle Oscar is that Vicky and Al dated before Al married Erica." I got out a mug and measured my favorite coffee, Bustelo, into a filter.

"Maybe you should have herbal tea instead," Steve said. "Or milk."

"Am I going too fast for you? Erica is Rita's mother. Vicky's sister. Al, Rita's father, went out with Vicky, but he married Erica. And Vicky married Dave. Zara's father. Erica and Al. Vicky and Dave. Or so I thought! And I thought that Uncle Oscar was vague and disoriented. Disoriented in time. Confusing the present with the past. But he isn't. He's right. The old romance has rekindled. What a mess!"

"Soap opera," Steve said. "Oh, Quinn called. The story he's telling Rita is that he burned his hand moving the grill. And Zara found a picture of Frank Sorensen online. She sent the link. It's a group picture of hockey players."

"Waltham! Yes, hockey's big in Waltham and Watertown. There's a rink right near Pignola's."

"She thinks he's the same guy who tried to steal Izzy."

"John asked about that. And I've wondered. But I still don't understand why he'd take Willie if he'd already seen Izzy. Could Zara be wrong? Maybe she wants to think that it was Frank Sorensen. If so, then the guy who tried to steal Izzy is dead, and she doesn't need to worry that he'll try again."

"Like I said, it's not some close-up picture of his face. She could be seeing what she wants to see."

I nodded. "That's what Rita will think. And it probably doesn't matter." Then I resumed my narrative, which was of more interest to me than it was to Steve. "Elizabeth was scandalized. And shocked." I made my coffee and took a seat at the table. "Rowdy, your feet look very handsome. You're a good boy. Elizabeth has led a sheltered life. She wouldn't repeat what Vicky said. It was graphic, I guess."

"Did Elizabeth hear anything else?"

"Oh, she thinks that Willie barked a couple of times at about eight o'clock. She can't remember hearing him after maybe eight fifteen, but she's not sure. She's used to barking."

The phone rang. Caller ID read TREEN, TABITHA, but it might as well have read THE PEST, TABITHA. Still, shame on me. Tabitha is a fundamentally decent person who just happens to be obsessed with dogs. Well, yes, you could say the same about me. People probably have. Probably? They have.

"Tabitha," I told Steve. "I might as well get this over with. She never gives up. Hello?"

"Holly? I have to tell you that that horrible woman Cathy Brown has been spotted near Boston, and I want you to keep an eye out for her. I sent you a picture. Remember?"

What I remembered was a picture so blurry that no one could have identified anyone from it. "Yes," I said. "Did someone identify her from the picture?"

"No. You see, I sent that awful couple to Esme Ellis's puppy kindergarten. You know Esme, don't you? Very nice dogs. She breeds my lines. She teaches at a training center right near where they lived, in New Jersey, and I have to tell you, Esme could not say enough good things about my lovely puppy, Cheyenne, but those people just brought her there twice, and then they dropped out, and Esme was at a shopping mall right near you—her daughter lives in Lexington, is it? Concord?—and Esme saw that horrible Cathy there. The Burlington Mall. That's where it was. And when Esme went up to this horrible Cathy, she, Cathy, took one look and hightailed it. So, I want you keep your eyes open for her."

As I hadn't had a chance to say, I did know Esme Ellis, who was a reliable person. If Esme had said that she'd recognized the woman, then she had. Esme, of course, had met her, whereas I'd seen nothing more than a useless photo. "Tabitha," I said firmly, "the Burlington Mall isn't all that near Cambridge. I've driven by it, but I don't go there. A lot of people do shop there, though, people from all over the place. There's no reason to believe that this Cathy—"

"Holly, you need to take another look at that picture. I'll send it to you again. I want you to memorize her face. It just makes me sick to my stomach not to know where my baby is. Holly, I need you to help."

"I'll keep my eyes open." The promise was sincere. I'm not in the habit of wandering around with my eyes closed.

chapter seventeen

An hour later, when I'd called Leah to make sure that Kimi was all right, Zara and I were at the kitchen table searching eBay for the stolen wedding presents and finding nothing. Izzy and Rowdy were enjoying rainy-morning snoozes at our feet, and Sammy, who'd also had a pedicure, was dozing in the kitchen crate. Steve was out in the rain walking India and Lady.

"Little Frankie must've stashed—" Zara started to say when Steve, India, and Lady burst through the back door followed by Rita and Quinn. Before anyone said a word, I knew that there was a crisis: Quinn's hair showed signs of having had hands run through it, and although both Rita and Quinn were wearing rain coats, Rita hadn't bothered to protect her coiffure from the weather. Her agitation had evidently squelched her morning sickness: her complexion was more red than green.

"Uncle Oscar, the old rascal!" Rita exclaimed. "John isn't here?"

"He hasn't come down yet," I said. "I guess he's still asleep. Or maybe he's in the shower."

"Sleep," Rita said. "That brings us to the reason for this visit. Did anyone notice how awake Uncle Oscar was last night?"

"Wouldn't you like to sit down?" I suggested. "We'll get another chair from the dining room, or we could all move into the living room." Our kitchen is smaller than I'd like, too small for five people and five dogs. Rowdy must've shared my opinion. Instead of getting up to say hello to Rita and Quinn, he remained under the table. "Would you like coffee? Herbal tea?"

"Holly, please stop playing hostess," Rita said. "I asked whether anyone had noticed how lively Uncle Oscar was last night."

"He was charming," I said.

Zara looked up from her laptop. "He was his old self."

"Drugs," Rita said.

"Provigil," Quinn added. "He helped himself to my samples."

I laughed.

Rita glared at me. "He read the patient-information insert in the little box."

"That's the drug the police found. The one the burglar stole." I felt oddly reluctant to utter the word *body*. "Isn't that the drug that keeps people awake? I don't know why you're so upset. Uncle Oscar read the insert and realized that it might be good for him. He took it. It worked." I paused. "He *is* okay, isn't he?"

Rita was unforgiving. "Holly, this is no time for frivolity."

"All I did was ask whether he was all right."

"As a matter of fact," Rita admitted, "he's asleep."

"The point," Quinn said, "is that it's a prescription drug that shouldn't be used without supervision, especially in someone his age."

"It's like the billboards," Zara commented. "You know? Teens who abuse prescription drugs usually get them from family members. We could do a new billboard. Ancient uncles who abuse prescription drugs—"

Rita cut her off: "It's not funny, Zara."

"It's just Uncle Oscar's little foible," Zara said quietly. "Don't worry about it." She returned her attention to her laptop.

"The little foible," Quinn said, "is kleptomania."

Rita corrected him. "It isn't kleptomania. He never shoplifts."

"That we know of," Zara said.

"A sterling-silver serving spoon," Quinn said. "Tiffany Audubon."

Rita was dismissive. "That was ours. Which reminds me, Quinn. We need to remove it from the list we gave to the police."

I remembered seeing Uncle Oscar pocketing the pods for Rita and Quinn's coffeemaker. "K-cups for your Keurig? But maybe there's a coffeemaker in his room."

"There isn't," Quinn said.

"We're hardly going to begrudge Uncle Oscar a few cups of coffee," Rita told him.

"An earring of my mother's," Quinn countered. "My Mont Blanc pen. Loose change. Bose headphones."

"I wondered where those had gone," Zara said. "And the loose change might be his."

"Chanel sunglasses," Quinn said.

"Oh," said Zara, "that must've been when we were driving up here. I thought they'd fallen out of the car at a rest stop."

Rita smiled at Quinn. "You see? He's just a harmless magpie."

"Magpies," said Quinn, "are kleptomaniacs."

"There's no need to pathologize a little quirk," Rita said.

To interrupt the diagnostic dispute, I asked, "How did he get caught?"

"The cleaning service was changing his sheets," Rita said. "He'd put his little treasures under the mattress. The cleaners told us."

"They didn't want to be accused of stealing," Quinn said pointedly.

"And how," I asked, "did Uncle Oscar react?"

Rita was horrified. "He'd be so ashamed!"

"Mortified," Zara agreed. "We always just reclaim our belongings."

"And return other people's," Rita finished. I had the dizzying sense of being whirled around in the vortex of a family madness. "But we're very upset about the Provigil," Rita continued. "That could've been serious."

Quinn seconded her. "Fatal."

"We need you to make sure that he couldn't possibly have access to any other prescription drugs. All of you." She fixed her gaze on Zara.

I'd been about to say that Steve and I didn't have any prescription drugs in the house, but to avoid embarrassing Zara, I said nothing.

"We're warning everyone," Quinn said tactfully.

"We'll be careful," Zara said. "And we'll tell John."

Having warned us to keep prescription drugs away from Uncle Oscar, Rita and Quinn were about to leave when the back doorbell rang. Steve got the door and ushered in Vicky, Monty, and MaryJo.

As if she'd read my mind, Vicky said, "We won't stay! We're going to the Gardner Museum. John's driving." With undisguised pride, she added, "We texted each other a few minutes ago. He won't need any breakfast. We're going to have lunch at the Gardner. Brunch. *Texted*. Do I have that right, Zara?"

Vicky wore what I suspected was a genuine Burberry trench coat. Monty was sensibly garbed in a black raincoat. Half his size, MaryJo wore turquoise plastic and clutched her big black patent-leather purse to her middle as if she suspected that one of us might snatch it.

Zara ignored her mother, who said, "Does anyone want to come with us? Monty and MaryJo didn't know what the Gardner was. Can you imagine? Holly, maybe you don't know, either."

Condescending bitch. I didn't say so, and Izzy didn't say so, either, at least not in English, but she rose from the floor and stationed herself at Zara's left side, her eyes on Zara's face.

Before I could think of a polite way to say that I'd been to the Gardner Museum many times, John appeared from upstairs. "Good morning, Holly, Steve, Zara. Sorry I kept you waiting, Aunt Vicky, MaryJo, Monty."

I wondered whether the pharmaceutical company trained its representatives to utter people's names as often as possible. Clean-shaven, freshly showered, John was dressed with the kind of casual elegance you see in ads for high-end menswear. His slickness obviously didn't grate on Izzy's nerves the way it did on mine. At the sound of his voice, she left her post at Zara's side, woofed, and, wiggling all over, did her best to run to John, who was making his way past the table toward Vicky, MaryJo, and Monty.

By then, there were nine people and five dogs in the kitchen. The combined body heat and the moisture emanating from those who'd been out in the rain made the air feel tropical. Although India and Lady were, as always, clean, they nonetheless gave off the distinct odor of wet dog, a scent that Vicky's strong perfume, John's cologne, and Monty's usual minty scent failed to mask. The lingering smells of breakfast and coffee added to the miasma. I felt queasy and suffocated. All color had drained from Rita's face. My own discomfort and my sympathy for Rita may explain my inaction.

Also, Vicky, Monty, MaryJo, and John were about to leave, to be followed promptly, I assumed, by Rita and Quinn. Vicky was buttoning the top button of her trench coat, and MaryJo had balanced her big purse on the edge of the table to leave her hands free to pull up her hood.

For whatever reason, I did nothing to stop Izzy's effort to dash to John, who had reached the back door and had his hand on the doorknob, nor was I quick enough to prevent Rowdy from barreling after her. More alert than I was, Steve was shepherding India and Lady out of the crowded kitchen when in her determination to reach John, Izzy slammed into a corner of the table and knocked MaryJo's big black patent-leather purse off balance and onto the tile floor.

Pandemonium! First the gunshot, and then screaming, shrieking, bellowing and barking. And the source of that gunshot? Who the hell expects a harmless little bird of a woman like MaryJo Youngman to go around with an ancient single-action revolver in her purse? And a loaded single-action revolver at that? Fully loaded: all six chambers. Not me! And I grew up in Maine, where a lot of people are armed—with hunting rifles, shotguns, and modern handguns that don't discharge when they're dropped, which is to say, almost all handguns.

But I've leapt ahead of myself. When the purse hit the floor, MaryJo and Monty must've immediately realized that her ridiculous, outmoded, dangerous Wyatt Earp-style revolver had gone off, but the rest of us were more focused on the effect than on the cause, the principal effect being a bleeding wound in Vicky's right calf. At first, I didn't even realize that Vicky had been shot. She was screaming, but so were Rita and Zara. Quinn was swearing, and Monty was shouting at MaryJo, who was crying. Izzy was jumping around and barking. And from his crate, Sammy was adding to the noise by imitating Izzy's woofs and emitting his own yips and yowls.

The gunshot must have registered on me as just that, a gunshot, but all I can remember from those first few seconds is the sound of the shot reverberating in my ears; and a frantic need to get my hands on Rowdy, who was in the middle of the commotion, and to assure myself that Sammy, Steve, India, and Lady were safe. Steve, who is blessed with a calm temperament and is used to emergencies, finished the task of removing India and Lady from the kitchen.

A glance at Sammy showed me that he was unhurt: he'd risen to his feet and was pawing at the door of his wire crate. In my terror that Rowdy had been injured, I momentarily forgot the million hours that he and I had spent working on a reliable recall, but when I discovered that Rita and Quinn were unintentionally blocking my route to Rowdy, I finally sang out, "Rowdy, come!" And guess what? The handsome boy took a shortcut under the table and even had the presence of mind to sit directly in front of me. The dog is sang-froid personified. Caninified? Dogified? He is too cool for words, even too cool for invented words.

When Steve returned, he quietly took charge. First, perhaps unnecessarily, he warned everyone to stay away from MaryJo's purse. Then, he said, "Zara, it'd be a good idea for you to take Izzy upstairs and spend some time with her. Low-key time. John, maybe you could go with them. Holly, you need to crate Rowdy in the dog room, and then take Sammy there." The dog room is a former guestroom that's right near the kitchen. It has big crates for all our dogs and also provides storage for dog supplies. "Rita, MaryJo, Monty, let's clear some space here. You could go to the living room, and Quinn and I'll see what we can do for Vicky."

By the time I'd crated Rowdy in the dog room and had returned to the kitchen for Sammy, no one was there except Steve, Quinn, and Vicky, who was moaning. She'd taken a seat, and Steve had our big first-aid kit open on the table. Quinn was kneeling in front of her.

"It's just a graze," Quinn said.

Vicky slammed a fist on the table. "I want a doctor!"

"I *am* a doctor," he reminded her.

Resilient creature that he is, Sammy *woo*ed at me when I opened his crate and snapped a leash onto his collar, and as I led him to the dog room, he bounced merrily along. After I'd crated him there, I got a big handful of liver treats, doled them out to everyone, and took a careful look at India and Lady. I don't want to malign Sammy and Rowdy by suggesting that they're insensitive—they aren't—but they're malamutes, and malamutes are tough. Although the German shepherd also has a reputation for toughness, I think that it's a reputation based more on Hollywood than on reality.

In any case, India notices everything and takes everything seriously. When worry is warranted, India worries. Our timid little pointer, Lady, scares easily. Fortunately, though, she draws strength from India, to whom she looks for direction. I took a moment to speak reassuringly to India and Lady, and I gave Lady a few extra treats, too. A highly stressed dog will usually refuse food, all food, even liver. When Lady accepted her treats, I felt relieved.

As I passed through the kitchen on my way to the living room, Steve said, "An antique revolver." He shook his head.

"No longer loaded, I hope," I said.

He nodded.

In the living room, I found Rita sitting rigidly upright in the middle of the couch, with Monty and MaryJo seated facing each in the chairs at either end of the couch—and not just facing each other, but facing off.

"What did you think you were doing?" Monty demanded. "You could've killed someone."

MaryJo was tearful but defiant. "I've heard terrible things about big cities. I've never been in one before."

"The most dangerous person in this city was you," her husband informed her. "That revolver is an antique."

"I know it's an antique! It's a valuable antique. I saw one just like it on *Antiques Roadshow*. It belonged to *my* great-grandfather, didn't it? And it's the only one I own. The others are all yours."

At an evident loss for words, Monty uttered only one: "Loaded."

"Well, what good would it do otherwise?"

In tones of cold reason, he asked, "For this whole trip, MaryJo? You've been carrying it around in your pocketbook this whole trip?"

"Just when I was going to be on city streets. Most of the time it was in my suitcase."

"Loaded."

"No. Monty, I do know how to load and unload it, you know."

"MaryJo, everyone knows that you know how to load it. We've seen the results of that."

In a pitiful little voice, MaryJo directed a question to Rita and me as well as to Monty. "Are they going to arrest me?"

"If the police were going to show up," I said, "they'd be here by now. Your purse muffled the sound, I think. Anyway, a sound like that could've been a car backfiring. And our neighbors on both sides of us are on vacation."

Rita finally spoke. "How is Aunt Vicky?"

"Quinn says it's just a graze," I reported.

"Good. Then I would like to go home and go to bed and fall asleep and wake up and find that this entire morning was nothing but a nightmare." She rose to her feet. "Holly, I can't even begin to apologize. I don't even know where to start."

Monty took his cue from Rita. "Our apologies." To my surprise, after standing up, he lumbered over to me, engulfed my hands in his, squeezed, and said, "God bless you and Steve. We'll pray for you. Won't we, MaryJo?"

She nodded.

I didn't care whether or not she prayed for us. I just wanted her to leave. In fact, I wanted everyone to go away, everyone except Steve and the dogs. I wanted to go away myself. The thought even crossed my mind of hustling Rowdy and Sammy into my car, driving to Maine, and staying there until the wedding was over and all of Rita's and Quinn's relatives except Zara and Uncle Oscar had gone home. Steve, however, would've refused to go with me, and I simply couldn't abandon Rita.

chapter eighteen

The best cure for a reeling head is a long walk with a strong dog. Fresh air, aerobic exercise, great company, and love! Steve said that one walk in the rain had been enough for him and that he wanted to repair the damage that MaryJo's bullet had done to one of our kitchen cabinets.

"A purification rite," I said.

As if to confirm Rita's frequent statement that Steve is not psychologically minded, he said, "No. I just want to fix the cabinet." Given a choice between a husband who psychologizes about purification and a husband who fixes cabinets, I'd pick Steve any day.

Although I'd have liked Rowdy's company, he is convinced that rain is the liquid form of mustard gas, a chemical-warfare agent hurled downward by ancient Arctic gods who are targeting Alaskan malamutes. Consequently, he takes pains never to expose himself to it. Nothing much bothers Sammy, who was happy to see his red dog pack, in which I stowed bottles of water, a folding water bowl, clean-up bags, and—in case we encountered loose aggressive dogs—an aerosol boat horn and a can of citronella spray.

Because the mustard gas, uh, pardon me, rain was still pelting down, I wore rain pants as well as a hooded rain jacket, and I put on hiking boots instead of running shoes.

I'd decided that instead of taking one of our familiar home-based routes through Cambridge, Sammy and I would pick up the river walk in Watertown and hike upriver along the Charles. The industrial, light-industrial, and formerly industrial area bore no resemblance to the Maine coast, where I longed to go, but the river trail was less obviously urban than were the streets of Cambridge and would support the illusion that I was getting away.

If I were a better person than I am, I'd have invited Zara and Izzy to accompany us, but as it turned out, fate forced me to issue the invitation: just as I was crating Sammy in my car, Zara and Izzy came down the steps to the driveway, and I had to ask Zara whether they wanted to come along, as they did. Because they'd been setting out for a walk anyway, Zara was dressed in a yellow rain slicker and matching rain boots, and Izzy wore her service-dog vest. In no time, we'd crated Izzy next to Sammy, whom Zara mistook for Rowdy.

Although I liked Zara, I felt a little irritated, not because Zara confused Rowdy and Sammy, but because I'd wanted to be alone with Sammy, and I was aching to burn off tension by moving at his exhausting pace. Even though Zara was a young, fit dog walker with a young, fit dog, I was convinced that Sammy and I would have to slow down to avoid outdistancing them. As if to prove me right, the first thing Zara did when she got into my car was to pull out her phone, question me about our destination, and then tell all of her social-network friends what we were up to. I envisioned a hike interrupted every two minutes by Zara's need to record and broadcast our progress.

Still, as we left my neighborhood and headed toward Watertown, Zara put away the phone, and I felt reconciled to human company. Neither Izzy nor Zara, I was happy to hear, had been traumatized by the gunshot or the ensuing chaos. Steve, Zara told me, had gone upstairs to check on her and had filled her in on what had happened.

"Izzy takes things in stride," Zara said. "That's one reason she's such a great service dog."

A perfect service dog would have stayed next to Zara instead of zooming across the crowded kitchen to get to John and thus accidentally precipitating the fiasco, but I didn't say so. In most ways, Izzy was a terrific service dog. Besides, if MaryJo's handbag had contained nothing more than the usual collection of cash, credit cards, cosmetics, and assorted junk, the consequences of Izzy's deviation from service-dog perfection would have been negligible.

"Are your dogs all right?" Zara asked.

"They're fine. Their ears are probably ringing, but the dogs didn't understand the significance of what happened. And what *could* have happened."

"Lucky dogs! Who would've thought that MaryJo was Pistol-Packin' Mama?"

I laughed. "Not her husband, for one. Monty is furious at her."

"What on earth was she thinking?"

"That big cities are dangerous."

Having spent a record five minutes or so without using an electronic device, Zara again extracted her phone from one of the capacious pockets of her slicker and busied herself with it. "We're right near a place called Eastern Something Bakers. It has great reviews."

"Eastern Lamejun," I said. "Yes, it's great. Lamejuns are Armenian pizzas, more or less."

Far be it from Zara to ignore an online recommendation; we just had to take a little detour. In spite of the rain, the day was fairly hot, so to avoid leaving Sammy in the car, I waited while Zara got Izzy out and ran into the store.

Returning with a large bag, Zara put Izzy back in the car, got into the passenger seat, and said, "I didn't get anything perishable except some feta for our lunch. The lamejuns are frozen, so they should be okay, and I got pita bread and olives."

"Well done." I had no doubt that she'd checked into Foursquare, too, and had updated her Facebook status by reporting on her whereabouts and her purchases. I wondered whether she'd already described the events of the morning but decided to find out later when I took at look at Facebook myself.

"Before Izzy, I might've had a hard time doing that," Zara said. "Simple thing, huh? Check out an ethnic bakery. Buy a few things. Nothing to it. *Now* there's nothing to it. Izzy, you are the best!"

Miraculously, we made it to the parking lot just beyond Watertown Square without having a cyber-power command us to stop at any five-star destination. Although Zara must have been as aware as I was that Frank Sorensen's body had been pulled from the river somewhere nearby, neither of us mentioned the significance of our location. Because that parking area served an outdoor pool as well as the riverside trail, it was usually full in the summer, but the rain had kept swimmers and trail-users home, and I had no trouble finding a space. When we got the dogs out, I delayed us by fastening Sammy's red pack and going through the tedious business of shifting gear back and forth between the saddlebags to balance the pack. Zara took pictures of Sammy, Izzy, and me and instantly posted them who knows where, possibly everywhere, online.

As we set out, neither Izzy nor Sammy showed any sign of residual stress from the events of the morning; on the contrary, they were both eager to move, as I was myself. The rain had tapered to foggy mist. The vivid colors of Zara's yellow slicker, Izzy's matching vest, and Sammy's red pack popped out of the gray-green background.

The sight of Zara and the dogs, so bright and healthy and beautiful, impelled me to apologize to Zara for our surroundings. "I should've warned you that this trail isn't exactly Central Park."

"It's fine."

"It's all weeds."

Flourishing to our left, to our right, behind us, and ahead of us were tall weeds, short weeds, weedy trees, weedy brush, weedy vines, weeds of all sorts, weeds great and small. The ground between the path and the river was thick with dense vegetation and unpruned trees, some listing at weird angles, some bending over to dip themselves into the river, which was swollen and muddy from the rain.

Zara was kind. "I have a friend who gathers weeds in Central Park. She says that they're food. And medicinal herbs."

I laughed. "I have friend like that, too. She'd turn this stuff into ointment or make wine with it. That's elderberry over there, I think. But there's probably not a lot you can do with wild morning glory. Zara, don't touch that! There's poison ivy in there."

The lower stretch of the Charles, where it separates Boston from Cambridge, is wide and impressive. Here, it was a river, not some piddling stream, but it looked unimportant and dirty; and the ugly white cinderblock pool building, the trashy vegetation, and an abundance of rusty chicken-wire fences combined to create a rubbishy gestalt worse than the sum of its unappealing parts. Why had I brought us here when we could easily have gone to Harvard Yard?

Beyond a footbridge that crossed the river, the trail took us close to a small cove thick with lily pads and the foulest of fowl, Canada geese. Although no sensible person who has ever set foot on ground made slimy and revolting by a flock of Canada geese ever feeds those damned birds, a short man carrying three big white plastic shopping bags was on the bank tossing torn-up pieces of bread into the water. The geese were squabbling among themselves, snatching up the bread, and gobbling it down. I thought of Ecclesiastes: "Cast thy bread upon the waters;

for thou shalt find it after many days." Well, after many days, this bread wouldn't be recognizable as such, but the defecatory habits of Canada geese being what they are, the unfortunate feet of thee and everyone else would be doomed to find this bread again, and in no time at all.

The man, who was facing the geese, wore baggy jeans so long that they brushed the muddy ground, and a lime-green rubberized rain jacket. The hood was down, and his hair was plastered to his head. As we approached, he turned to us, and my attitude softened. His round face showed the distinctive signs of Down syndrome. His smile was pure joy. Gesturing to the geese with one bag-laden hand, he said loudly, "They're hungry."

All thoughts of goose droppings forgotten, I smiled back. "They like you to feed them."

The quarreling geese had attracted the attention of both dogs. Izzy, I suspected, was more eager to plunge in and take a swim than she was to chase the birds. Sammy, however, had gone rigid all over, his predator's eye fixed on the geese and, secondarily, I thought, on their doughy snack. I could almost hear him order lunch: *I'll have the raw, feathery goose special, please, with a side of sodden bread.*

"Leave it," I told him.

The man transferred his attention from the geese to the dogs. Pointing at Izzy, the gentlest of animals, he said hoarsely, "Black dogs bite! Don't touch!"

The reaction was odd: Sammy was big and substantial, and to people more familiar with movie depictions than with Northern breeds, malamutes look like wolves. In contrast, Labs look harmless, and the public perception of the breed is benign.

I started to correct him. "Not this black—"

Quicker than I was, Zara said, "Some black dogs do bite. I guess you know one who does. We'll go ahead."

"We'll catch up with you," I told her.

Once Izzy was out of sight, the man turned his attention to Sammy. The beautiful smile reappeared.

Carefully setting his bags on the ground, he stretched out both hands.

"Would you like to pat him?" I asked. "He's friendly. His name is Sammy. Come over here. We don't want Sammy to eat the bread."

"For the geese."

I nodded. "Not for dogs."

Still holding both hands out, the man approached. Now that he had stopped casting bread upon the waters, the geese had settled down, so Sammy shifted out of predator mode. His plumy white tail sailing over his back, his dark eyes gleaming, an honest-to-dog smile on his face, he took slow, small steps toward the man, who shoved a clenched fist in front of Sammy's black nose. Instead of sniffing, Sammy responded by scouring the hand with his big pink tongue. The man's eyes widened, and he silently opened his mouth as if he expected words to flow out on their own. Then he burst into laughter that intensified when Sammy added his own peals of *woo-woo-woo*.

"Sammy likes you." Why say what my dog had just said? "It's okay to pat him."

The man held out his other hand and thumped Sammy twice on top of the head. According to the experts, it's not the ideal way to pat a dog. The same experts warn that dogs don't like to be hugged. Some dogs, yes. But what the experts overlook is canine brilliance in reading human facial expression, body language, and intentions. Geniuses at decrypting our codes, dogs understand what we mean even when we express ourselves awkwardly; and they care more about the genuineness of hearts than they do about the gaucherie of our thumps and pats and squeezes. Sammy upped the tempo of his tail-wagging.

"We'd better get going," I said. "We need to catch up with my friend. Bye!"

As we left, the man called out, "Bye-bye, Sammy!"

I'd lingered longer than I'd intended, but Zara would understand. Even so, I let Sammy set the pace and hurried along with him. Somewhere ahead of us, a dog barked. The single woof could've come from any medium-size or big dog, possibly Izzy, possibly another dog. Canine yelps of pain, menacing roars, or the growling curses of a dogfight would've sent me flying. As it was, Sammy and I continued briskly along the wet, gloomy path, and I felt no alarm at all until Zara shrieked from somewhere ahead of us, how far I couldn't tell.

"Izzy! Izzy! Izzy, come! Izzy, here!" Then, "Holly! Holly, help! Help me!"

And finally, a wordless scream.

chapter nineteen

Sammy and I ran so fast that we nearly collided with Zara, who continued to scream until I put my free hand on her shoulder and spoke firmly. "Zara, I'm here." I must have sounded as if I were talking to a panicked dog. "I'm here." Then I stated the obvious: "You fell, and Izzy is loose."

Splotches of mud covered the front of Zara's yellow slicker. Dirt streaked her face. Although her battered-looking hands suggested that she'd tried to break her fall, her left cheek, too, was red and raw. Her eyes were wild, and she was gasping for breath.

I looked around in search of a bench or a fallen log, but found no place she could sit. "Tell me what happened." Her silence was so frustrating that I felt tempted to shake her. I waited. Eventually, I said, "You fell. Did you trip? And let go of Izzy's leash?"

She shook her head.

"Someone pushed you. Did you see who it was?"

Once she started speaking, her words flew out so fast that I had to strain to understand her. "We were just walking along, and all of a sudden, someone slammed into my back and knocked me to the ground. It was like being hit by a brick wall. One second, I was walking along, and the next second, I was flat on my face. I can't even remember falling. Izzy, come! Izzy!"

"Zara, did you see who it was?"

"No."

"Did he grab Izzy's leash?"

"I don't know. Holly, what if I let go? That's one of the things they teach us. They said that you never let go of a dog's leash. Never. What if I did?"

"If you did, it was because you couldn't help it. And if you let go, maybe she's loose and we can find her. Let's see where it happened, okay? Sammy, let's go."

For once, Sammy's sunny attitude irritated me. In his place, Kimi would've understood that something was dreadfully wrong. She might even have known what it was. Because Rowdy was Izzy's special buddy, Rowdy's presence would have attracted Izzy, and he'd have noticed her absence and maybe even helped to find her. Sammy, who was beautiful beyond beautiful, had Rowdy's lovely almond-shaped dark eyes, Rowdy's perfect ear set, Rowdy's gorgeous head.

Looking at Sammy, I thought, Why couldn't you have inherited your father's brains, too? Then I felt guilty. "Sammy," I murmured, "I'm sorry. You're not brainless. You're just optimistic. Your water bowl is always half full. And you have way too much faith in me."

Zara, meanwhile, was shrieking for Izzy.

"Zara," I said sternly. "Zara? Zara, stop for a second. When you call her, try calling the way you usually do." I wanted to tell her to take a deep breath, but I hate, hate, hate being told how to breathe. Of all the bossy, intrusive pieces of advice that one person can give to another! You can tell me to calm down or to keep quiet or to stop hollering, but how I breathe is my own damned business. "Just use your ordinary voice," I said.

Unprompted, Zara took a deep breath. Sounding more or less normal, she called, "Izzy, come!"

Half reluctantly, I joined in. "Izzy, come!" Dog is my native tongue. A loose dog who's ignoring his owner will sometimes respond to my firm, happy *Rover, come!* by sprinting right to me, much to the embarrassment of his owner, to whom he says, "She speaks my language. Why don't you?" Well, no, not in those exact words. Still.

I had no desire to play the game of dog-handling one-upmanship with Zara, but I had to do everything within my power to get Izzy back. I gave it my best: "Izzy, come!"

My puzzled Sammy looked at me as if to say, *Why are you calling me when I'm already here?*

When we reached the spot where Zara had been shoved to the ground, I felt like a lone Dr. Watson in need of Sherlock Holmes. To my eye, there was nothing to see except a few marks left by Zara's hands. Or boots? Holmes, having observed a dozen significant disturbances, would've deduced that her assailant was a corpulent redheaded Freemason who'd once lived in China or a dog who'd failed to bark in the night. I did notice, though, that there were no rocks or roots that could've tripped Zara, who was too well coordinated to have stumbled over her own feet.

We could've examined the thick, bushy weeds and low branches for signs that someone had lurked nearby, but for the moment, we cared only about recovering Izzy.

"We'd better call the police," I said.

"I don't want to talk to them. Izzy, come! Here! Izzy, here! Holly, she's been stolen."

"The experts on finding lost dogs always say that you should never assume that a dog has been stolen. We need to keep looking."

We followed the trail upriver for five or ten minutes. Zara continued to call for Izzy, and with an increasing sense of futility, I did, too. Soon after we reversed direction, we ran into a gray-haired couple with waterproof binoculars hanging on their chests. The birders listened politely but hadn't seen any dogs at all. Assured that Izzy was friendly, they promised to catch her if they could and to call the number on her ID tag.

"We know not to chase loose dogs," the man said. "We have crackers and cheese with us. We can use that. Good luck." Two drenched runners in neon-pink Spandex responded to my question about a black dog only by shaking their heads while speeding by. When we reached the little cove, the geese were still there, but the smiling man had left. As we passed the swimming pool and when we reached the parking lot, we encountered four or five people who heard me out and wished us luck.

By then, Zara was incapable of asking the simple question of whether someone had seen a black dog. Her hands were trembling, and her face looked like a death mask. Belatedly, I realized that we should have left something that bore Zara's scent at the place where she'd been assaulted, the place from which Izzy had vanished. If Izzy was loose, she might return there and stay near Zara's possession. I was, however, too worried about Zara to retrace our steps or to search elsewhere.

"Let's get you home," I told her. "Then I'll make some calls." In response to her oddly suspicious look, I added, "I want to call animal control in Watertown and Waltham, and since that footbridge goes to Newton, I'd better call Newton, too. "

It proved a lot easier to crate Sammy in the car than to settle Zara in the passenger seat. I had to open the door for her, and when I'd persuaded her to get in, I had to fasten her seat belt for her. Although I'm always a careful driver, I was particularly cautious on the way home, mainly because I was fighting the urge to floor the accelerator and race back to Appleton Street as quickly as possible. Zara's state of mind—more accurately, her state of mind and body and spirit—was beyond me. She needed help that was in Rita and Quinn's province and not in mine.

So eager was I to find professional help for her that when we passed Rita and Quinn's house, I was tempted to pull in. All that stopped me was the fear that Vicky might be there; I couldn't take the chance of inflicting Vicky on

Zara, especially now. To my disappointment, neither Steve's van nor John's rental car was in our driveway; I'd hoped that either Steve or John would be available to help.

Getting Sammy out of the car, I wondered what to do if Zara insisted on going up to Rita's old apartment and isolating herself there. To my relief, she let me guide her to my kitchen.

"You look cold," I said. After turning off the air conditioner, I ran upstairs for a blanket that I wrapped around her. Then, feeling like a Barbara Pym character, I insisted on making her a cup of sugary tea and made one for myself, too. Sitting opposite Zara at the table, I took a sip of tea and said, "I know quite a lot about finding lost dogs."

"Izzy isn't lost."

"Zara, Frank Sorensen hasn't come back from the dead. And please try to remember that Willie was found— and pretty quickly. Izzy has ID tags. Someone may call any minute." Then I asked an apparently innocuous question: "She's microchipped, isn't she?"

Our five dogs are chipped, of course. Even my cat, Tracker, who never leaves the house, is microchipped. Chipping is routine.

Zara shook her head.

I was so surprised that I blurted out, "She's not?"

Zara must have heard the question as an accusation. "I was afraid that they cause cancer."

"Does she have a tattoo?"

"What?"

"It's what we did before microchips. Rowdy has one. Some people still do them."

"No. I've never even heard of tattooing dogs."

"Zara, if you have to pick only one form of ID for a dog, a collar with tags is your best choice." It takes two seconds to remove a collar and throw it out. I didn't say so.

"Someone could take her collar off. And she's a black Lab! There are millions of them."

"With no white anywhere. That's a little bit distinguishing. Lots of black Labs and Lab mixes have at least a little white somewhere."

My words weren't comforting. If we'd been in an English novel, the blanket and the sweet tea would've helped. As it was, Zara was still shaking, and her face was still white.

"Zara, is there a medication you should take?"

Her expression was blank. I handed her a tissue, not because she needed one but because I had the idea that crying would somehow be good for her.

"If you don't mind," I said, "I'm going to call Quinn."

Summarizing Steve's and my take on Rita's about-to-be husband, Zara said, "He's a pompous ass, but he's kind."

"I won't quote you to him."

She didn't smile. The levity was misplaced, anyway.

When I called Quinn and spoke briefly to him, I told him only that Izzy was missing—lost or stolen—and that Zara could use his help.

"He's coming right over," I told her.

"Holly, someone's been following me."

Sammy had been dozing on floor. I called him to me. "Who?" I asked Zara.

"I never see him. Or her."

"Then how—?"

"I just sense someone. A presence. You know that feeling of being watched?"

I nodded. Kimi can awaken me from sleep by looking at me, or so it seems. In truth, what awakens me is the sound of her exhalations and inhalations or the breeze of her breath on my skin. I don't believe in ESP. I wanted to know whether Izzy, too, had sensed the presence—In Dogs We Trust—but I didn't have the heart to ask.

"Zara, I want to call the ACOs. Animal control."

"She isn't lost."
"We don't know that."
"I do."

chapter twenty

When Quinn arrived, he was at his best: kind, thoughtful, and blessedly low-key. While he and Zara conferred in our living room, I called the ACOs in Waltham, Watertown, and Newton, and I e-mailed Lab Rescue. I made sure to let everyone know that Izzy was a service dog and that she'd been wearing a yellow service-dog vest.

Feeling vaguely guilty, I didn't specify that she was a psychiatric service dog. Want to hear my reasons? Zara's psychiatric difficulties were a personal matter that she alone had the right to disclose. Izzy's specialty was irrelevant; the disappearance of any service dog merited immediate attention. Despite all the good publicity given to service dogs for veterans and others with post-traumatic stress disorder, the stigma of mental illness might make the search for Izzy low priority.

Okay, were these merely rationalizations and not reasons? I hoped then and hope now that they were reasons. Here's the kind of thinking I feared: if your problem is only in your head, why rush to get your service dog back? *Only?* As in *only a dog? Only:* the ultimate diminishment. If Izzy's task had been to see or to hear for Zara, or to predict seizures or a dangerous drop in blood sugar, I'd have said so; it would never have occurred to me to do otherwise. Was I as guilty as everyone else of *only* thinking?

Rita's signature tapping on the back door jolted me out of my reverie. Without preamble, she said, "In case you wondered, I'm keeping Vicky out of the way. Whatever's going on, Zara will be better off without her. So, what *is* going on?"

I filled her in and finished by saying, "Zara's convinced that Izzy's been stolen. I think she's probably right." After hesitating, I added, "She says that someone's been following her. Well, she says that she's had that *sense*."

"She's never been paranoid before. Not that I know of. I don't know what to think."

"Maybe Quinn will have some ideas. If you can just keep Vicky away, that'll help. Where is she?"

"At home."

"And MaryJo?"

"She and Monty are there, too."

"Really?"

"There's a big literature on the responses of disturbed people to *real* calamities—fires in mental hospitals, that kind of real crisis. Interestingly, those kinds of external emergencies sometimes produce surprisingly practical, rational responses. That seems to be what's going on with Vicky."

"She isn't having hysterics?"

"In one sense, yes. She's heavily invested in this new image of herself as someone who's been *shot*. In fact, she wanted to hear all about the great-grandfather who owned the gun. Oh, the drama!"

"In a way, that's good, Rita. What if Vicky refused to be in the same room with MaryJo?"

"Then maybe Vicky would move to a hotel. If only! No, she'd probably insist on inflicting herself on you."

I had to smile. "It's not going to happen."

Quinn and Zara emerged from the living room. He had an arm around her shoulders. "Zara would like to go upstairs. We're declaring it a mother-free zone. Doctor's orders."

Zara managed a token smile as they left.

"Quinn is going to be a good father," I said.

Rita was smug. "Yes, I know."

Quinn returned in almost no time, and seconds after he'd closed the kitchen door, he had to open it again to admit the shooting victim herself, who paused dramatically, pointed a finger at a chair, and announced, "*That's* where I was gunned down."

"How are you doing?" I asked flatly.

Vicky swept a hand to her throat. "I am putting up a brave front. In that spirit, I am treating MaryJo—my very own personal Bonnie Parker—to a manicure and a pedicure and possibly a massage at Soignée, and I wondered whether the two of you and Zara would like to come along."

Rita's face fell. "Aunt Vicky, that's supposed to be my treat. In case you've forgotten, Quinn and I are getting married in three days, and Soignée is—or was—going to be my treat for the day before the wedding, *my* girls' day out."

"Well, we can just go back again!"

"And get manicures and pedicures all over again? The day after tomorrow?"

Instead of standing by helplessly and watching the quarrel escalate, I intervened. "Vicky, thank you, but we have a crisis here. Izzy is missing."

"Who?"

Quinn said, "Izzy. Zara's service dog."

"Service dog! Let me tell you something. There is nothing basically wrong with Zara. She just loves making a fuss over nothing. She always has. And she loves embarrassing people, especially me, with that dog and its silly costume. Quinn, I'm surprised that she's fooled *you*. Aren't you supposed to be a psychiatrist?"

"I am a psychiatrist. I know mental illness when I see it." Quinn's delivery was deadpan.

The verbal bullet didn't even graze Vicky, who demanded, "And just where is my daughter?"

Rita answered. "Upstairs in my old apartment."

"I'm going to go get her and make her stop this ridiculous mental hypochondria."

Vicky started toward the door, but Quinn got there first. Grasping Vicky's elbow, he ushered her out. With a nod to me, Rita followed.

chapter twenty-one

Here's proof that I'm only half malamute: a purebred would never have forgotten to eat lunch. When Steve got home, I belatedly noticed that I was famished. A purebred malamute wouldn't have left the bag from Eastern Lamejun in the car, either. On the contrary, a malamute would've ripped open the bag, the boxes, and the plastic bags and devoured the lamejuns, the pita, and everything else except possibly the olives right there in the car. It may be just as well that I'm half human. Malamutes have no respect for gracious living.

Although Steve had stopped at McDonald's on the way back from the hardware store, he accepted my offer of a second lunch. Sammy is Steve's first malamute. I felt happy to recognize a sign that Steve was already experiencing the effects of migratory malamute DNA.

He and I were sitting on the towel-padded benches of our picnic table. Lady and India were conducting the sort of olfactory investigation of the yard that dogs enjoy in damp weather. Sammy and Rowdy, being malamutes, were conducting an optimistic study of our lunch, which consisted of lamejuns heated in the oven, spread with yogurt, and rolled up. The dogs were too well trained to leap up and steal the food out of our hands or off the table, but a long stream of saliva descended from Sammy's mouth, and Rowdy was eyeing the paving stones in the hope of snatching dropped morsels before Sammy got them.

After checking on Zara, I'd given Steve an update. Now, at his insistence, I provided a detailed account of the events preceding and immediately following Izzy's disappearance.

When I'd finished, he said, "Let's start with what we know. Not what we *think*. What we *know*."

"I understand the difference."

He smiled. "Okay. Frank Sorensen tried to steal Izzy. He lived in or had lived in Waltham. That same day, that evening, he broke into Rita and Quinn's house. And— *and*—until earlier that day, Zara and Izzy had been staying with Rita and Quinn. While Frank was in the house, robbing the house, he was hit with a poker. He stole some sterling silver and some drug samples. At the same time, Willie disappeared and then ended up at Enid Garabedian's house. In Watertown. Right near the Waltham line. Frank ended up dead. His body was found in the Charles near Watertown Square.

"Today, Zara was knocked over and Izzy disappeared not all that far upriver from the Watertown dam. Izzy is a service dog, but when you and Zara called her, she didn't come. Would you say that she has a reliable recall?"

"By my extreme standards, a really reliable recall means that the dog comes every single time no matter what." I repeated: "No matter what."

"India."

"Your India. My Vinnie." Vinnie was my last golden retriever. "Our other dogs? In the ring"—the obedience ring—"Rowdy and Kimi are reliable. Loose in the woods if a deer runs by? No. That's why I keep them on leash. Lady? Typically, she'll run to you or to India whether you call her or not, so that's not exactly a recall. Sammy?"

Hearing his name, Sammy lifted his great head and eyed Steve, who laughed. "The roulette-wheel brain.

Where it stops, nobody knows, right, Sammy? You know, Holly, he's a beautiful dog. Aren't you, Sammy?"

"Of course he is," I said. "He looks just like Rowdy."

"Izzy? How's her recall?"

"She's less reliable than India or my Vinnie, but by normal standards, yes, Izzy comes when she's called in spite of ordinary distractions. Today, I think that she couldn't."

"I think so, too. Look, Holly, all these things are no coincidence. Frank Sorensen tried to steal Izzy. He burgled Rita and Quinn's house and probably took Willie."

"Willie had been at Angell until that day. Izzy and Zara had been staying at Quinn and Rita's."

"And someone actually has stolen Izzy. Then there's the Waltham and Watertown connection. "

"More than that. Waltham near the Watertown line, Watertown near the Waltham line, everything near the river."

"No coincidence," he repeated.

"Steve, you know what I think about coincidence."

He grinned. "The infamous Holly Winter theory that coincidence doesn't exist."

"Not at all! The theory—the fact—is that if you trace back apparent coincidences far enough, you'll find that that they're intimately connected by a common thread and that the thread is invariably—"

"—dogs."

"—the unifying force in this otherwise random and senseless universe. Would you like some coffee?"

We cleared the table, made coffee, and returned to the yard with our mugs.

Resuming where we'd left off, Steve said, without conceding the universal truth of my so-called theory, "In this case, the shared element happens to be—"

"—dogs. You see?"

"No. One dog. Izzy."

"What about Willie?"

"They're both black dogs."

"But he's a Scottie!"

"A black Scottie. A black dog. And one small geographic area. But there's something else that jumps out."

"Frank Sorensen is dead. Why do I have to keep saying that? He tried to steal Izzy, but he did not rise from the dead and steal her today. You want fact? What we know for sure? Frank Sorensen was not Jesus."

He ignored me. "If the unifying theme is Izzy, then Frank Sorensen had an accomplice."

"His brother," I said. "Gil. Or someone else."

"Why would someone—anyone—want to steal Izzy?"

"Money. That's the obvious reason. Ransom. Zara could obviously pay it. But why here? In Cambridge? And—"

"Let's slow down. Why don't you review what you know about Izzy."

"Zara got her from a shelter."

"Zara *says* she got her from a shelter."

"Good point, Steve. Yes. Okay, you can tell to look at Izzy that she's a quality dog. Horrible phrase. That she's from a show kennel. She's not from working lines, and she's no pet-shop Lab. Dogs from show lines do end up in shelters. Not all that often, but they do."

He nodded.

"She's not microchipped, and that's odd. Zara hasn't chipped her because she's afraid that chips cause cancer—"

He sighed. "They—"

"Of course they don't. But most shelters routinely microchip. And you know what else is strange? I just realized this. Adopters who really love their dogs usually remember everything about adopting them. The typical happy adopter has a long, detailed story about noticing the dog on a website or first hearing about the dog, looking at other dogs, choosing this one—or feeling chosen—and so on.

"So, wouldn't you expect Zara to have a long story about adopting Izzy? I'd expect to hear all about going to the shelter, seeing other dogs there, realizing that Izzy was special, and so on. But all Zara has ever said to me is that Izzy came from a shelter. She's never even said which shelter it was."

Steve nodded. "Back to Zara's money."

"Well, that I *do* know about. Rita told me. The story is that Zara's grandfather on her father's side was a Wall Street type, an investment banker. He had tons of money. And when he died, he left it all to Zara and to her father, Dave. His wife, Dave's mother, was already dead, and Dave is an only child, and Zara is, too, of course. "

"His only grandchild."

"Yes. And Zara got more than Dave did, presumably because Dave didn't need it. He's some kind of high-powered lawyer. So, Zara got a lot of money, some of it in a trust fund and some it left to her outright. Anyway, in terms of ransom, she could obviously pay it. She doesn't brag about being rich, but she has a condo on the Upper West Side. And the car."

"The Benz," Steve said with a wicked smile.

"Thank you, Quinn. Yes, the Benz. I gather that she bought it during a manic phase when she first had Izzy. She didn't say *manic*, but that's what she meant, and then it turned out to be the perfect dogmobile, so she kept it."

"Holly, when Frank Sorensen tried to steal Izzy, how would he've known? How did he even know who Zara was? Never mind that she could pay ransom. If that was what he was after."

"Facebook?"

"Her Facebook page doesn't say she's rich. And it doesn't seem like he was a social-network kind of guy. A small-time crook like that?"

"Maybe he networked with other small-time crooks. For all we know, there's a Small-Time Crooks Facebook page. We could become fans! Sorry. This isn't a good time for frivolity. Seriously, almost everyone his age is on Facebook, and Zara probably accepts every Friend request she gets."

"How did he know that she existed?"

"I have no idea."

"We need to talk to Zara," he said.

chapter twenty-two

Although we had keys to the apartment, I knocked on the door, and both of us called Zara's name. I had no reason to believe that she had ever been suicidal. If she were a threat to herself, Quinn would never have agreed to leave her alone; would he? Besides, Izzy had been missing for only a short time. Zara would never, ever desert Izzy, would she? Still, I felt relief when Zara eventually answered the door.

Steve and I had agreed to confine our questions to the matter of Izzy's origin. If we so much as mentioned Zara's overactivity on Facebook, Twitter, Instagram, Pinterest, and such, we might risk making her feel at fault, as neither of us believed that she was. When I saw how dreadful she looked, I knew that we'd made the right decision. She was alarmingly pale and so shaky that I wondered whether she was taking a medication that made her tremble.

"Were you asleep?" I asked. "I'm sorry if we—"

"No. No, it's okay."

We followed her to the living room, which still had most of Rita's furniture. Without inviting us to take seats, Zara flopped onto the couch and wrapped herself in a blanket. The surest sign that Zara wasn't herself was the near absence of electronic devices: the only gadget in sight was a single phone that sat on an end table by the couch. Although Zara was a guest in our apartment, I was reluctant to sit down without an invitation, so I stood there feeling like a door-to-door salesperson on the verge of trying to sell her products that she didn't want.

Steve, however, took a seat on the edge of the couch right next to Zara and rested a hand on her shoulder. "No calls?" he asked in his low rumble. "No messages?" He could have been examining a badly wounded animal, as, in effect, he was.

"No."

"Zara, there are a couple of things we need to ask you about, a couple of things about Izzy that don't add up. And I don't know whether they've got anything to do with what's going on, but we've got to explore everything." Without calling Zara a liar, as I'd have come close to doing, he said, "First of all, microchips. These days, just about any shelter microchips dogs as matter of routine."

Zara's eyes were cast down.

"Then," Steve said quietly, "there's what you can tell about Izzy by looking at her. Correct size. Beautifully proportioned. Wide skull, clean-cut head, good pigment, otter tail, overall look. She's a breeder dog. But then there's another thing. You know, Holly and I do malamute rescue, and I see a lot of rescue dogs in my practice, and when an adopter bonds with a shelter dog, I hear a lot about where the dog came from, how the owner happened to get the dog. I hear the stories. But what you've got to say about adopting Izzy is just about nothing. So, I've got to wonder."

Zara shifted around and pursed her lips.

"So," Steve finished, "if there's more you'd feel comfortable telling us, we'd like to hear it."

She pulled herself upright on the couch and blew her nose. "I can't. I'm just not free to say. But you're right. She didn't exactly come from a shelter." Her speech was slow and almost mechanical. "Someone gave her to me. She really did need a new home, though, so she's a rescue dog. She's *like* a shelter dog. I wasn't lying."

Steve nodded. I hoped that Zara would expand on the little she'd said, but she didn't.

Eventually, I asked, "Is there anything I can get you? Tea? Coffee? Something to eat? Do you want one of us to stay with you?"

She refused the offers and said that she just wanted to lie down. Dismissed, we went back downstairs. As soon as we got there, Steve took India and Lady and left for the Charles River trail to hunt for Izzy. "Just in case we're wrong," he explained.

Alone with Sammy and Rowdy, I had a sense of helpless anger. Instead of voicing my frustration and fury to some inevitably judgmental human being, I made a cup of strong coffee, sat at the kitchen table, and addressed the dogs. All dogs are great listeners, but Alaskan malamutes are ideal confessors because they're in no position to make harsh judgments about others. Given the opportunity, malamutes will steal food off your plate, out of your hands, or even right out of your mouth. They revel in breaking the necks of cute little furry animals. Malamutes not only catch songbirds on the wing but swallow their avian prey whole—feathers, feet, beaks, and all.

Furthermore, even my own malamutes are capable of breathtaking pettiness: Rowdy and Kimi, the best of canine friends, once had a snarling, if blessedly bloodless, battle over one minuscule morsel of liver biscotti that Rowdy found and Kimi wanted. In case you wondered, Kimi won. The girls usually do.

"So, boys," I said, "why won't Zara answer simple questions about Izzy's origins? Especially now! And why can't she accept comfort and company?" Dogs are such geniuses at decoding human intentions that even if I'd shouted, Rowdy and Sammy would've understood that they weren't the targets of my wrath. Still, my tone was sweet. "And whose fault is it that Zara has so many problems? And has to take medication? Maybe not *all*

Vicky's fault, but partly hers, the nasty *bitch*—in the nontechnical sense. No reflection on Kimi, India, or Lady.

"And then there's MaryJo and her antique revolver. I mean, so what if it was her great-grandfather's? Who cares? What kind of pitiful excuse is that for reckless stupidity? And Monty! Monty should have kept that revolver locked up. She's his wife. He must know what she's like. While we're at it, since John is supposedly so close to Zara, he should be here now to hold her hand and maybe to rouse her to action. Yes, *what* action? I have no idea.

"But I can tell you that if one of you vanished, I'd be out there doing something. Anything! And on the subject of who should and shouldn't do what, I should never have let Zara and Izzy out of my sight on the trail. Mea culpa, boys, mea maxima culpa."

The dogs' attention was beginning to wane. I dug into a pocket and gave each of them a little treat. "Thank you for listening. Okay!"

The dogs did not grant me absolution; since they believe me to be incapable of sin, they didn't have to. Besides, I hadn't finished confessing. Among other things, I hadn't said how furious I was with Rita, not only for tolerating Vicky's noxious presence, but also for getting pregnant to begin with and, worse, for insisting on marrying Quinn. Rita would be a superb single mother. Steve and I would be terrific godparents.

What did she need Quinn for? If she wanted a child, fine; and from a dog breeder's viewpoint, in other words, from *my* viewpoint, Quinn was a strong, healthy, intelligent, good-looking male, a suitable sire, but damn it! As Zara had said, he was a pompous ass. A sperm donor is one thing. A husband is quite another.

chapter twenty-three

Maybe Rita is right about talking cures: my discussion with the dogs—and with myself—left me energized; after venting my sense of helpless anger, I was ready for action.

For a start, I took Rowdy up to Rita's old apartment, knocked, waited, and then presented him to Zara, who retreated to the couch, where she curled up. "Rowdy isn't a service dog, of course," I said, "and he isn't *your* dog, but any dog is better than none, and Rowdy is better than most." A gross understatement, but there's a limit to my insufferable bragging about my dogs. Really there is. There is, isn't there? Anyway, even a perfect dog, Rowdy, for example, isn't a perfect service dog because there's no such thing as a generic service dog. Each service dog is trained to meet the handler's specific needs, so perfection lies in the match between the dog and those needs.

I expected Rowdy to barge in and nudge Zara or maybe to lick her face or hands, but instead, he stationed himself next to her and simply watched her. I knew immediately that Rowdy was right: Zara needed a strong, calm presence. He had set himself the task of meeting that need.

Returning home, I posted on Facebook about a missing black Lab. I didn't identify Izzy, but I was quite precise about the area where she'd disappeared. I checked my voicemail and found no messages from the ACOs or Lab rescue. The only e-mail of note was yet another message from Tabitha the Pest about Cathy Brown, the "evil wife," as Tabitha called her, the woman who'd bought the puppy, Cheyenne.

As I hadn't known, the woman was a nurse. After hearing that she'd been seen in Massachusetts, Tabitha had found her—or, I thought, another nurse with the same common name—in the Massachusetts database of registered nurses. According to the listing, Cathy Brown lived in Waltham. Tabitha, who'd searched WhitePages.com and who knows what else, went on to list sixteen addresses in or near Waltham for Catherine Brown, C. Brown, C. G. Brown, and so on. Could I possibly do Tabitha the favor of doing a quick drive-by? Typical Tabitha! One quick drive-by, okay. One drive-by might be quick. But sixteen? I mean, *sixteen?*

I replied by telling Tabitha that my dearest friend was getting married in three days, that I was her matron of honor, that my husband was the best man, that two of her relatives were staying with us now, and that more houseguests were arriving soon. *And there are complications that I won't go into,* I added. *In other words, this isn't the best time, but I'll do my best.*

I'd no sooner sent the message than Steve, India, and Lady returned. They were not, I might add, followed by Izzy.

"No luck?" My question wasn't one.

"Nothing. I talked to people. No one had seen her. She likes other dogs, so I thought that Lady and India might attract her." He shrugged.

"I think that we wait for a ransom demand," I said. "I just hope that there is one. And if there is—"

Steve finished my thought. "Zara's a wealthy young woman, but that doesn't necessarily mean that she can raise a lot of cash in a hurry."

"And even if she can—" I left the sentence unfinished. Even if Zara paid ransom, Izzy could be dead. We had, in fact, no proof that Izzy was still alive. "Steve, there must be something we can do. The accomplice? The brother? If that's who it was. If there even was one."

"It could've been a girlfriend."

"Frank took her out for a night on the town breaking into houses?"

"His driver."

"That's possible. He broke in, grabbed the stuff he was going to steal, got clobbered, and then when he didn't reappear, she got worried and went in after him. And got him back to the car."

Steve looked skeptical. "And while she was at it, she acquired a pet."

"Why not? Willie is very appealing. He's cute."

"While her boyfriend's bleeding from a head wound?"

"If you put it like that. Yes. You know, I just thought of something. When I talked to Elizabeth McNamara, she said something about bad language. She was in a hurry, so I didn't ask much, but that doesn't sound like Rita's and Quinn's relatives. They have their faults, but obscenity isn't one of them."

"What exactly did Elizabeth say?"

"I don't remember. She immediately started talking about Vicky. She'd overheard that phone call I told you about, Vicky's end of it, Vicky talking to Al, and she was shocked. All I remember about the bad language is just that she mentioned it. For all I know, the person she heard swearing was a woman, in which case it could've been a girlfriend. It could even have been Vicky. I'm going to call Elizabeth."

When I reached Elizabeth, she at first assumed that I was calling to report that her house, too, had been burglarized.

"No, Elizabeth, it's not that at all. Your house is fine. I'm just calling to find out a little more about something you said about overhearing bad language. We're trying to find out whether the burglar had an accomplice, and we wondered whether you might've heard the two of them, the burglar and someone with him. Also, did you tell the police about what you heard?"

Although my questions were not, for once, about dogs, Elizabeth, being a real dog person, began to answer me by talking about dogs. "I said *very* little to the police because The Baby happened to jump on one of them, and do you know what he said? He said to get *it* off him. *It!* Never trust a person who refers to a dog as *it!*"

"Certainly not. I never have and never will."

"Good. So, after that, I just got rid of those terrible men. Besides, I thought they'd ask me to repeat what I'd heard, and I wasn't about to pronounce those words, was I?"

"I don't blame you. Elizabeth, could you tell who was speaking? A man? Two men? A man and a woman?"

"Oh, two men. Actually, I know this will sound funny, but for a split second, I mistook one of them for Kevin Dennehy. But it was just because of the Boston accent. Kevin never uses language like that, and it wasn't Kevin's voice, anyway. Now *there's* a policeman who'd never call a dog *it.*"

I agreed. When I got off the phone, I immediately went online to see whether I could find an address for Frank Sorensen's brother, Gil. His name turned out to be Gilberto, and the address I found, 55 Peach Street, Waltham, was the one Zara and I had driven by. Although I had no conscious recollection of having done more than glance at Tabitha's list of possible addresses for her puppy buyer, Cathy Brown, the image of that list must somehow have imprinted itself on my mind. Consulting it and actually reading it this time, I had no difficulty in finding the same address, 55 Peach Street, Waltham, next to "C. Brown."

My head was spinning. The points leading to the conclusion were whipping around, but in the midst of the swirl, the conclusion itself was clear: Izzy was Tabitha's missing puppy.

chapter twenty-four

My first impulse was to jump in the car and drive to 55 Peach Street. What stopped me was the fear of being recognized. Someone—Frank or Gil Sorensen or Cathy Brown—had presumably cased Rita and Quinn's house before the burglary and followed Zara in person and on Facebook. I'd been in and out of Rita and Quinn's house all the time. Zara and I had gone places together, and many of the recent photos she'd posted included me. Consequently, I was in no position to show up at the door of 55 Peach Street and try to pass myself off as a stranger selling religion or requesting donations to a good cause.

In fact, I knew better than to show my face on Peach Street at all.

Instead, I made a phone call. "Tabitha? Holly Winter. I owe you an apology."

"It's about time." Tabitha is not the most gracious person I've ever known. "You did the drive-bys?"

"No, but I know what happened to Cheyenne."

"My God! She's dead!"

"No. No, I, uh, think I can find her. I just need a little more information about Cathy Brown. Cheyenne is registered to her and her husband? They're both the legal owners? What's his name?"

"No, they bought her together, but she's registered to Cathy. They have different last names. He's Wilson. John Wilson."

No wonder Izzy had gone berserk when she'd seen John: she'd once been *his* dog. I am too stupid to live. Well, maybe I'm not too stupid to live, but I'm too stupid to live with malamutes. My poor dogs. "Tabitha, you've been right all along. I must've sent those people to you. Indirectly. I must've given your name to a friend who gave it to them. I'm sorry." People ask me for names of breeders all the time. I must have given Tabitha's name to Rita, who'd given it to John.

"You should be. They're liars and cheats. The last time I talked to that horrible woman, she said that Cheyenne was with her husband, who was living at their house. They'd split up. But when I went there, no one was home, and there was no sign of a dog. I looked. Nothing in the yard. I looked in the windows, and I could see the whole kitchen, and there was no crate, no toys, no bowl, nothing. And when I was leaving, some neighbor told me that the puppy wasn't there anymore."

"Tabitha, I did not know these people. I did not recommend them. I leave it to breeders to screen their puppy buyers."

"I did! They seemed fine. They owned their house. The yard *was* fenced. A doctor and a nurse? They seemed fine."

"He's not a doctor. He's a drug-company sales rep."

"He said he was a doctor. You see? I told you they were liars."

"I believe you," I said.

As soon as I got off the phone, John Wilson—pardon me, *Dr.* John Wilson—had the misfortune to show up, and even though he was Rita's cousin and my houseguest, I had no inclination to go easy on him.

"Izzy is missing," I said, "Izzy, who is Cheyenne, the puppy you and your wife bought from Tabitha Treen. You got Tabitha's name from me via Rita. I know that I never gave it to you directly. And then for some unknown reason, you gave Cheyenne to Zara, you left her breeder worried sick about where the puppy was, and you persuaded Zara to lie about where Izzy had come from. And you know what? Zara is not a particularly good liar. She's bad at supplying details. She doesn't create a credible picture. Her story was that Izzy came from a shelter. Period. With no embellishments. But you know what Zara's good at? Loyalty. Keeping a promise. She didn't tell me the real story. I had to work it out for myself."

John was still standing by the back door. "Holly, you haven't heard my side."

"I'm listening."

"My wife, my ex-wife—"

"Cathy."

"Cathy. Cathy had a big substance-abuse problem, and that was just one of a lot of problems she had. Men. Money. She spent my money, she spent money we didn't have, she lost her job, and when we split up, she robbed me blind."

"The puppy?"

"For the first couple of months we had Cheyenne, Cathy was okay. She even took her to some class. And then it started. She'd forget to feed Cheyenne. She'd leave her locked in a crate. Forget to take her out or just not do it. And the worst thing she did was just open the front door and let Cheyenne out. When the back yard had a fence! Cheyenne could've been killed by a car. And then Cathy'd be drunk or high, and she'd fall all over Cheyenne. It was disgusting. And after I kicked Cathy out, I had the locks changed, but she broke in and stole Cheyenne. I managed to get Cheyenne back, but I knew I had to do something, so I gave her to Zara."

"What do you know about Frank and Gil Sorensen?"

"Wasn't Frank Sorensen the dead guy? Rita's burglar."

"Yes. What else do you know about him?"

"Nothing."

"Did Cheyenne belong to you and your wife? Was she registered to both of you? Or just to one of you?" I found myself speaking as if Izzy were two dogs, the one she'd been in her previous existence, Cheyenne, and the one she was now. In a sense, of course, Izzy really had had two lives.

"Both of us," John said. "I paid for her. I wrote the check."

Since Tabitha had no reason to lie about the registration, John was lying. Or maybe he'd forgotten. Pet people never attach the importance to American Kennel Club registrations that dog people do.

"Are you in touch with Cathy?"

"If I knew where she was," John said, "I'd go after her and get my diamond ring and my money back."

chapter twenty-five

The ransom call came just after I'd fed Rowdy and taken him out. When I returned him to Zara, she played her recording of the call. I closed my eyes and listened hard. The caller's voice was as unmistakably male as his accent was inimitably Boston. To my ear, the man's *parking*, with its baaing *a* and missing *r*, was identical to Kevin Dennehy's *pahking*, and the *o* in *lot* and *dog*—*lawt* and *dawg*—sounded like Cambridge, too.

The man's *t*'s thought about becoming *d*'s but changed their minds just the way Kevin's did. Within a few blocks of my house there was probably a Harvard sociolinguist who could've stated with certainty that particular features of the accent were unique to the South Shore, the North Shore, East Boston, Southie, Revere, Medford, Cambridge, or, of course, Waltham. I'm not that good. All I knew was that the accent was the real thing. The letter *r* is easy to drop, but Boston vowels are impossible to fake. Poor Hollywood! Actors almost never even get close. Two who get the accent right are Matt Damon and Ben Affleck in *Good Will Hunting*. Why? Damon and Affleck both went to Cambridge Rindge and Latin.

"Gil Sorensen," I said to Zara. "I'll bet that's who it is." Although I had no idea where he'd been when he'd placed the call, I pictured him sitting on the steps of the shabby house on Peach Street.

"He's reading it, isn't he? He wrote it down, and he's reading it."

"And not very fluently."

This was the first time I'd seen Zara without makeup. During Rowdy's and my absence, she'd washed her face and brushed her hair. She looked pale and very young.

I took a seat on the couch next to her. Rowdy resumed the position he'd evidently decided was his: he sat next to her, his body relaxed, his expression gentle and open. She rested a hand on his shoulder.

"Why is the ransom so small? Why isn't he asking for more money?" Her voice was soft and weak. "He calls me Rich Bitch."

The demand was for only about a third of the price of a car, and that's the kind of car I'd buy, not the Mercedes that Zara drove. The man had told her that unless she did what he said, her dog would die; if the police were involved, her dog would die. He'd instructed her to put the money in twenty-dollar bills in a white plastic bag and to come alone the next day at six to a parking lot—*pahking lawt*—off Pleasant Street in Watertown, near Pignola's.

She was then to walk toward the river, pass some tennis courts, keep heading toward the river, and drop the bag by an old desk. Although he'd clearly been reading from a script, he sounded disconcertingly uncomfortable about giving explicit directions. Zara had had to ask him whether he meant six in the evening. He'd said yes. She'd also asked whether he meant the Pignola's parking lot. He'd said no: "the pahking lawt nee-uh the tennis cohts and the Sons of Italy." Fortunately, I knew exactly the parking lot he meant. He'd ended more or less as he'd begun: with a death threat, and a credible one.

"Desk?" Zara asked me.

"People dump things there," I said.

"The money's easy. There's a branch of my bank in Harvard Square." She paused. "If I can—"

"I can get some of the cash if that'll help."

"No, it's not that. But thank you. I've got enough. But how do I get to the bank without Izzy?"

"Zara, please remember that you're not in this alone. I'll do anything I can, and so will Steve and Rita and Quinn. We're with you."

"No! Don't tell them! If you tell them, they might call the police. Holly, please! Don't tell anyone!" At her side, Rowdy stirred. Then he shifted an inch or two and rested his head on the couch next to her.

Although I had no intention of being the only person who knew about the ransom demand, I avoided giving Zara a direct response. "We'll work out the details tomorrow morning. The important thing to remember is that I'll do anything I can to help."

Zara leapt to her feet, pacing back and forth, peering out the windows, taking a seat, leaping up again, and pacing like a caged animal. Without Izzy, I thought, Zara felt caged. Rowdy trained his eyes on my face in search of instruction. I met his gaze, shrugged, and mouthed, "Good boy," in the hope, I guess, of reinforcing my connection with him and telling him that nothing was required except his presence. As to what, if anything, I should do, I had no idea. My knowledge of dog behavior and dog training offered little initial guidance. Yes, Zara was suffering from acute stress; she was, as it's said, over threshold. Rowdy's presence hadn't kept her stress level down, nor had my promise to help in any way I could. As I watched her pace, I realized that although my intellectual understanding was letting me down, my dog trainer's intuition, together with common sense, told me not to stand passively by as her pacing became increasingly frantic and as her arousal level escalated: interrupt the behavior!

"Zara, stop!" I ordered.

And she did. Once she was no longer scaring me by pacing so frenetically, I knew what to do. When you're dealing with a dog-aggressive dog who goes bonkers at the sight of another dog, it's vital to let your dog know that protecting him is *your* responsibility and *not* his: since you are his strong, bold, trustworthy protector, he need do nothing except relax and let you do your job. And you'd better be good at it! If an unwelcome dog appears, you need to remove your dog from the situation or, if need be, press the trigger on your citronella spray, blast your air horn, and use your dog-trainer voice, too, until that canine enemy turns tail and vanishes off the face of your dog's earth.

"Zara, you're too stressed to think straight right now. You're too frightened for Izzy. I'm worried, too, but I'm less stressed than you are, and I'm going take charge. We've got this evening and tomorrow to get through. There are plans that have to be made, and I'm going to make them. You don't need to. I am a strong, capable person. I'm going to listen to what you want. We aren't going to tell everyone about the ransom demand. But we're going to have a plan, and we're going to stick to it, and we're going to get Izzy back. Do you hear me? We're going to get her back."

chapter twenty-six

B ossiness comes naturally to me. For one thing, I grew up with golden retrievers who were so used to obeying my martinet mother that they obeyed me, too, even when I was barely old enough to tell them to sit, stay, and heel. For another thing, I've lived with dogs and trained dogs ever since those early days. In contrast to my late mother, who favored the jerk-and-drag methods of her time, I'm an enthusiastic participant in the positive-methods revolution in dog training.

Still, I use positive reinforcement in the form of food, praise, play, and yet more food as a means to an end, and that end is the same one I've always sought, namely, dogs who do what I tell them to do when I tell them to do it, thereby behaving like canine ladies and gentlemen.

So, benevolent despot that I am, I felt comfortable taking charge.

My first decree was that we needed to eat and, eventually, to sleep. By *we*, I meant only Zara and me. For all that John was our houseguest, I was so annoyed about his duplicity that I'd have wished starvation and insomnia on him, but as it happened, he was going to a Red Sox game with Quinn, Steve, and Monty. Neither Rita nor Quinn referred to the outing as a bachelor party. Rita called it a pre-wedding male-bonding ritual. Out of my hearing, Quinn probably did, too.

Quinn wasn't a bachelor-party type—and a good thing, too, since so far as I could tell, he'd have had no friends to invite. It was flattering and troubling that he'd chosen Steve as his best man. Yes, Steve is wonderful, but Quinn hadn't known him for long; he and Steve saw each other almost exclusively when Rita, Quinn, Steve, and I got together; the two of them didn't hang out without Rita and me. Worse, Quinn didn't hang out with anyone else, either. What kind of man has no friends? But the Sox game was progress, I told myself, and since Quinn had paid more money than I can imagine to some scalper for four seats right behind home plate, Steve was actually looking forward to the evening. You know that line in the Robert Frost poem? Frost said that boughten friendship was better than none at all, so let's hope he was right.

As an aside, let me mention that although the poem, "Provide, Provide," is supposedly about an old hag who was once a Hollywood star and has hit hard times because she failed to provide, it's possible that in the devious, multilayered manner of poems, it's also about the poet, and if that's the case, the reason he had to think about buying friends instead of making them was that no one wanted to hang out with a guy who used weird words like *boughten*; so, Frost should have advised his readers to provide by talking like normal human beings.

Anyway, because I wanted a little time alone to mull over my plans, I didn't raid our freezer but walked down the block to our local fancy-food emporium, Formaggio—properly, Formaggio Kitchen—for a rotisserie chicken, a collection of delectable side dishes and cheeses, and a loaf of French bread. By the time I got home, my mind was clear. Among other things, I'd decided to tell no one but Rita about the ransom call. I hadn't worked out exactly how to avoid telling Steve, who, honest and open and straightforward man that he is, would've wanted to inform the police. Searching for a way to conceal everything about the ransom from him, I finally hit on an improbable and elusive but perfect strategy: for once in my life, I'd keep my mouth shut. Why tell Rita? I trusted her completely. Also, as a psychotherapist, she had tons of experience in keeping secrets.

On the way home, I met Steve, who was walking to Rita and Quinn's.

"No news?" he asked.

"No," I lied. "You're taking one car, aren't you?"

With a wry smile, he said, "Quinn's Lexus. But John's meeting us there."

"He's from New York. Has it occurred you that he could be a Yankees fan?"

"Knowing him, I wouldn't be surprised." In Boston, those are damning words.

"It's a good thing we're playing the Orioles. What if you had to go to a Yankees game with a Yankees fan?" I told him that I intended to watch the game on television and promised to keep an eye out for him. "I'm going to stay in Rita's old guestroom," I warned him. "I don't like the idea of Zara being alone on the third floor, even with Rowdy. I'll take Sammy with me."

When I got home and checked on Zara, she said that she wanted to take a shower—a good sign, I thought—and agreed to watch the game with me. She wasn't a big baseball fan, but when she watched, she rooted for the Mets, not the Evil Empire, as I'd have predicted even if I hadn't already known.

"We're both thinking of nothing but Izzy," I told her, "but we have to get through. It's less than twenty-four hours now. You can do it."

From my own kitchen, I called Rita, who sounded flustered. "MaryJo is starving. Vicky doesn't want to eat before eight. MaryJo wants to watch the game so she can see Monty on television. Thank God for Uncle Oscar! He says that anything is fine with him. And he's very sweet with Willie."

"Rita," I said, "I need to swear you to secrecy."

"Consider me sworn," she said.

"Izzy has been kidnapped. Dognapped. Zara has had a ransom call. You can't tell anyone."

"Holly, call the police!"

"I can't. Izzy is Zara's dog."

"How is Zara doing?"

"Rowdy is with her. He's helping her get through, I think."

"I'm coming over."

She hung up. Five minutes later, she was at my door, and ten minutes after that, we were in her old apartment, which still felt to me like hers. The fan was running in the bathroom, and outside the bathroom door, Rowdy was in a sphinxlike down. He associates bathrooms with water and therefore hates them. Still, he was watching out for Zara. When she appeared in her bathrobe with a towel wrapped around her head, Rita said that she knew about the ransom call and asked all those therapist questions about how Zara and I were feeling about everything,

But when she'd finished, I actually felt better than I had before, and then Rita turned sensible and practical. She told Zara to dry her hair and get dressed, and when Zara reappeared, Rita had her play the ransom call. As I listened for the second time, I again envisioned the caller on weedy Peach Street.

"Working-class guy," Rita said. "It's a lot more money to him than it is to you. And he's smart. He isn't asking for more cash than you can raise in a hurry. You can raise it, can't you? I can help. If you're determined to pay him." Just as I'd done, Rita made no mention of what was so painfully missing in the call: the sound of a dog barking or, indeed, any other indication that Izzy was still alive.

"Absolutely," Zara said. "If I can get to the bank. How am I going to get there? I'm not used to going anywhere without Izzy. I'm not used to leaving home without her. Or to being home alone without her, either."

Rita, Zara, and I were seated around Rita's table, on which I'd spread the takeout from Formaggio. Rowdy was sitting at Zara's left side. Her hand was on his shoulder, and she was digging her fingers deeply and rhythmically into his dense coat.

Rita said, "Izzy has a whole beautiful wardrobe of those vests. Put one on Rowdy."

"No!" I protested. "You can't pass him off as a service dog. That's—"

"It's perfectly ethical," Rita said. "It's not like trying to sneak a pet onto a plane by pretending he's a service dog. If Zara needs him to go where she needs to go, then he *is* her service dog, at least for the moment."

Zara and I spoke simultaneously: "That's true."

"Legally, it *is* true," I said. "Dogs don't need certificates or whatever to be service dogs. If you have a disability, and your dog lets you do whatever you need to do, then he's your service dog." I smiled at Rowdy. In his own fashion, he smiled at the chicken on the table. "Zara, if you don't watch out, he'll steal our dinner. In every other respect," I added, "he's the perfect dog."

"It would be helpful," Rita said, "to have a detailed plan about what we're going to do. This evening. Tomorrow morning. Afternoon. Not just about delivering the ransom, but a plan, a schedule, if you will, for the time until then. It'll make it easier to get through." Then she talked incomprehensibly about binding anxiety.

I said, "Let's eat." Channeling Rowdy?

When we helped ourselves to the food, I, as usual, filled my plate. Rita, who was eating for herself and my godchild, took more substantial helpings than she'd have done a few months earlier, when she'd been watching her weight. Zara took a chicken wing, a small piece of Brie, and a thin slice of bread. Zara and I drank sparkling water from the refrigerator, and Rita had a big glass of milk. Being half malamute and blessed with an enviable metabolism, I ate with my usual gusto. Rita ate as if it were her duty to do so, as it was. Zara pushed her food around and sipped water. Rowdy drooled.

As we ate—or in Zara's case, didn't eat—we agreed that I'd spend the evening with Zara. Although Zara had no interest in the Sox or the Orioles, we'd watch for Steve, Quinn, Monty, and John in their just-behind-home-plate seats at Fenway.

"Zara, do you have something to help you sleep?" Rita asked. "In case you need it."

"I'm a traveling pharmacy. I'll drug myself to oblivion. And I have guided imagery on my iPhone." She paused. "Does Rowdy sleep on the bed?"

"If you want him to. He's not supposed to get on the bed unless he's invited. Just pat the bed and give him permission. But if the room is hot, he might end up on the floor."

We ran through a rough schedule for the next day. As Rita pointed out, there was a branch of Zara's bank near Fresh Pond, so Zara wouldn't even have to go to Harvard Square to get the cash she'd need. I couldn't imagine strolling into the bank and withdrawing thousands of dollars, but when I asked a tentative question, Zara said that her money was hers; that what she did with it was none of the bank's business; and that even so, in the morning, she'd call someone she knew at her bank in New York.

Because Rita's parents, Erica and Al, were arriving and were going to stay in Rita's old apartment with Zara, she and I would tidy things up and prepare the guestroom for them. Then we'd go to Rita and Quinn's to review the service and the vows they'd written for the wedding and to try on the dresses we'd be wearing. We'd already had a fitting, but Rita wanted to be sure that the alterations had been done correctly. Once Al and Erica arrived, everyone would gather for a late lunch at Rita and Quinn's.

"And then," said Rita, "the three of us are going to deliver the ransom."

Zara almost shouted: "Oh, no, we are not! I'm going by myself."

"No, you're not," said Rita.

"You're not," I said. "I'm going with you."

"No, you're not."

"Yes, I am."

Thanks to a certain Monty Python sketch, I realized that we were merely exchanging contradictions and that if Rita and I intended to persuade Zara of the folly of going alone, we'd have to elevate the discussion to the level of argument.

"Do you intend to take Rowdy with you?" I asked.

At the sound of his name, Rowdy looked at my face. People always say, "Doesn't Rowdy love you! He watches you all the time." He does love me, but he watches me because he's been carefully trained to make eye contact. In return, I watch him. We exchange positive reinforcement. I give him bits of liver. He gives me the pleasure of seeing his gorgeous head, his blocky muzzle, his all-but-black almond-shaped eyes, his heavy bone, his big snowshoe feet, his plumy white tail, his gloriously healthy and shiny double coat, and all the rest, the best of the rest being his charismatic aura of power.

Rowdy? Rowdy has star quality. Rowdy is a *presence*.

Where was I? Oh, so then I said, "Rowdy is not going without me. You remember in the Bible? Ruth to Naomi. 'Whither thou goest, I will go.' Where Rowdy goes, I go, and if you want him along, you're going to be stuck with me, too."

"Holly, that's not fair," Zara protested. "Besides, Naomi wasn't Ruth's dog. Naomi was her mother-in-law."

Ignoring the nitpicking, I said, "You are more than welcome to take Rowdy with you, but only if I'm there, too."

"Zara," Rita said firmly, "if you insist on going all by yourself, it's possible that you'll get to this parking lot and then discover that you are, in fact, unable to get out of the car and deliver the ransom. You have to have backup."

"Me," I said. "If you can't deliver the ransom, I'll do it. Rowdy can wait in the car with you, and I'll go in your place."

Rita banged a fist on the table. "Holly, you and Zara don't look a thing alike. This Gil person is going to take one look at you and realize that you're not Zara. Let's remember that he and his brother must've been watching all of us. That's how they planned my burglary. They watched us, they watched our houses, and they followed Zara on that damned Facebook and who knows where else."

"Blame Facebook," Zara said. "Blame me! It's my fault."

"It's not your fault," I said. "Rita doesn't mean that."

"Of course I don't," Rita said. "All I mean is that the safe assumption is that he knows what we look like. Among other things, he saw you today when he stole Izzy, and since he'd obviously been following you, he must've seen Holly, too."

The three of us exchanged glances.

"I'll wear Zara's clothes," I said. "And a hat."

"I look much more like Zara than you do," Rita said.

I objected. "Rita, delivering ransom just isn't—"

"It's obviously not something I've ever done before, but you haven't either, Holly, and there's no reason to believe that you'd be any better at it than I'd be."

"I'm more, uh, temperamentally suited to it than you are, Rita."

Rita laughed. "Just don't tell me it's because you have big, rough dogs."

"Well, it is."

"And Willie is easy? Who's always saying that Willie has real terrier character?"

"He does," I admitted, "but we're not talking about dogs."

"Holly, do you know what you just said? You actually said that we're not talking about dogs. This? From you?"

Zara raised both hands high in the air. "I surrender. Peace, please. Truce. White flag. But you're both going to have to ride on the floor of my car."

"Rowdy and I are going with you," I said. "We can decide about Rita tomorrow."

chapter twenty-seven

After Rita left, Zara and I turned on the TV and tried to spot Steve, Quinn, Monty, and John among the hundreds of fans seated behind home plate. Yes, why peer at the screen and struggle to see people we'd just seen in person and would see again in the flesh in no time? Senseless. But the humble fact of being on television seemed to confer fleeting stardom or would do so, anyway, if we could catch sight of them.

Our task was challenging because we were watching on Rita's little portable TV, which for many years had represented her apology to herself for owning any TV at all. She'd used this one mainly to watch PBS, of which she was a generous financial supporter, a member of an elite circle of wealthy donors who gave big bucks to fund the production of soap-operatic melodramas that masqueraded as highbrow British theater-on-film. I wallow in those soaps, too. I just like watching them on a big screen.

Anyway, we managed to catch sight of Steve or possibly of a tall man we identified as Steve, so we decided that the men on either side of him were Quinn and Monty. Our little game was a moderately successful distraction, and the Sox-Orioles game was engaging, too, at least for me. I brought Sammy upstairs and sat on the floor idly working on his coat with my Chris Christensen 27mm T-brush, a tool that could've been designed for those of us who groom big hairy dogs while watching television, since it grabs undercoat and holds onto it instead of flinging it all over the place. I ate some ice cream and persuaded Zara to have a little, too. In the sixth inning, the game was tied, but it held no interest for Zara, who decided to go to bed.

Rowdy and Sammy needed to go out, as did India and Lady, so I told Zara that I'd take care of the dogs, return Rowdy to her, and watch the rest of the game before settling myself in Rita's guestroom. Since Zara had taken some kind of sleep medication, she expected to fall asleep soon. We agreed that she'd leave her bedroom door ajar so that Rowdy could enter the room without awakening her and leave during the night if he wanted to.

"Don't worry about the television," Zara said. "It won't keep me awake. If I hear it at all, it'll be cozy. It'll remind me that I'm not all alone."

I was tempted to tell her that tomorrow night at this time, Izzy would be back here with her, but I couldn't bring myself to offer what might turn out to be false comfort.

After all four dogs had had a quick trip to the yard, I got a nightgown and my e-reader and returned to the third floor with Rowdy and Sammy. The Sox-Orioles game was still tied. Standing just outside Zara's room, I heard nothing at all. I did some speedy calculation: Twenty minutes to get there. Then five minutes. Ten at the outside. Twenty minutes to get back home. So, forty-five or fifty minutes. Staring at the TV screen, I decided to let fate decide: If I caught sight of Steve, I'd go. If not, I'd ditch the plan.

And there he was, just behind home plate, my hunk of a husband, unmistakable, with Monty on one side, and Quinn on the other. Even if they left Fenway right now, I had time or almost enough time, anyway. Besides, the game was tied. They weren't leaving yet. Yes, I had enough time—if I left right now.

Zara was asleep and was probably going to stay asleep. If she awakened, there was no chance that she'd check the ID tag on the dog she'd assume was Rowdy. Even so, I took a moment to switch the dogs' collars. I felt only a hint of guilt about the deception. In Zara's eyes, Sammy and Rowdy looked identical, and as a stand-in for Rowdy, Sammy would be, if anything, even more attentive and more outright cuddly than Zara expected. Besides, I had no choice. Sammy was observant, but he'd alert to the presence of cats, dogs, raccoons, skunks, and any other creatures, including people.

If Izzy were present, Rowdy, however, would not only perceive her presence but would also communicate his perception to me; I trusted Rowdy and only Rowdy to tell me whether Izzy was still alive.

After leaving my nightie and my e-reader in the guestroom, I led Rowdy out the door and down the stairs to the kitchen, where I snapped a leash on him and grabbed my purse and a little black waist pack stocked with dog-walking essentials. Then, as quickly as possible, I took Rowdy to my car, crated him, started the engine, found the Sox game on the radio, and set off for 55 Peach Street in Waltham.

Because there was no traffic, the trip took us seventeen minutes. Turning onto Peach Street, I scanned for a parking spot, found one almost immediately, and pulled into it. Then I got Rowdy out of the car and disguised us as ourselves: fastening the little pack around my waist and leashing Rowdy, I became a credible dog walker, and Rowdy, as always, made the perfect dog.

My Cambridge snobbery had led me to expect that Peach Street, aka Weed Street, would have only a few streetlights, and weak ones at that, but the illumination was better than I'd expected, more than sufficient to show that the burdock, chickweed, and other trash vegetation was still flourishing.

Although the night was warm, no one was sitting on any of the diminutive porches or front steps. The bluish light in the windows suggested that everyone was inside watching television. As if to compensate for my snooty expectation about the streetlights, Rowdy hurled himself into an egalitarian display of appreciation for Peach Street by lifting his leg on one tall weed after another. Truly, the dog is the better half of myself.

Although I was eager to get to 55 Peach, I kept Rowdy's leash loose and let him meander and sniff and anoint as he pleased; I wanted his attention focused on his surroundings and not on me. Even more than usual, my own attention was on him. If Izzy was in the vicinity, it was remotely possible that she'd passed this way. Rowdy didn't seem to think so. He checked out the bases of streetlamps and utility poles with nothing more than his usual interest. His ears were relaxed, and his plumy tail waved casually over his back. A runner, a slim woman in yellow Spandex, sped down the street in the direction from which we'd come. Otherwise, we saw no one.

We crossed a narrow side street that intersected with Peach. Checking the numbers on the houses, I saw that we were almost at our destination. When we reached the house at number 55, I saw that it was as dilapidated and depressing as I remembered. The ugly aluminum awning still sagged over the front door, to the right of which were three doorbell buttons and three mailboxes. A bare bulb mounted above the door cast dim light onto the concrete steps and the hard-packed, weed-infested remains of a tiny front lawn. The windows on the ground floor and the top floor of the house were dark. On the second floor, the front windows showed the flicker of a TV screen. Parked in a driveway next to the house were two small dark sedans. Rowdy showed no more interest in this house than in the others we'd passed.

Headlights approached from our rear. My heart responded with a few extra beats. Feeling foolish, I positioned myself in back of Rowdy to block the driver's view of my big eye-catching dog. The car passed.

Feeling silly, I cast nervous glances to the left and right before climbing the steps with Rowdy at my side and taking a close look at the mailboxes and the push buttons. The mailboxes were of three different styles—which is to say, three different styles of cheap and dented metal. The labels on the mailboxes and under the vertically mounted doorbell buttons were, however, stylistically consistent: ragged scraps of paper Scotch-taped to the mailboxes and beneath the buttons showed names printed in block capitals. The top button was labeled SMITH; the middle button, BROWN; and the bottom button, SORENSEN.

As I was verifying that the same three names, with no initials, also appeared on the mailboxes, I was startled by a sound from inside the house: the light beat of footsteps descending a staircase and heading for the front door—in other words, right toward Rowdy and me. Tightening my grip of Rowdy's leash, I all but flew down the concrete front steps and, in a panic, hustled Rowdy across the weedy little ex-lawn, past the two cars in the drive, and around the corner of the house, where I came close to colliding with a row of trash barrels.

Their presence, however, proved useful. Silently patting my thigh, I guided Rowdy to shelter behind the barrels. Once we were in the deep shadow of the house, I quickly lowered my right hand in front of Rowdy's face, and good boy that he is, he understood my awkward signal and dropped to the ground. Crouching beside him, I peered around the closest trash barrel.

Striding toward the cars was a man who should've been at Fenway with Steve, Quinn, and Monty. In spite of my sense that I was seeing someone I'd assumed to be elsewhere, I had no difficulty in recognizing John Wilson, Rita and Zara's cousin—one member of the couple who'd bought Tabitha's puppy, the man who'd given Izzy to Zara and had made her promise to swear that Izzy had come from a shelter, the man who'd once been married to Cathy Brown, the same C. Brown who lived right here.

I remembered what John had said when I'd asked him whether he was in touch with his ex-wife: "If I knew where she was," he'd said, "I'd go after her and get my diamond ring and my money back." The liar! He'd known exactly where Cathy was. Had he been telling the truth about trying to recover his ring and his money? If so, maybe he'd just succeeded. Maybe he hadn't. I didn't care.

What I cared about was Izzy, who adored John and who reacted to him with noisy glee. If she'd barked, I'd have heard her. If she'd yipped softly or whined or even breathed loudly, Rowdy's sharp canine ears would've picked up the sound. But if Izzy were nearby, Rowdy'd have detected her scent before John appeared, wouldn't he? The silence in spite of John's presence confirmed what Rowdy had already told me: that if Izzy was here, she was undetectable. I'd hoped to find proof of her presence. What I'd actually found was that Izzy might be here. And might not. The Sorensen apartment, the one of the ground floor, was dark. Of the two cars in driveway, one was John's. The other might belong to Cathy or to the unknown Smith who lived in the third floor. Gil Sorensen might be elsewhere. Izzy might be with him. I just didn't know.

chapter twenty-eight

In retrospect, I realize that the next day was the day when everyone got caught. Well, everyone but Rowdy and me. We arrived home from Waltham before Steve returned from Fenway; and when we reached the third-floor apartment, Zara was still asleep; so, I had no difficulty in restoring Rowdy's and Sammy's collars to their rightful owners, thereby destroying the evidence of our disappointing excursion to Peach Street. The next morning, Zara was filled with praise for Rowdy, who, she said, had helped her make it through the night.

I was up a good two hours before Zara showed up in my kitchen. By then, I'd fed the dogs, let them out in the yard, let them in, taken a shower, dressed, run up the street to the Hi-Rise for fresh bread, and commiserated with Steve about the Red Sox, who'd lost in the fifteenth inning. I'd left a note for Zara telling her that Rowdy was with me and that I'd expect her for breakfast. Although she had a fresh-from-the shower look, her eyes were puffy, but she'd taken the time to blow-dry her hair and put on makeup, and she wore a pale-green linen pants outfit suitable for her trip to the bank. When she entered the kitchen, Steve politely rose to his feet, hugged her, and tried unsuccessfully to get her to eat more than toast for breakfast.

When he asked what was on our agenda today, my guilty startle almost made me spill my coffee, but I covered up by saying that we were going to run a few errands, get the guestroom in the apartment ready for Rita's parents, and go to Rita and Quinn's to try on our dresses one last time and to go over the wedding ceremony in case anything needed editing.

"We're all having lunch there," I reminded Steve.

As I was about to say more, John Wilson came downstairs. As usual, his hair was carefully styled, and he was so clean-shaven that I almost wondered whether he'd waxed his face instead of using a razor. He wore a seersucker suit with a white shirt and a red tie.

"Hey, Steve," he said in that slick voice of his, "sorry about not showing up at the game. I got a last-minute call from one of the higher-ups in the company." He glanced upward and raised a hand toward the heavens as if to suggest that the higher-up was none other than the Almighty himself.

John's pants immediately caught fire. His nose grew five inches. If only.

Steve smiled. "When you didn't meet us at the gate, Monty scalped your ticket."

I expected John to ask how much the ticket had gone for so he'd know how much to ask Monty or Quinn to reimburse him—for a ticket that had been Quinn's gift to begin with. To avoid having to listen to John, I cut him off by offering breakfast. Since I was eager to get Zara to the bank, I hoped that he'd refuse, but he accepted, and we somehow got through the twenty minutes that it took him to eat his yogurt and toast and to drink two cups of coffee. Particularly hard to take were his nauseating expressions of concern about Izzy's whereabouts and his fake sympathy for Zara.

I was almost overwhelmingly tempted to ask him outright what, if anything, his ex-wife knew about the dognapping. Was she complicit in it? And what about his own involvement? Having apparently given his ex-wife's dog, Cheyenne, aka Izzy, to Zara, was he now involved in stealing Izzy and returning her to the same ex-wife? Yes, the ex-wife who was living in the same building formerly inhabited by the late Frank Sorensen and evidently inhabited by Frank's brother, Gil. I had the sense to keep my questions and my speculation to myself, and since I have the opposite of a poker face—everything shows—I busied myself by tidying the kitchen, taking out the trash, and making unnecessary little trips up and down stairs, all the while wishing that John and I were both dogs and that instead of being a civilized human hypocrite I could confront him in honest malamute fashion by snarling, leaping, slamming him to the floor, and pinning him until he shrieked for mercy.

John eventually left for what he said was a business appointment, and soon thereafter, Steve went out to do errands. When they'd gone, I drove Zara and Rowdy to the bank. At her insistence, we took along one of Izzy's service-dog vests. Because Rowdy was much bigger than Izzy, we'd adapted a red vest of Izzy's by using safety pins to fasten it to the red yoke of Rowdy's dog pack. The result looked only a little makeshift.

In any case, when we got to the bank, which was a small branch near the Fresh Pond traffic circle, I parked close to the entrance, and Zara decided that she could go in alone. If I'd been entering a bank with the intention of withdrawing a large amount of money in twenty-dollar bills, I'd have taken an oversize tote bag or even a suitcase. Zara, however, had done online research on the height and weight of currency and carried nothing more than one of her usual large purses. As she walked to the bank entrance, she stood tall, her shoulders back, her head high, and it seemed to me that she looked brave, elegant, and young. Strangers probably envied what they saw as her poise and self-confidence. No one, I felt sure, would ever look at her and realize that she needed the help of a psychiatric service dog.

In Zara's absence, I checked weather reports on the radio and on my phone, mainly to find forecasts for the day after next—that is, for Rita and Quinn's wedding day. The ceremony and the reception would both be indoors, and Appleton Chapel was only a short walk from the Harvard Faculty Club, but all of us were hoping for the perfect weather that everyone wants for weddings, indoors or out. All sources agreed that today's overcast skies and high humidity meant that we'd have rain in the late afternoon or early evening. But the next two days were supposed to be sunny, with highs in the mid-seventies.

Because of my inexperience in withdrawing large amounts of cash, I somehow expected that Zara would have to consult with the branch manager, present multiple forms of ID, sign complicated documents, and otherwise wade through time-consuming formalities. I even imagined that when she finally left the bank, a coterie of kowtowing bank employees would line up to bid her an obsequious farewell and to escort her out the door.

As it was, she returned in only a little more time that it would've taken me to withdraw a couple of hundred dollars.

Possibly to compensate for the bank's failure to provide appropriate fanfare, Rowdy, who'd remained in his crate, greeted Zara's return by addressing her with a long series of syllables emitted with the intonation of someone whose native language is American English. The most characteristic malamute vocalization is a resounding *woo-woo-woo* or, in the case of dogs who can't pronounce their *w*'s, *roo-roo-roo*. In addition to the almost universal *woo*-ing, many malamutes utter what are obviously declarative sentences, detailed questions, and expressive exclamations and comments. Malamute talking, as it's known, makes generous use of the consonants *r* and *w*. Favorite vowel sounds are *ah* and oo. In spoken malamute, so to speak, the *ah* sounds remarkably like *I*, and the *oo* sounds correspondingly like *you*, so a talkative malamute like Rowdy ends up saying things like *Ah rah rah wah rah, oo oo* oo?

And what does he mean? Typically, *I have a strong opinion about what's going on, don't you-you-you?* If I may venture to translate the string of syllables that Rowdy uttered to Zara as she got into the car, he said, "You were gone longer than I like, and I really like you! Did you get what you wanted? And are you happy to see me, too?"

Zara flopped back in the seat and laughed.

"Did it go okay?" I asked.

She patted her handbag. "All set. I just wish that we could deliver it right now."

"I do, too. We'll stay busy. It won't be long now." Wishing that I felt as confident as I sounded, I added, "You'll have Izzy back in no time."

chapter twenty-nine

"**N**o *obey*, of course," Rita said.

Zara and I were seated with Rita and Quinn at their kitchen table. Spread over its surface were copies of traditional marriage services with large sections of text crossed out. A reference to the "dreadful day of judgment" had been slashed, as had a lot of other religious material. God had survived, presumably by divine intervention. Phew!

"No one obeys anyone anymore, anyway," said Zara.

"My dogs do," I said. "They obey me. They even obey my commands. Most of the time. But we're very unfashionable."

"What's au courant?" Leave it to Quinn to ask that question.

"Cuing. Instead of promising to love, honor, and obey you could promise to love, honor, and reliably respond to cues."

"Everyone responds to cues," Rita said. "We can't help it."

"Then it's a safe promise."

"This looks good," Zara said. "Overall. But this bit you've added about psychosocial context is sort of jarring."

"What's jarring about it?" Rita asked. "Marriage does take place in a psychosocial context."

"It jars with 'plight thee my troth.' And it also clashes with the *Jane Eyre* part—'If any man can show just cause why they may not lawfully be joined together, let him now speak, or else hereafter forever hold his peace.'"

"Zara, we changed that," Rita said.

"To *any person*," Quinn said.

"We're keeping it," Rita said. "I love *Jane Eyre*."

"Then *psychosocial context* has to go," Zara decreed. "The *Jane Eyre* is better, anyway."

"So long as there's no first Mrs. Youngman stashed in the attic," I said.

"Holly, stop!" Rita protested.

"If there were," Quinn pointed out, "we'd hardly have kept that part of the—"

Although Quinn's mother's voice came from the front hall, her enraged holler drowned Quinn out. "Monty, I am disgusted with you! Polluting your lungs like that! Your body is a temple, and you swore before God that you would quit desecrating it, so besides lying to me, you lied to God. What kind of Christian are you?"

Tiny MaryJo all but dragged her fleshy husband into the kitchen. Pointing her index finger at him, she addressed Quinn. "Look at your father! His doctor ordered him to quit smoking, and he promised God to quit, and he swore that he had, and now this! Sneaking around like some teenager. That's what you were doing when you left that nice restaurant, isn't it? That's why you were gone so long. You weren't in the little boys' room, were you! No, you were sneaking out to smoke cigarettes."

Ah hah! Minty Monty. His mysterious absence from Vertex. Now I understood.

Attracted by the shouting, Vicky appeared from upstairs, but for once, she remained silent. Or maybe even she couldn't get a word in.

Monty made an effort to defend himself: "At least I didn't shoot anyone, MaryJo."

Mistake.

Angrier than ever, MaryJo said, "You did worse than that! You exposed your unborn grandchild to toxins!"

Rita exhaled audibly.

Quinn was at his most doctorly and authoritative. "This has gone far enough."

"I didn't mean to say it!" MaryJo switched from yelling to wailing. "I'm sorry! I'm so sorry. Rita, I'm sorry. It just slipped out. But we couldn't miss it, could we? When you were so sick every morning—"

My attention had been focused exclusively on the little drama. Zara, however, had slipped away to admit Rita's parents, Erica and Al, who'd arrived at the kitchen door. I'd met both of them before when they'd visited Rita. In appearance and manner, Erica had none of her sister Vicky's brittle artificiality. She wore her silvery hair in a medium-length blunt cut with baby bangs, and her makeup was minimal. Rita always complained that her mother was dumpy and dowdy. Erica was, I admit, short and plump, especially around the middle, and her style was simple and conservative—today, she wore a navy-blue cotton twin set and pearls—but she was pretty.

In fact, Rita and Zara both looked like her, and she had the warmth that they shared with Uncle Oscar. Rita complained that her mother was censorious and had a Victorian outlook. The Victorian part was accurate in the sense that Erica loved Dickens, but I love Dickens, too, and I'm hardly repressive or prudish. Al, Rita's father, was a tall, good-looking man who, I suddenly realized, bore a disconcerting resemblance to—you guessed it—Quinn Youngman. I'd never before noticed the similarity, mainly, I thought, because I'd never before seen them together. Furthermore, Al happened to be wearing a dark-blue polo shirt trimmed in red and pale blue, a shirt that had come from Orvis, as I knew because Quinn Youngman owned exactly the same shirt and had dropped the Orvis name when I'd admired it. Worse—much worse—Quinn was wearing that polo shirt right now.

Rita's glance moved from Al to Quinn and back again. A look of horror crossed her face.

Pointing at Al and Quinn, Vicky screeched in that metallic voice of hers, "Isn't that the cutest thing! Twins!"

Ignoring Vicky, Erica stared at Rita and said softly and flatly, as if addressing either herself or no one, "Morning sickness." Then she spoke directly to Rita. "Morning sickness. And you chose not to tell your own mother."

Al spoke up. "Erica, you seem to have forgotten that Rita has a father, too. Rita, this is wonderful news. Wonderful. Quinn, we're delighted."

"*You* may be delighted." Erica's eyes flashed. "Rita, at your age!"

"Erica, shut up!" Vicky said.

"That's a very vulgar expression," Erica told her sister. "Just what I expect from you." Turning again to Rita, she said, "So, you told your aunt and not me?"

"She didn't tell anyone," MaryJo said. "I guessed, and I let it slip. I'm so sorry. But Monty and I are just thrilled, aren't we, Monty?"

He beamed. "Couldn't be happier."

Erica said, "All the more reason you shouldn't have—"

Al cut her off. "Erica, that's no way to talk to Vicky. You owe her an apology."

"Mother," Rita said, "you owe *me* an apology."

Erica sank into an empty seat at the table. Although her jaw was almost locked, she somehow managed to grind her teeth. "Rita, I never expected you of all people to have to get married. I am mortified. And at your age!"

"As you have pointed out, Mother, I *am* of childbearing age. Otherwise, my age has no bearing on anything, and I do not *have to* get married. I am more than capable of supporting and raising a child on my own. Many people do."

"Dear God," said Erica.

MaryJo took a seat next to Erica, bowed her head, and placed a hand over Erica's. "We know where to turn, don't we?" she said.

Erica looked dumbfounded.

"God forgives Rita," MaryJo continued. "And the rest of us need to, too. You know, Jesus said, 'He that is without sin among you, let him first cast a stone at her.' No one needs to blame her, and I'm certainly in no position to cast the first stone." She lowered her voice and shot a meaningful glance at Quinn. "I was in the family way with Ishmael when Monty and I got married."

She'd have done better to shoot someone again.

chapter thirty

The responses were almost simultaneous but far from unanimous, except in the sense that MaryJo had managed to offend or anger almost everyone, including me.

"That quotation is about the woman taken in adultery," I said. "That's—"

"Who said anything about adultery?" Vicky snapped.

"You were pregnant?" Quinn demanded. "And you never told me? You didn't think I had a right to know?"

Al was red in the face. "What's this fundamentalist horseshit!"

"Ishmael?" Rita asked. "Who is Ishmael? Quinn, I didn't know you had a—"

"No, he doesn't have a brother," Zara said.

"MaryJo," said her husband, "we've agreed never to mention that. I've never held it against you."

Zara said, "Who cares? No one cares anymore."

"I do!" Erica said.

"Why would you hold it against me?" MaryJo asked. "I could hold it against you, couldn't I?"

"Good for you," said Vicky.

"I care about having my daughter compared to the woman taken in adultery," said Al. "In fact, I'm not listening to this." With that, he stalked out.

"Ishmael," Rita repeated.

Zara looked up from her phone, in which she'd taken refuge. "It's Quinn's real name."

"And how do you know?" Rita asked.

"MaryJo let it slip the other night at Holly and Steve's. When Uncle Oscar had us all singing. You'd left."

Erica stared at Rita. "This is no time for a woman in your situation to make a fuss about his name. Who cares?"

Rita turned green. "Who cares? Who cares who the hell he is as long as he's going to make an honest woman of me? Is that your implication, Mother?"

I've seen more peaceful dogfights.

"Erica, you disgust me," her sister said. "I've listened to more than enough of this. I'm going for a walk."

In the hope of getting rid of yet more relatives—the fewer, the better, Zara and Uncle Oscar excepted—I offered to show Rita's mother, Erica, to the room in our house where she and Al would be staying and to help her with the luggage. As it turned out, Erica and Al had stopped at our house first, and Steve had shown them to their room. Happily, Uncle Oscar succeeded where I'd failed, not in the sense of thinning out the concentration of relations, but in the sense of distracting people from the multiplicity of animosities. He and Willie had been outside on the patio, and when Uncle Oscar entered the kitchen, Willie trailed after him. Erica rose and gave Uncle Oscar a big hug, and Rita sank to the floor to commune with Willie.

If asked, Rita would have maintained that psychotherapists were the best defense against quarrelsome relatives. But where did she turn now? Did she call her psychiatrist? No, she did not. She turned to her dog, who, I might point out, didn't give a damn that she was pregnant, that Quinn hadn't told her his real name, that Vicky had told Erica to shut up, that Erica had implied that Vicky was vulgar, that MaryJo had revealed her knowledge of what was supposed to be a secret, or any of the rest of the human overcomplexity for which there was and always will be one cure: the perfect simplicity of dog love. Willie cared that Rita was right there with him. He cared that he and Rita loved each other. He didn't give a damn about anything else.

But Uncle Oscar's presence had an effect, too. I had the feeling that the family felt ashamed to behave badly in his presence. Rita rose from the floor and set about organizing lunch. Probably to avoid having the various antagonists placed in close proximity at a table, Rita announced that we'd eat buffet style. She had Zara clear the pages of wedding vows from the table, and before long, we'd set out plates, silverware, napkins, and ready-to-serve platters of food from the refrigerator. Quinn took charge of drinks. He and Rita said nothing to each other, and when we'd filled our plates with salads, cold seafood, cheeses, and bread, Quinn headed for the dining room, and Rita went out to the patio.

I resolved to stay near her. She looked small and vulnerable. Until she and Quinn moved in together, that is, until no time ago, she'd spent her whole adult life living alone, always with a dog for company, but without another person. She'd longed not just for a partner but for a husband. Now, she was surrounded by people in various states of anger and distress, and I knew her well enough to know that she was rethinking her decision to marry Quinn. Ishmael. Whoever he was. Whereas someone else might've made light of the resemblance between her husband-to-be and her father, Rita was doomed to make heavy of it, so to speak. As she put out food and asked for help with little kitchen tasks, thoughts of Oedipus and Freud were, I felt certain, dancing through her head like visions of toxic sugarplums.

Like Caesar's Gaul, our group was divided into three parts. Quinn, Monty, and Erica settled at the dining room table; MaryJo and Uncle Oscar stayed in the kitchen; and Zara, Rita, Willie, and I went outdoors to the patio. I'm not counting Vicky, who was presumably still taking a walk, or Al, either. I had no idea where he was. I can't imagine what Quinn, his father, and Rita's mother talked about. Maybe they kept asking one another to pass the salt.

MaryJo did busywork in the kitchen. I heard her unloading the dishwasher. Out of the corner of my ear, I heard her tell Oscar that she was happy to find that Rita's mother was a good Christian woman. I wondered whether MaryJo knew that Uncle Oscar was Catholic and, if not, whether she'd be shocked if he told her so. To avoid finding out, I closed the door to the kitchen before I joined Rita and Zara at the wrought-iron table.

Rita, who is usually civilized, speared a shrimp with her fork as aggressively as if she were committing crustacean murder. The shrimp was already dead, of course. It had come from a beautiful seafood platter from which I'd helped myself to poached salmon, mussels in dill-mustard sauce, and giant sea scallops. Eyeing me, Rita broke the shrimp in half and fed a big piece to a grateful Willie. "Never feed the dog at the table," she said defiantly.

I smiled. "He's your dog. If you want him to beg for food, that's your choice."

"I *do* have choices."

Falling back on banality, I said, "Those are yours, too."

Rita patted her still-flat abdomen. "But I'm choosing for two."

"Rita, what do you want me to say? How about a platitude? Most of the important choices that all of us make have consequences for other people, but the choices are still ours."

"The marriage license probably isn't even legal. I'll bet that he lied about his name on it."

Zara looked up from her tablet. "He's Quinn in the Mass. Medical Society database."

Unmollified, Rita said, "Then maybe his medical license is invalid, too."

Glancing at the tablet, I saw that Zara had moved from the Massachusetts Medical Society website to a page about the kidnapping of the Lindbergh baby.

I spoke more sharply than I intended. "Zara, stop! You're scaring yourself. This is not a comparable situation. Rita, tell her to stop reading about the Lindbergh kidnapping."

Rita snapped at us. "Both of you, stop! The death of a baby is the last thing I want to think about. How *could* you?"

I apologized. "And I shouldn't have looked at the screen, Zara. The sites you visit are none of my business. I'm sorry."

"You sound like MaryJo." Zara glanced toward the kitchen and spoke softly. "'I'm sorry, I'm sorry, I'm sorry.'"

"I am so tired of that woman's hostility," Rita whispered.

"Mine?" I asked.

"MaryJo's," Rita murmured. "Those mistakes of hers? That woman leaks hostility. Those slips? Those are *motivated*. Including that gun in her purse. I almost prefer Aunt Vicky. At least she doesn't pretend that her barbs are accidental, and she never says she's sorry."

Zara gave a sardonic smile. "You can count on my mother not to apologize."

Rita yawned. "Maybe instead of marrying Quinn, I'll divorce my whole family." Looking down, she added, "And start fresh. But I'll keep you, Zara. And Uncle Oscar. And maybe my father." She yawned again and looked up at the sky, which was low and gray. "This humidity is affecting my thought processes. I need a nap. What time are we leaving?"

"I don't think you should go with us," I said, "after this—"

"—fiasco," Rita finished. "Let me see how I feel after my nap. What time?"

"Five fifteen," I said.

Simultaneously, Zara said, "Five."

I echoed her. "Five."

Since I'm incapable of accepting hospitality without saying thank you, I told Rita that the food had been delicious. Zara told her the same thing. Then she and I managed to say goodbye to everyone.

Once we were outside, we both, I think, felt tempted to sprint to my house and might have done so if the humidity had been less than unbearably tropical. My head was spinning, and I felt mildly unwell, as if the toxicity in Rita's house had actually poisoned me. I could hardly wait to get home.

chapter thirty-one

I opened the kitchen door to find Steve standing at the counter contemplating a tub of OmniThrive. Rowdy and Sammy, who adore OmniThrive, were bouncing around with telltale smirks of recognition on their faces. Telltale smirks? Tattletale smirks.

Steve whacked the tub. "This is half empty."

"I'm not giving it to India and Lady," I said. "And everyone swears by it. Look at Rowdy's coat! This is the best it's ever been in August. Kimi's is amazingly good, too, and so is Sammy's."

"Just which veterinary schools did *everyone* attend?"

"Everyone in malamutes. And look at the dogs' pigment! It's beautiful."

"It always was. Holly, we've been through this before. You don't know what's in this stuff. Or where it came from."

"It's made in Ohio."

"And where did the ingredients come from? You don't know that. But this is all beside the point. The point is that you know I don't want you giving this stuff to the dogs, and you said you wouldn't."

If you're a wise dog-person wife, you don't admit to your husband that you care more about your dogs' coats than you do about your honesty with him.

"I'm sorry. But your objection to OmniThrive is totally irrational. The dogs really are *thriving* on it. It's an excellent source of zinc, and a lot of Northern-breed dogs have low zinc levels."

"If we were worried about their zinc levels, we'd test for it." His eyes were sad. "Holly, you went back on your word."

"I'm sorry. Look, Steve, we'll talk about it later. I need a shower. Everything at Rita's was horrible. MaryJo and Monty guessed that Rita is pregnant, and MaryJo let it slip when Rita's parents were there. Erica's response was just as mean and prudish and critical as you could imagine, and MaryJo said that when she and Monty got married, she was pregnant with Quinn, except that she called him Ishmael. So Rita found out that Quinn has been hiding his real name, and I think it's possible that she'll call off the wedding. There's more, but that's some of it. The whole atmosphere was so poisonous that I need to take a shower and wash my hair."

Before he could respond, I hightailed it upstairs. My need to decontaminate myself was, by the way, genuine. Zara felt the same way, as she'd told me while we'd been walking home. She, however, hadn't broken her word to anyone, at least so far as I knew, and she didn't bear the guilt I did about failing to tell Steve about the ransom demand and about my intention of helping Zara to deliver the money. Then there was the business of sneaking out last night and seeing John leaving his ex-wife's apartment.

I'd told no one about my little recce, and I certainly hadn't admitted to Zara that I'd switched dogs on her. On that topic, I'd even gone so far as to drag my innocent, honest dogs into the deception by switching collars. What I needed wasn't so much a shower as a ritual bath.

When I got downstairs, Steve had gone out and had taken India, Lady, and Sammy with him. Rowdy was alone in the kitchen. I'd offered him to Zara on our way home, but she'd said that she was going to take a shower and would be all right by herself.

"You had a narrow escape, my boy," I told Rowdy. "If you'd gone with Zara, she might've tried to lure you into the bathroom, and you know what's there, don't you? Yes, water! God forbid."

Rowdy sat directly in front of me and met my gaze.

"But you're only a little safer with me because we're going out, and I hate to break the news, but it looks like rain. With luck, though, you won't have to leave the car. You'll just have to be there for Zara, who is so, so scared and for good reason, maybe more than she knows. But we know, don't we?"

It was tempting to hear his *woo-woo* reply as a statement of agreement, but in the spirit of honesty, I have to say that he may have been asking for liver treats.

"We didn't see the slightest sign of Izzy last night. I didn't see anything, you didn't smell anything, and neither of us heard anything."

"*Roo*," said Rowdy. Translation: *If you don't happen to have liver handy, cheese will do.*

"I love you, Rowdy," I said and added blasphemously, "I am weak, but you are strong, buddy."

Although I was sorry that Steve had vanished while we were in the middle of an argument, even a stupid one about OmniThrive, his absence meant that I could leave without having to concoct an excuse. Still, it bothered me that he hadn't left a note the way he usually did. On the off chance that he'd left voice mail or sent me a text, I checked my smartphone, where I found nothing but a one-word text from Zara: *Ready?*

Almost, I replied.

Rita? she shot back.

Not here.

A second later, I heard Zara's footsteps on the stairs. It was typical of her to have texted me when she'd been almost at my kitchen door. As we'd previously arranged, she wore the same yellow rain slicker and matching boots that she'd had on when Izzy had been stolen. If she needed me to deliver the ransom, it would be easy to switch rain gear, including boots, since we wore about the same size shoes.

On the assumption that the dognapper would be watching from nearby, it also seemed wise for me to avoid wearing the slicker I'd had on when he'd seen me. If Zara felt able to deliver the ransom herself, I'd never have to leave the car, and the dog thief wouldn't see me at all; and if she needed me to substitute for her, he'd see me only in her outfit and mistake me for her.

But what if Zara left to deliver the cash and didn't return? What if the instructions for reclaiming Izzy included unknown complications that would require my help? What if I were forced to show myself? My best bet, I decided, was to look as anonymous as possible by enveloping myself in a long and voluminous unisex garment, namely, Steve's army-green rubberized rain poncho, which had the advantage of being the sort of fashion-free, rainproof camouflage favored by the birders who frequented the banks of the Charles even in downpours. To complete the look, I paired the poncho with ugly army-green Wellies that I'd owned since high school and had worn perhaps twice.

Zara approved. "Androgynous and anonymous. You could be anyone."

I removed the poncho, checked the time, and prepared to give Rowdy his dinner. Although it was an hour before we'd really need to leave, Zara and I were impatient to be on our way. I, in particular, was eager to be gone before Steve returned. I had no desire to lie to him about the purpose of our trip but couldn't tell him the truth, either. I measured dry food into Rowdy's bowl, poured in a little water, and defiantly mixed in a scoopful of OmniThrive.

In expectation of dinner, Rowdy doesn't leap quite so high in the air as Kimi does, but he shrieks as piercingly as she does. And when he whirls in circles, you'd swear that he'll turn into malamute butter in the manner of the tigers in the objectionable children's book that no one reads anymore.

"Down," I told him. Tail flying, eyes glistening, he hit the floor.

Putting the bowl in front of him, I said, "Okay." To Zara, I said, "Thirty seconds maximum, usually less. I've timed him."

During the twenty seconds it took Rowdy to empty his bowl, I got his lead and my dog-walking waist pack from the hooks on the kitchen door, fastened the lead to Rowdy's collar and the pack around my middle, and grabbed my purse, my phone, and Steve's poncho. "Let's go."

"I know we're early," Zara agreed. "But what if we get a flat tire?"

Zara's car, which was in our driveway, still had two big crates in the back. I crated Rowdy, got into the front passenger seat, and watched as Zara fiddled with a variety of controls that I didn't understand. Faster than I'd have thought possible, the humidity dropped perceptibly, and in response to the sudden comfort, I closed my eyes and sank into the luxury of the leather seat. As I was wondering whether this little power nap would revitalize me and prepare me for any crisis that might lie ahead, I was jolted out of my reverie by frantic tapping on the window to my right.

"Let me in!" Rita demanded. "I have to get out of here. I'm going with you." Her hair was almost standing on end, and her eyes were wild.

Zara threw some switches, lowered the window, and told Rita that the doors were unlocked. Even so, I got out, ushered Rita into the back seat, and closed the door before again settling myself in the front seat.

Out of breath, Rita was almost panting. "I'll explain. Just go! Get me out of here! I won't be in your way. I won't interfere."

While Rita was still speaking, Zara backed out the driveway and onto Appleton Street, and then turned left onto Concord Avenue.

"Rita, what's up?" I asked.

"Just when you think that things can't get worse, they do," she said. "Zara, I'm sorry to blurt this out, because it concerns you, too, but—"

"My mother and your father. I already know."

"What?" I said.

"Uncle Oscar knows, too," Zara said.

"I've heard him hint—" I started to say.

Rita interrupted. "And no one told *me*?"

"Maybe you could just tell us what happened," I suggested.

"When I got up from my nap, not that I slept, there they were, right in the upstairs hallway, *my* hallway, Aunt Vicky and my father."

"In flagrante delicto?" Zara spoke lightly. "Right there in the hallway?"

"No, not quite in flagrante, but close enough. Zara, does my mother know?"

"Probably. I'm sure that my father does. That's why he's not here yet, why he's not getting here until just before your wedding."

"*Wedding*," Rita spat.

"How did you leave things?" I asked.

"I didn't. I just ran out. I was going to get in my car and go, I don't know, anywhere, but my parents' rental car was blocking mine, and I couldn't face going back inside, and I don't want to be alone, anyway. Oh, God! Willie. I put him in his crate, but—"

"Is Quinn still home? I asked.

"Yes."

"If you don't want to talk to Quinn, you should text him," Zara said. "Just tell him to take care of Willie."

Silence.

"I don't know—" Rita murmured.

"What?" Zara said.

"It could be awkward," I said.

After taking an audible breath and exhaling, Rita said, "Zara, you may find this incredible, but I do not know how to send text messages. Leah showed me, but I don't remember what to do, and for all I know, the battery in my cell phone is dead. I practically never use the damned thing."

"I'll do it," I offered.

"What if Quinn asks where I am?"

"I won't reply if you don't want me to."

"I don't. And if he calls you, don't answer."

After sending Quinn a text telling him to take care of Willie, I set my phone to DO NOT DISTURB and dropped it in my purse. "Done," I said.

"He'll remember anyway," Rita said. "He loves Willie, and he's very responsible." She paused. "In certain respects."

By then, we were on Mount Auburn Street in Watertown, perhaps a half mile from Watertown Square.

"Zara," I said, "we're early. Do you want to pull over and wait?"

"No. I want to get closer than this, close enough so I can walk there if we get a flat tire."

"I can go in your place," I reminded her.

"I can do it." Zara's jaw was set, her face wooden.

I tried to sound soothing. "Let's review the plan. Zara, first you drop us at Pignola's. Then you go to the parking lot. I'll point it out when we drive by. There are two. One is next to an indoor skating rink. A hockey rink. That's the one closer to Pignola's."

"Hockey," Zara said. "Yes. Remember that picture of Frank Sorensen I found online? He was with some other hockey players. It could've been taken at this rink."

"His brother probably played hockey, too," I said. "It's big in Waltham and Watertown. That's why he thought of this place. He knew it from hockey. I wondered. Anyway, the other parking lot is for the tennis courts and the picnic area. That's the one he meant. No one's going be playing tennis or having a picnic in the rain, so go right to the end of the parking lot and walk toward the river."

"He didn't say to go to the river," Zara objected.

"You won't. Beyond the tennis courts, you'll see a grassy area with picnic tables and benches, I think, and beyond that, there's a steep slope down to the river. There's no path that I know of. Along this section of the river, the hiking trail is on the opposite bank. On this side, it's all overgrown, and there's trash and litter, and I think that that's where the desk must be. I don't know how far down. It could be near the top, but if it isn't, be careful. The ground is going to be slippery from the rain, and there'll be branches you could trip on, so watch your step. Take your time. Don't run."

And that was when Rita precipitated an ill-timed quarrel.

chapter thirty-two

"**I** still think that you should call the police," Rita said.

"No!" Zara had panic in her eyes.

"I won't," I promised, "and Rita can't because her cell phone is probably dead, and she doesn't know how to use it, anyway."

"Yes, I do, but, Zara, I think that Holly and I should stay in the car instead of waiting at Pignola's. The glass back here is practically black. No one will see us."

"No! He said *alone*."

I said, "We'd still be visible through the windshield or the front-door windows. Zara, please keep your eyes on the road."

"We'll get on the floor behind the front seats," Rita countered.

"I should've come all by myself," Zara snapped.

"No, you shouldn't have. We're doing everything right. It's important to have a backup plan," I reminded her, "and I'm your backup plan."

"I'm not," Rita said. "I'm just making you more anxious."

"What you're doing," Zara said, "is pissing me off."

Ahead of us, a traffic light turned yellow. "We're almost there," I said. "Go slowly and watch on your left. I'll show you the two parking lots, the one you want and the one you don't, although it doesn't matter all that much which one you use."

"It does if he's watching."

"There! On the left. That's the one. And this next one with the sign for the skating rink? When you come back, you're going to pass that one. Okay?"

"Got it."

"Holly," Rita said, "Would you like to hazard a guess about how many maps of this area she's looked at? Including that business about dragging that little figure around and seeing movies. You see? I'm really quite tech-savvy."

"Zara," I said, "take us to the parking lot beyond Pignola's, not this one. Yes, this turn. And pick us up here. We'll wander around and keep an eye out for you, and if you get instructions about Izzy and you're delayed, we'll just keep waiting. You know, we can always take a cab home."

As Zara pulled up near the entrance to Pignola's, I said, "You can still change your mind and let me go in your place."

"No. I can do it."

When Rita got out, I grabbed Steve's poncho, pulled it over my head, and then got Rowdy out of the back of the car. The second I closed the rear door, Zara drove off. Liberated, Rowdy shook himself all over and eyed me with the happy expectation that I'd get him out of the rain, which was falling steadily.

"Sorry, buddy, but no dogs allowed. Human customers with colds, not to mention strep, tuberculosis, and leprosy, yes, but not you. It's a crazy world."

Rita's beautiful tan trench coat had probably been billed as water-repellent rather than waterproof. Its fabric already looked wet. She wore open-toed sandals.

"Rita, go inside," I said. "We'll be back soon."

"Where do you think you're going?"

"I'm taking my dog for a walk."

"Holly, I know that look of yours."

"Rita, when that man stole Izzy, he knocked Zara to the ground. He could do worse this time. Besides, I wouldn't mind getting a look at him."

"What makes you think he'll be there?"

"He won't let that money sit around for long. He'll pick it up pronto."

"What if he sees you?"

"What if he does? I'm an androgynous dog walker. Now, get out of the rain."

"I'm going with you."

"No, you're not. Go inside. This isn't your kind of thing. It isn't your kind of thing at all."

chapter thirty-three

My parting remark to Rita was meant as a casual statement of fact: a clandestine foray in the wet outdoors was, in reality, no more her kind of thing than dream interpretation was mine. Besides, she wasn't dressed for rain, and she couldn't have begun to keep up with Rowdy and me. Especially when we're in a hurry, we walk faster than most people run.

We started out on the sidewalk in front of Pignola's. As I knew from having checked out dog-walking possibilities, beyond the industrial buildings and blacktop directly in back of Pignola's was the kind of steep, heavily overgrown drop-off I'd described to Zara. It was terrain that would have forced us to bushwhack slowly over fallen trees and past weedy shrubs, whereas on the smooth sidewalk, we reached the turn-off for the skating rink in almost no time. The skating rink was closed for the season, and because of the rain, no one was playing tennis in the long stretch of public courts that ran between this area and the end of the parking lot that Zara had been instructed to use.

Rowdy and I stopped for a second so I could get my bearings. To our right was the wooded slope that ended at the river, and to our left were the tennis courts. The wide swath of land ahead of us was set up as a small park. In front of us was a large pavilion, a roofed structure with no walls. In the pavilion and along a blacktop path were a dozen or more deep-green park benches, all unoccupied. Beyond the tennis courts were picnic tables at which no one sat.

On either side of the asphalt path, close-cropped weeds and bare spots served as a lawn; and tall trees intended to provide shade had insect-eaten leaves, sparse branches, and slimy-looking green trunks. Refuse flourished: candy wrappers, scraps of paper, orange peels, apple cores, bits of plastic, and torn bags were everywhere, as if litter were an invasive species given to rampant self-sowing and exuberant growth.

Although I saw no one and heard no one, I tucked in my chin, pulled the hood of the poncho forward, and hoped that my face would disappear in the fabric. Feeling foolish, I reminded myself to act like a generic, genderless dog walker. The Wellies helped: in themselves, they were unfeminine, and when I clomped along in them, so was my gait. There was no disguising Rowdy, but the absence of an audience dampened his show-dog compulsion to flaunt himself, and the rain washed away his good spirits. His tail was down, his expression, woebegone.

As we followed the asphalt past the tennis courts, I was alert for even the slightest indication that Rowdy detected Izzy's presence: the twitch of an ear, a glance to the left or right, the hint of a bounce in his step, or any other sign, no matter how subtle. I saw no change in Rowdy. The bright yellow of Zara's rain slicker and boots would've stood out. I scanned everywhere and saw no sign of her.

Beyond the tennis courts, I moved to the right. At the edge of the steep slope, I looked toward the river and easily spotted the broken remains of a cheap fake-birch desk that had been thrown down the incline, where it had collided with the massive trunk of a dead but upright tree. Before or after the crash, the desktop had separated from the legs and from what must once have been shelves.

Broken pieces projected from under the remarkably intact writing surface, which lay tilted, one end on the ground, the other in the air.

Beneath the desktop was a clean white plastic bag: Zara had delivered the ransom. Zara herself wasn't in sight. Neither was anyone else.

To see the dognapper without being seen, I needed to move quickly. Still, I paused to pick out a hiding place and to plot a route to it; without a plan, Rowdy and I could find ourselves thrashing around in the underbrush, losing sight of the broken desk, and advertising our presence. Thirty or forty feet downhill from the broken desk were the decaying remains of what must once have been a magnificent tree. When a storm, or perhaps gravity alone, had snapped the massive trunk, the upper half had crashed top-first to the ground but had remained attached to the trunk. Together, the two parts formed an upside-down V. Around, under, and through this structure grew the thick-stemmed vines and weedy brush endemic to this stretch of the riverbank.

In effect, the shattered tree and the wild vegetation created a rough natural hunting blind. As for a good route to this observation spot, there was none. Pressed for time, I settled for the simple plan of continuing to move parallel to the river before heading down the incline and uphill to the hiding place.

Now that I knew where we were going and how we were going to get there, I was in a tearing hurry. Smacking my lips and patting my thigh, I urged Rowdy forward and, less than a minute later, headed toward the river. Since any route through the underbrush was as bad as any other, I chose one almost at random and concentrated only on avoiding the thorny canes that would've wounded Rowdy's feet.

In spite of the rain, or maybe distracted from it, Rowdy interpreted our plunge into the New England jungle as an adventure and threw himself into it with his usual power and zeal, and without my concern for minimizing the noise we made. Twigs and branches snapped as he bounded past them and as my ungainly boots crushed them underfoot. Six feet ahead of me, at the end of his leash, Rowdy dove beneath a horizontal branch that sprang back and whacked me mid-thigh. Clambering over the branch, impeded by the poncho, I almost fell, and in struggling to regain my balance, I slipped on wet leaves and hit the ground.

Clinging to Rowdy's leash, I panted for breath, got to my feet, and whispered a stern, "Easy!"

In reply, Rowdy threw me that same look of puzzled pity that he gives me when we're hiking up a nearly vertical hill and I, sissy that I am, insist on following the switchback trail instead of heading directly upward to the summit.

But at least he studied my face, and when he did, I smiled at him and mouthed a silent, "Good boy! Easy does it."

By then, the poncho had trapped so much body heat that I resisted the impulse to yank it off only by reminding myself that its sickly army green blended smoothly into the damp foliage and the moss-ridden trees and fallen limbs around us. Pausing, I saw that Rowdy's hell-for-leather-leash dash had positioned us a welcome twenty feet or so from my goal, the dead tree with the snapped trunk. The blighted woods and undergrowth were so silent that I was wary of moving, but we'd already made noise by crashing downhill.

And I wanted to reach that blind, where I'd be close enough to get a good look at the man who retrieved the ransom—if the ransom was still there. Had I missed him?

Patting my left thigh, I coaxed Rowdy to my side and stepped forward. Attuned to me, he moved more silently than I did as we made our way to the shattered tree, which was even more thickly shrouded in vegetation than I'd seen from the top of the slope. Viewed from up close, the vine I'd noticed revealed itself as a tangled mass of woody stems and lush foliage, a thick web evidently woven by some weirdly vegetative and psychotic spider.

Huddling down, I lowered my hand in front of Rowdy's face in the familiar drop signal and then squirmed and yanked at the voluminous poncho until I'd fashioned a waterproof seat for myself. I also managed a small tent that covered most of Rowdy's body and would prevent him from advertising our presence by waving his flag of a tail.

Encased in this makeshift tent with my big, damp dog, I sweated and waited, my eyes trained on the broken pieces of the desk and on the slope above it.

chapter thirty-four

Soon after Rowdy and I had settled ourselves in the shelter of the vine-infested tree, my eye caught a flash of movement at the top of the slope. Seconds later, a man in dark jeans and a cobalt-blue windbreaker started down through the wet undergrowth and tangled vines so fast and so carelessly that he lost his footing and crashed to the ground.

Cursing loudly, he scrambled to his feet; brushed himself off; and having learned a lesson, picked his way slowly to the broken desk.

Because I'd seen photos of the late Frank Sorensen, Little Frankie, I'd irrationally expected Gil Sorensen to be an older version of his hot and handsome brother. Could this weirdly proportioned man possibly be Gil? Except for his blonde hair, he looked nothing like Frankie. On the contrary, he looked like a repulsive clown. He had long, skinny legs; short, skinny arms; and a tiny head perched on a grotesquely thick neck. His forehead took up half his face, his mouth was wide, and his nose miniature.

When he reached the broken desk, I could see his eyes, which were a vivid and oddly familiar blue, and his pendulous ear lobes, in each of which was a diamond stud earring.

Bending from the waist, he picked up the white plastic bag. As he stood upright, a woman's voice called from above: "Gil, you bastard, I knew you were up to something."

With more caution than Gil had exercised, the woman followed the route he'd taken. Even on that slippery, vine-choked terrain, she moved with an eerie grace that was all the more remarkable because her long violet-indigo trench coat almost touched the ground. I'd have tripped on that robe-like garment and tumbled downhill, but she seemed almost to float, as if she were an elf princess or a woodland goddess whose powers included levitation and whose principal attribute was extraordinary beauty. She had delicate features and a mass of dark wavy hair. In one respect, however, she resembled Gil: her eyes were that same mysteriously familiar shade of violet-blue.

Her hair. Her eyes. Her extraordinary beauty. Something Steve had said? Yes. When all of us had gathered for dinner at our house, we'd been talking about the burglary, and someone had asked whether we'd noticed any strangers in the neighborhood. Steve had replied that he'd seen a woman who looked like the young Elizabeth Taylor.

I'd assumed that he was joking about noticing no one except a gorgeous woman. It now seemed obvious that he actually had seen such a woman: *this* woman, a dark-haired woman with violet eyes, a woman who bore a strong resemblance not to the harridan of *Who's Afraid of Virginia Woolf* and not to Elizabeth Taylor's hard, jaded Cleopatra, but to the fresh and incredibly lovely star of *National Velvet*. Steve hadn't been joking: He'd seen this woman in our neighborhood.

But he couldn't have heard her. That voice! She had the rusty-gate croak of a grackle. Vicky's voice was high, loud, and irritating. This woman's was harsh, nasal, and guttural, and by *guttural*, I don't just mean throaty; I mean that she sounded like something out the gutter. Sluttural? Is that a word?

"Gimme the goddamned bag, Gil!"

Gil did nothing: he held onto the bag and remained silent.

"Gimme that bag now, or there'll be no more goodies from Nurse Cathy."

Cathy. Cathy Brown. John's ex-wife. Tabitha's puppy buyer.

"Your goodies did my brother a wicked lot of good," he told her.

"It wasn't me that hit him. It was you."

"It wasn't. I swear to God, Cathy, I keep telling you, I found Frankie that way. I shoulda never trusted you."

"All's I did was try and shut him up."

"I shoulda taken him to the hospital."

"So's he could go back to jail? They'd've seen he was using. And none of it would've happened if you'd stuck to the plan, you and Frankie."

"I did, goddamn it! I waited in the car, but Frankie didn't come out, so I had to go find him, didn't I? And there he was, all covered in blood, with a poker laying on the floor, and he wasn't making sense, and that's why I ended up with the wrong dog."

"Gil, any moron can tell the difference between a Lab and that ankle-biter."

"It was a black dog, and it was the only dog there."

"Bullshit! Gil, I watched that house, and there was no Scottie there. I watched, and I planned, and that crazy cousin of John's put everything online, photos included. I had this fucking thing planned to the second. I mapped the neighborhood and whole layout of the house, and all you and Frankie had to do was wait for my call to tell you they were at the restaurant. Then you break the window, Frankie goes in, he gets my dog and gets out. It was so fucking simple! Go in. Get my dog. Get out."

Rowdy stirred. I rested a hand on his big forepaws and met his gaze. He wasn't, I thought, reacting to the word *dog*. Rather, Cathy's enraged croak distressed him—and probably hurt his sensitive ears.

Cathy returned her attention to the bag in Gil's hand. "What the hell is that? Let me see it." As she took a step toward him, her hand darted out.

He stepped back. "Cathy, don't play games with me, or I'll have a little talk with your old folks' home about where the pain meds are really going."

This time, she moved quickly and snatched at the bag, but Gil reached out and shoved her, not hard enough to knock her off her feet but enough to make her scramble to stay upright. Once she regained her balance, she twisted her mouth, spat at Gil, and got him right in the face.

As Gil roared and lunged, the pathetic fallacy kicked in: thunder pealed, and the drizzle turned to heavy rain. In response to the violence or the downpour, Rowdy stirred again, and I decided that instead of waiting to find out whether he'd voice his discontent, I'd take advantage of the shouting and fighting to slip away. Rita and Zara would be worried about us, and I had no fear of missing anything. Gil obviously wasn't going to reveal Izzy's whereabouts; the dognapping was a private scheme, an independent enterprise that he'd kept secret from Cathy, as secret as he and the late Frankie had kept the theft of Rita and Quinn's wedding presents.

I gathered Rowdy's leash in my hand. Gil and Cathy were preoccupied with each other, and the thunder and hard rain offered auditory camouflage. Still, I moved as smoothly as the terrain allowed and used my body and Steve's poncho to block the sight of Rowdy's giveaway tail. The steep climb up the sodden slope was easier than the descent had been. In what felt like only a minute or two, we emerged from the trashy woods.

Instead of retracing our steps past the picnic area, the benches, and the pavilion, we headed to the parking lot that Zara had been told to use. This route struck me as faster than our original one, if only by a minute or two. We'd been gone longer than I'd intended; I'd meant only to get a good look at the man as he collected the ransom.

If Zara and Rita were angry with me, it would be for good reason.

The parking lot was long and wide, with a strip of weedy grass and a few skinny Norway maples in the middle and a double row of parking spaces on either side. Eight or ten cars and a few pickup trucks were parked at the far end. Since I no longer needed to avoid attracting attention, I was free to run—or as free as the Wellies allowed.

Eager to get out of the rain, Rowdy bounded across the asphalt with me and then, to my annoyance, came to an abrupt halt. Worse, he adopted a stance that I knew all too well. By stiffening all four legs and holding his head and tail perfectly still, he announced, in effect, that he was no longer composed of living tissue, bone, and blood, but had suddenly and miraculously become a concrete dog, a stone dog, or possibly, in a fashion reminiscent of Lot's wife, a canine pillar of salt.

"Rowdy," I said, "this is no time to pull that mala-mule act. Let's go!" I patted my thigh, smacked my lips, and took a step forward.

Rowdy moved not one millimeter.

"What *is* this?" I demanded. "You hate rain." I tried sweet talk: "Don't you want to get out the rain? Get nice and dry? Come on! Let's go!" Reaching under the poncho, I dug some desiccated treats out of the right-hand pocket of my jeans. "Here you go, pup!"

Rowdy refused the food.

"This is ridiculous," I said. "What's going on?" The question wasn't one. It was a complaint. Then the impossible registered on me: Rowdy? *My* Rowdy? Refusing food?

Curiosity replaced irritation. "Rowdy, what is it? Show me what it is."

chapter thirty-five

The second the words left my mouth, I was chagrined to realize that I sounded as if I were talking to Lassie: *What is it, girl? What is it?* If Rowdy had taken my sleeve in his mouth and led me off to rescue a child who'd tumbled into a well, I'd have been as embarrassed for him as I already was for myself, but he spared us the cliché.

Only when I turned my attention to where it should have been all along—on Rowdy, of course—did I notice that he'd slammed on our collective brakes at the rear of a battered blue station wagon, the kind of big American model that you almost never see anymore, and that his eyes were fixed on that rusty rattletrap. Research on canine social cognition, as it's called, demonstrates that dog are adept at following the human gaze: dogs look where we look. What's equally true is that we dog people follow the canine gaze: we look where dogs look. In other words, dogs and people share a gaze-based system of synchronizing attention, a system based on mutual respect: each species respects the other's judgment about what's worth watching.

At first glance, though, the blue station wagon wasn't much to look at. It had ordinary Massachusetts plates, a dented rear fender, and bald tires. No one was seated in it.

Now that Rowdy had directed my attention to the battered vehicle, he was no longer a stiff-legged mala-mule.

He rose up, planted his front paws on the rear fender, and made a plaintive sound midway between a whine and a yip, a vocalization outside his usual repertoire.

I'd heard that cry of concern once before, not from Rowdy, but from Kimi. The occasion was unforgettable because Kimi's distress had been my fault: Stupidly, thoughtlessly, unforgivably, I'd played a recording of wolf cubs in Kimi's presence. Her response had been immediate and frantic. She'd dashed around making that heart-wrenching cry and had eventually zeroed in on the speaker from which the voices of the cubs emanated. Then, for once in her self-confident life, she'd had no idea what to do. Belatedly catching on, I'd pushed the off switch. The little wolves, recorded in their den, had reacted to the intrusion of the recording equipment by screaming for help, and Kimi had been hell-bent on rescuing them. I'd assumed that Kimi's vocal response had been maternal: strictly female. I'd been wrong.

Peering through the back window of the station wagon, I saw that the rear seat was down. Piled on the flat surface were cheap synthetic blankets so grubby that it was impossible to tell whether they'd originally been pale yellow, baby blue, cream, or maybe even white. In the middle of the pile was a big lump.

I rapped on the window. "Izzy! Izzy!"

The lump stirred.

As frantic as Kimi had been when she'd heard those distraught cubs, I yanked at the tailgate latch and then checked all four doors. The doors were locked. The rear windows were closed, but the two front windows were cracked open maybe half an inch. If the day had been ten degrees warmer, there'd have been no movement under the pile of blankets.

According to that famously reliable news source, Facebook, a sign sometimes displayed in front of dog-loving churches reads IF YOU SEE A DOG IN A HOT CAR, YOU HAVE GOD'S PERMISSION TO BREAK A WINDOW.

With my bare hands? The trash strewn around the parking lot didn't include bricks, and there wasn't a rock in sight. If you see a dog in a hot car, I guess that God gives you permission to steal whatever you need to break a window. Rowdy reluctantly ran with me to the vehicles parked at the far end of the lot.

One of the pickups had a truck cap, and the bed of a second pickup was empty, but in the third I found what felt like a godsend: a rusty iron bar. I snatched it and dashed back to the station wagon.

Keeping Rowdy behind me, I raised the iron rod and slammed it into the window by the driver's seat. Around the hole left by the rod, hundreds of miniature cracks appeared and spread like a dreadful rash. When I dealt the glass another blow, chunks and shards tumbled onto the driver's seat.

For a second, I half expected to hear the shouts of some justifiably irate stranger to whom I'd say—what? "I'm so sorry, sir, but my dog insisted—"

"Sure, lady. Did he eat your homework, too?"

But Rowdy *had* insisted. And as I stuck my hand in the car, unlocked the front door, opened it, and then unlocked and opened the rear door, the blankets moved. I pulled off the top blanket and a second one to reveal Izzy, who lay frighteningly still, her eyes closed. Under my open hand, her rib cage was hot to the touch, and the only beat I felt was the pounding of my own heart.

She opened her eyes.

"Down," I told Rowdy.

Just as I was leaning in, slipping my hands and forearms under Izzy, and bracing myself to lift her, Zara's unmistakable car pulled in behind the station wagon. In seconds, she was beside me.

"Izzy's alive," I said. "I think she's dehydrated. Maybe drugged. This doesn't look like heatstroke. We need to get her to your car, and then you drive to Steve's clinic. Never mind a crate. Just get one of the back doors open. I'll explain everything later."

When Zara had done as I asked, we used one of the filthy blankets as a stretcher to transport the almost comatose Izzy. I retrieved my purse from the front of Zara's car. "I'll call Steve, but if he isn't at the clinic, someone else will be. Where's Rita?"

"She wasn't at Pignola's. I thought she was with you."

"Never mind. I'll find her. We'll take a taxi. Go!"

As soon as Zara drove off, I released Rowdy from his admirably solid down-stay and hustled him away from the battered and now badly damaged station wagon. Since Izzy was no longer my responsibility, I wanted to distance myself from Gil as quickly as possible. Avoiding the exposed parking lot, I headed to the tennis courts and then toward Pignola's before pausing to call Steve. Our conversation was brief.

"Zara's on her way to your clinic with Izzy," I said. "Could you get there as soon as possible? And let them know to expect Izzy. She looks drugged, but that's just a guess, and I think she's dehydrated, I'll explain later. Can you leave now?"

"I'm on my way," he said.

The call ended. That's when Rita screamed for help.

chapter thirty-six

For the record, I am contributing to what is primarily Holly's narrative only at her insistence. In using the word *insistence*, I am grossly understating her pestilential and pestilentially cheerful persistence. There is no question in my mind that Holly herself would attribute both her unrelenting perseverance and the irrationally happy attitude that accompanied it to her experience in training dogs. If confronted, she would laugh and then find a way to work in the word *doggedness*. If you know Holly, it goes without saying that she attributes everything about herself to her life with dogs, so why make an exception?

Oh, my, it's clear that in blaming Holly for extracting from me the promise to provide a statement of my actions and observations after she left Pignola's, I am avoiding doing precisely that. The role in which I am most comfortable involves persuading others to construct meaningful narrations of their lives. The narrative of my own life is something I prefer to keep strictly between my analyst and me; it is not for public consumption. *Consumption*: an oddly oral lexical choice, one to be taken up with one's analyst, perhaps? *Analyst, analysis*: oddly anal?

Obsessive procrastination! So, when I told Holly that my own narrative was private, she said that no one was asking for my *life* narrative and that all she wanted was an account of events that occurred when I was present and she was not. Holly, I might note, is less psychologically minded than she likes to imagine, as is evident in her near obliviousness to the connections those events have to disturbing revelations about my family of origin, most notably my parents; the hormonal fluctuations I was experiencing; and the crisis in my relationship with Quinn induced by his passive-aggressive mother's having spilled the news that I did not know the real name of the man who had fathered the child I was carrying.

When I explained my understandably conflicted state to Holly, she said that I should pretend that I'd been orphaned at birth and had recently availed myself of the services of a sperm donor; or that I should do anything else necessary to recover from what was plainly a simple case of writer's block.

To begin. When Holly set off with Rowdy, leaving me at Pignola's, her parting words were, "This isn't your kind of thing at all," a statement that I naturally took as an insult, as if my passion or métier were what? Shopping? Dream interpretation? Well, since I am a clinical psychologist, my métier does occasionally involve a certain amount of dream interpretation, but I nonetheless felt undervalued and dismissed. In addition, I was so worried about Holly's overconfidence that I even considered chasing after her to take her up on her dangerous attitude, which bordered on brinksmanship, but I knew from experience that if I challenged her, she'd say, "Relax! Dog is on my side. I'm perfectly safe."

As proof that Holly was ridiculously sure of herself and sure of Rowdy, let me point out that her phone was in her purse on the floor of Zara's car. Now, I'll be the first to say that Rowdy is a wonderful dog, but he has his limits, one of which is that as a substitute for a cell phone, he is utterly useless.

So, making sure that my own cell phone was in my purse, I set out after Holly with the intention of maintaining my distance and, if necessary, calling the police, at least if my cell phone's battery was charged. I was not dressed for outdoor adventure. Contrary to what Holly likes to imagine, I do own a few outdoorsy outfits, the wardrobe being all that remains of a relationship I once had with a birding enthusiast who shared his ornithological passion with me and his sexual passion with others as well. I ditched him and two unflattering hats, but I kept the binoculars and an assortment of rather attractive khaki pants and jackets as well as a pair of Italian hiking shoes, which I was not wearing now, when I needed them. I was not, thankfully, wearing pumps, but my cute sandals had little wedge heels. (I see no reason to permit pregnancy to turn me into a frump, and flat heels are so unredeemably *dowdy*.) My trench coat was one I'd chosen more for style than for comfort in the rain, and raining it was.

I started out not all that long after Holly left, but I walked so much more slowly than she did that she and Rowdy were out of sight. I remembered where she had told Zara to turn, and when I got there, I walked as casually as possible through a largely empty parking lot, which ended in a row of tennis courts. Holly and Rowdy were nowhere to be seen, which I thought was a good place to be—nowhere to be seen—so I walked around the tennis courts, and when I caught sight of a gazebo or pavilion, a roofed structure open on all sides, I took shelter in it and sat quietly on a park bench to watch and listen.

Listening is something I am ill-equipped to do, thanks to my hearing loss and in spite of my unobtrusive and absurdly expensive hearing aids, which are supposed to give me more or less normal hearing but do not. Let me amend that. As a therapist, I *listen* exceptionally well. What I have a hard time with is *hearing*.

Sitting quietly on the sheltered bench, I had the leisure to sort matters out. It's one thing to realize that one's family of origin is dysfunctional in a general sense, but it's quite another to discover that one's father is engaged in adolescent acting-out by having a sordid affair with his sister-in-law. I also pondered the implications of that liaison for Zara, whose supposedly biochemical disorder and whose successful adaptation to it had obvious psychological meaning. The unfaithful mother? And the service dog, the *dog*, the traditional symbol of—what else?—fidelity!

Then there was the entire matter of Quinn, whose name change, reflecting as it did the rejection of one personal identity and the selection of another, bothered me not at all, but whose deception and—let's call it what it is—whose sneakiness rankled in the present and boded ill for the future.

At that point, I heard or thought maybe I heard shouts or cries or some such, although it was impossible for me to identify the sounds accurately and, contrary to the claims of hearing-aid manufacturers, completely impossible for me to tell which direction the sounds came from. Although I couldn't be certain, it seemed to me that I'd recognize Holly's voice, as I did not, but I couldn't be sure.

Just in case I needed to summon help, I removed my cell phone from my purse and checked to see whether the battery was charged. With regard to the cell phone, I want to point out in my own defense that I am not a complete Luddite. I know how to use my computer to send and receive e-mail, and I occasionally look things up by using Google. My limited use of the cell phone is my choice. I prefer to reserve the cell phone for emergencies, not that they actually occur, and I more or less know how to use the cell phone to place calls.

Answering calls is not a problem because almost no one has the number. Quinn does. Holly and Steve do, as does Holly's cousin Leah, who helps me with technological challenges. In fact, I give out the cell number so seldom that I can never remember what it is, but I do know how to interpret the little picture of the battery to see whether the phone is dead or alive, and when I looked, the battery picture was half dark and half light, so I felt confident about dialing 911 if I needed to.

For good reason, I had much less confidence in my hearing aids than I did in the cell phone. The aids had fresh batteries, but the miserable devices dislike humidity, and even in dry weather, they are a poor substitute for good ears and consequently left me no choice except to take a wild guess about where the possibly imaginary noise was coming from and to move close enough to it to see what was going on.

Once I'd retraced my steps for only a short distance, the shouting was so loud that even I could hear it and could tell that its source was the heavily wooded area to my right, a hillside that dropped downward and was filled with trees, fallen logs, and miscellaneous bushes and vines. More to the point, plainly visible were a piece of broken furniture, clearly the desk where Zara was supposed to have left the ransom; and two people engaged in a shouting match, the first a sandy-haired, pinheaded, weirdly proportioned man I'd never seen before and the second a dark-haired woman I was shocked to recognize as Cathy Brown, my cousin John's ex-wife.

Since the man held the white plastic bag that Zara was supposed to deliver, I assumed that he was the dognapper. It required no assumptions to realize that Cathy was trying to get her greedy hands on the bag. The two of them were like a pair of children squabbling over a toy that one had and the other wanted. Oddly enough, although the man was by far the larger and stronger of the two, instead of using physical means to retain possession of the bag, he initially used a verbal weapon: a threat. I can't remember his exact wording, but the gist was that he'd tell her employers that she was stealing pain medication meant for the geriatric patients for whom she was responsible. John had once told me that Cathy had done exactly that at the nursing home where she worked when they were married.

Maybe for once he'd been telling the truth.

At that point, the confrontation didn't alarm me. Because I see couples as well as individuals in my practice, I'm used to arguments. My main reaction was relief that the noise I'd heard had come from these horrible people and not from Holly, who, I suspected, was somewhere in the vicinity. Unless she'd returned to Pignola's? If so, I'd probably have seen her when I'd been sitting on the park bench, especially because Rowdy was with her. He's hard to miss. So, it was because of Rowdy that I decided to look for Holly and, as a result, made the mistake of stepping down into the sodden mess of thick bushes and vegetable junk, and, ridiculously, hiding behind a tree trunk to gaze around.

The quarreling people were preoccupied with each other, so I wasn't especially concerned that they'd notice me. I was, however, worried that if Rowdy saw me, he'd greet me in his usual fashion by *woo*ing and even howling so loudly that no one could ignore him.

From my new vantage point, I still couldn't see Holly or Rowdy, but I had a clear view of the couple, whose conflict suddenly turned violent when Cathy reached out and made a serious effort to snatch the bag; and, presumably because his previous verbal threat had been useless, the man pushed her hard enough to throw her off balance.

Regressing before my eyes, Cathy spat in his face.

Holly has instructed me to devote particular attention to reporting the details of what followed. But first, I have to remark that Cathy's act of oral aggression, which may seem foolish, stupid, or risky, was entirely in keeping with her primitive narcissism; and that her narcissistic character disorder blinded her to the probable consequences of her aggression and, in brief, made her feel invulnerable, as subsequent events proved that she was not.

Holly would like to know who said what. For a few seconds, no one said anything. The only sound I heard was thunder, soon followed by hard rain. Then, almost as if he were imitating the storm, the man rumbled inarticulately and lumbered toward Cathy, who shouted, "Don't get rough with me, Gil."

Confirming my sense of a psychosexual undercurrent in the relationship, the man, Gil, said, "You like it rough, Cathy."

"Rough is all you're good for, you bastard," she told hm. "Is that the real reason you killed Frankie? Because you're good for nothing much in bed, but Little Frankie, who wasn't so little—"

Just as Freud would have predicted, the insult to his manhood, especially in the context of sibling rivalry, inflamed Gil. In what I feel justified in interpreting as an act of sado-sexual symbolism, he whipped around behind her, dropped the plastic bag, and wrapped both hands around her neck. She writhed briefly and went limp.

Because of my profession, I hear about all kinds of sexual fantasies and acts, and especially because of the immediately preceding insult, I thought that I was seeing foreplay or perhaps a sadomasochistic substitute for sex itself. In other words, perhaps defensively, I was slow to recognize the reality of violence, violence that I'd never witnessed before and hope never to witness again, and once I finally understood that Gil was strangling Cathy, I was frozen with fear and hideously, horribly reminded of Holly's parting words to me, a statement that I now saw as damningly and shamefully true: this was, indeed, not my kind of thing at all.

In my cowardice, I half expected Holly to stride out of the woods with Rowdy by her side and order Gil to let go of Cathy; and when Holly didn't appear, I tried to imagine what a brave person would advise an unarmed and yellow-bellied person like me to do in this situation. Holly, predictably, would advise me to conjure up the image of an immense dog of some protective breed, but since I'd have no idea how to manage such a daunting creature, the imagined advice was useless.

I was then visited by common sense based on self-knowledge: whereas I was not a physically courageous person, my years of experiencing and practicing psychotherapy had conferred on me a certain amount of wisdom; and the wise course now was to slip quietly away and call the police. No sooner had I formed that excellent plan than something all but impossible happened, something so entirely unexpected that when the fourth movement of Beethoven's Ninth Symphony rang out, it took me a split second to recognize this electronic rendition of the Ode to Joy as the ringing of my cell phone.

Although I managed to find the wretched gadget in my purse, I had no idea how to silence it and, worse, realized that I couldn't dial 911 while the phone was still ringing, as it was when that dreadful man dropped Cathy and began to clamber uphill toward me. As he did, I noticed somewhat incidentally that in his earlobes were my diamond earrings, my beautiful earrings, my purloined earrings, my wedding gift from Quinn.

But I was too frightened even to be angry; and although I could have sworn that I was suffering from laryngeal paralysis, I heard myself scream. Heartened by the sound, I found my voice and screamed again, this time voluntarily, and shouted for help.

chapter thirty-seven

Rowdy and I made it to the top of the slope in time to see Gil Sorensen slam into Rita, knock her to the ground, and deliver a hard kick to her middle that could've been meant to kill her unborn baby. As my whole body flushed with rage, my left hand tightened around Rowdy's strong, thin leather lead, and I envisioned myself plunging downhill, overpowering the man, wrapping the lead around his neck, jerking hard, and twisting the life out of him. I might equally well have imagined myself sprouting wings, flying down, and dropping a noose over his head. He was far too big for me to overpower, and I wouldn't even have the advantage of surprise. Did I expect him to cooperate by holding still while I draped the lead around his neck and choked him to death?

If you can't overpower a big dog and don't want to use force, what do you do? Outfox him, that's what. I rid myself of the encumbering poncho, caught Rowdy's eye, and grinned. Keeping Rowdy's lead loose, I went leaping and stomping and sliding down the slope while hollering and whooping a sort of rebel yell as voiced by the bloodthirsty offspring of a Scottish Highlander and a psychotic banshee: *Yee-ah-hooooo!*

Rowdy bounded ahead of me, and when we reached the startled Gil Sorensen, I raised my right arm and abruptly lowered it, and Rowdy did a flashy drop into a sphinxlike pose.

My effort to startle Gil Sorensen more than succeeded. He looked stunned. Before he had time to recover, I said, "The police are on the way. This is your only chance. Pick up that bag and get out of here. Don't take your car. Just go." I paused. "And walk. Don't run." On impulse, I added, "I can't always control this dog." The truth if it's ever been spoken.

The last I saw of Gil Sorensen, he was heading down through the overgrown woods toward the river, the white plastic bag clutched to his chest.

Cathy's body was motionless. Rita lay curled in a fetal position. Her eyes were open. She was breathing.

"Rita? Rita, he's gone. It's over."

"Holly—"

"Are you bleeding?"

"I can't tell. I just can't tell."

chapter thirty-eight

I'm tempted to skip ahead to the visit I paid to Enid Garabedian the next morning. Remember Enid? The woman who found Willie on the night of the robbery. Or didn't find Willie. I want to explain, but I have to linger briefly in those ugly, weedy woods to give proper credit to the medical and law-enforcement people who arrived en masse, especially to the EMTs who tried but failed to restore Cathy Brown to life and who, I hope, take comfort in knowing that when they whisked Rita into their medical van and rocket-propelled her to the ER, they were treating not just one patient, but two.

Although Quinn shares my gratitude, he maintains that the real credit belongs to evolution, which has equipped women of our species with strong musculature that protects fetuses from external blows. MaryJo had a fit when her son spoke admiringly of evolution and wouldn't stop crying until Quinn conceded that God deserved thanks, too. Rita blames herself for having rebelled against my warning about what wasn't her kind of thing, but she feels indebted to me for having rescued her.

The creature most deserving of thanks, especially as expressed in the form of pats on the back, is, of course, Rowdy, whose formidable appearance and striking demeanor stunned Gil Sorensen even more than my war cry did; and who was solely responsible for detecting Izzy's presence in the battered station wagon and for forcing me to find her.

Steve maintains that even without his ministrations, Izzy would probably have pulled through once she was hydrated and once the sedatives had worn off, but Zara insists that *probably* wouldn't have been good enough for her and for Izzy, and that without Steve, Izzy would have died.

Died.

Almost the first thing Enid Garabedian said to me when I visited her the next morning was, "My little Frankie was never a good swimmer, so it's no wonder he drowned, my beautiful little boy, but my Gil was a wonderful driver, so I'll never believe that terrible car crash was his fault, and I don't for one minute believe that my Gil stole that car, either. It's terrible to say these awful things about someone who's no longer here to defend himself."

Attila the Hun?

I handed Enid a fresh tissue, squeezed her hand, and said that I was sorry about her losses. I truly did hate to see her heartbroken. My sympathy did not extend to Gil, who had, in fact, stolen a car, crashed it, and perished.

On the table with the gilded-ivy lamp and the photo of the Yorkie, the framed snapshot of the two little blond boys at the beach was now draped in a band of black lace, a ragged strip that looked like trim cut off a nightgown or petticoat. Enid wore a black caftan. Her beautiful violet eyes were bloodshot. Her face was blotchy and wet.

In spite of her grief, Enid had insisted on supplying me with a cup of delicious coffee and a plate of baklava and a piece of Armenian pastry.

"More coffee?" she asked.

"No thanks," I said.

"You like the pastry? Nazook, it's called."

"It's delicious."

"I made it myself. You know, when Mr. G. first brought me home, his family was none too crazy to have him marrying a girl named Sorensen, and I was blonde then, like Gil and Frankie, but his mother took me under her wing—she knew I loved her boy—and she taught me about Armenian food, and took me to the shops, and I even learned a little Armenian. When Mr. G. passed, I could've gone back to my own church, but I didn't. I still go to the Armenian church. They'll be here, the ladies from the church. They'll bring food. But if I do say so myself, I'm a better Armenian cook than most of them."

I smiled. "I'm sure you are."

"Could I ask you to hand me that picture?" Enid pointed to the photo of Frankie and Gil.

I complied.

"My brother, God rest his soul, made me promise to look after them. Their mother died when they were practically babies. My sister didn't ask me to make any promises about their cousin, that Cathy, not that I'd've said yes even with my sister on her deathbed, God rest her soul. That Cathy was a bad girl. Pretty and spoiled. So pretty! But a bad girl and a bad influence on my boys. I won't have her in my house."

Having been strangled to death by her cousin Gil, Cathy wasn't going to turn up at Enid's door, but I chickened out of breaking the news.

"But my boys! My Frankie, so sweet, and Gil, not handsome like Frankie, but so generous, even when he couldn't afford it, not that he ever admitted it. Take that little Scottie dog. Gil told me a friend of his didn't want that dog anymore, but I knew that Gil found that little dog and decided to give him to me because he knew I missed my own baby Edgar Pooh. Gil didn't mean to do wrong. He just wanted a present for his auntie. But I didn't feel right about it. Gil hadn't even taken the tags off the Scottie's collar, so I knew the little one was somebody's pet. So I called."

"Thank you. It's good that you did." I pondered the gruesome question of whether Gil had presented his auntie with her gift before or after he'd dumped his brother's body in the river.

"I told you a fib," Enid confessed, "but I didn't want Gil getting in trouble. And I told him that the little Scottie ran away."

"Actually," I said, "as it turns out, the Scottie, Willie, does belong to someone who knew Gil. My friend Rita."

Enid beamed. "She sent me such a lovely basket of cookies."

Reluctant though I was to take advantage of Enid's mind-boggling gullibility, I pulled out my phone and showed her some pictures of Rita and Quinn with Willie. "Gil was taking care of some things that belong to Rita and her husband," I said. "Gil was doing them a favor."

Enid said, "That's just what he told me, but he didn't say who they were. He just said that his friends were moving."

"They're all settled in their new house now. I don't want to trouble you today, but whenever it's convenient, Rita would—"

"She'll want her very own things around her, just like I do." Enid swept her hand through the air, and her gaze landed on her china shepherdesses, tawdry tchotchkes, and garish bric-a-brac, all of which Rita would have consigned to the trash.

At Enid's insistence, I followed her outdoors and waited as she unlocked and opened a side door to the small garage. Entering, she flipped on bright overhead fluorescent lights that revealed a power mower, a small wheelbarrow, rakes, snow shovels, a circular saw, and, across the back wall, a long workbench with tools hung neatly above it on pegboards. Resting on the workbench were two ordinary brown paper grocery bags that proved to contain Rita and Quinn's sterling flatware and serving pieces.

Removing a sterling dinner fork and examining it closely, Enid confided, "I have to tell you that these are not of the very best quality. I saw the same pattern in Walmart in Framingham the last time my poor Gil drove me out there. But we do love what's our very own, don't we? It's just human nature."

I thought of her attachment to Frankie and Gil. "Yes," I agreed. "It is."

chapter thirty-nine

When I arrived at Rita's to find her in the back yard with Willie, Zara, and a healthy-looking Izzy, my first thought was that Quinn had moved out and taken his parents with him. As of the previous evening, the wedding had been on. In the unromantic setting of the ER, Quinn had dropped to his knees, declared his undying love for Rita, and pleaded with her to forgive him for being an idiot—his words—and to do him the honor of becoming his wife.

The curtain around Rita's bed had offered privacy from prying eyes, but not from my shamelessly eavesdropping ears. I knew that Quinn had fallen to his knees because I'd heard Rita tell him to get off them. The scene reminded me so much of the ghastly Mr. Collins's proposal to Elizabeth in *Pride and Prejudice* that I foresaw the same happy outcome: rejection. Or maybe my wish for that outcome made me imagine that the scenes resembled each other more than they did. Quinn's proposal hadn't been penned by Jane Austen, and neither had Rita's response.

In non-Janeist fashion, Rita began by admitting that she'd deliberately quit using birth control. Quinn was flattered. Rita went on to say that she'd done a lot of thinking about love, mortality, and the fragility of life and that she didn't want to squander the chance for happiness because of petty irritations about trivia. She loved Quinn, knew what a wonderful father he'd be, and wanted to marry him. Then the two of them got unbearably sappy, and I quit listening.

As I discovered when I presented Rita with her stolen silver and started to explain how I'd recovered it, the wedding was still on.

"Sit down," Rita said. "We need to talk."

Only then did I notice that both Rita and Zara looked peculiarly wide-eyed and stunned, as if they'd just stepped off a violent carnival ride that had spun them upside down, shaken their brains, and jolted their bodies into flaccid insensibility.

"What's happened?" I asked. "Izzy is okay, isn't she?" Izzy was sitting calmly at Zara's left side. Her posture was alert but relaxed. Her eyes were clear and bright. "She looks fine, but both of you look—"

"—gobsmacked," Zara finished. "Thunderstruck. Bowled over. Thrown for a loop."

"Zara," said Rita, "this is no time for word games."

"What's going on?" I asked.

Therapists can never just blurt things out. After supplying me with coffee and making me endure seemingly endless psychotherapeutic preliminaries about the ubiquity of family pathology, Rita finally revealed that her parents and Zara's were switching partners.

My response was inevitable: "What?!"

"Vicky and Al and Erica and Dave," Rita said. "*Bob & Carol & Ted & Alice*. Zara, it's an old movie."

Zara nodded. To me, she said, "I've suspected for a while."

"Not me," Rita said.

"They intended to make an announcement tomorrow at the reception," Zara said. "Rita and Quinn's reception!"

"You're joking," I said.

Zara and Rita spoke in unison: "We're not."

"Quinn and I thought about postponing the wedding," Rita said, "but we didn't want to. And we thought about going to city hall with you and Steve and Zara and Uncle Oscar and Quinn's parents, but it would feel like scurrying off. Besides, we want a celebration."

"You should disinvite them," Zara said. "The way you did John."

"John?" I asked.

"The skunk," Rita said. "The liar. Do you know that he and Cathy were never divorced? So he's the surviving spouse, and he can hardly wait to get his hands on whatever she owned. He's been in touch with her all along."

"I'm shocked," I said. "Shocked."

"He knew she wanted Izzy," said Zara, "and he never said a word to me."

"He was still in love with her," Rita said.

"And desperate for money," Zara added. "He got fired a month ago. I had to drag that out of him. I think it's true, but with John, you can never tell for sure."

"It all blew up when Quinn caught John trying to borrow money from Uncle Oscar," Rita said. "From Uncle Oscar! I was just furious. When we confronted John, he denied it. I never want to see him again."

"So what's the latest on your parents and the wedding?" I asked. "What have you decided?"

Zara answered for Rita. "The four of them are allowed at the wedding but not the reception. If they turn up at all, they're supposed to say that they have planes to catch."

"Where are they now?"

"Gone," Rita said. "At hotels. I don't know, and I don't care. Those people tried to hijack our wedding! They will not be at tonight's rehearsal and dinner, and they may or may not show up at the service tomorrow, and if they do, they'll leave right after it, and good riddance to them."

"And Monty and MaryJo?"

"We're not telling them," Zara said. "They know there's been a falling-out. That's all. And Uncle Oscar says he already knew. Or guessed."

"Where is everyone?"

"Steve's taken them all to play golf. Quinn, his parents, Uncle Oscar."

"Steve doesn't play golf," I said. "Miniature golf?"

"No," Rita said. "They're at some golf course in Newton. It was Uncle Oscar's idea."

Zara said, "He brought his clubs with him. It's a good thing I have a big car."

Rita said, "Uncle Oscar was quite the athlete in his day. He's had to give up tennis, but he still plays bocce with some other old Italian men."

"He uses the weight room at his retirement place," Zara said.

Rita stood up. "Speaking of Uncle Oscar, the cleaners were here again this morning."

Zara laughed.

Rita made a quick trip to the kitchen. Returning, she handed Zara a fancy-looking camera. "Yours, I think."

"Mine," Zara confirmed. "Thank you."

"Holly, I think this must be yours." She handed me the outdoor sensor for our weather station.

"Steve and I looked everywhere for this."

"Not quite everywhere." Rita laughed.

"Under the bed is his favorite spot," Zara said affectionately. "Sometimes, under the mattress."

With warmth and pride, Rita said, "As you already know, Holly, Uncle Oscar is our family packrat." She sounded as if she expected me to congratulate her on her family's good fortune in possessing someone to fill that role.

I said, "Does Uncle Oscar ever return the things he, uh, borrows?"

Zara was quick to correct me. "He doesn't borrow them. He takes them."

Rita answered my question. "Of course not. If he returned them, he'd have to say that he'd taken them, wouldn't he?"

"He could say that he'd found them," I suggested.

Zara was defensive. "He'd never do that."

Rita nodded in agreement. "Uncle Oscar wouldn't lie. It's John who's the family liar. Uncle Oscar is perfectly truthful."

"Perfectly honest," Zara said.

"And no one ever confronts him." Although I knew that no one did, I still couldn't quite believe it.

"We wouldn't want to embarrass him," Rita said. "Besides, there's nothing to confront him about, really. It's just his little foible."

"Exactly," Zara said. "It's just his little foible."

chapter forty

That afternoon was so hectic that I had no time to think through what I'd learned. The second I got home, my cousin Leah arrived with Kimi, who caroled a *woo-woo-woo* greeting to me and flung herself at my feet. My response to our reunion was more restrained than Kimi's, but I was as happy to see her as she was to see me. Before I had a chance to fill Leah in on everything, Steve got home, and then Buck, Gabrielle, and their dogs arrived from Maine with live lobsters and clams.

My father, as usual, turned my kitchen into booming chaos by bellowing like a moose while steaming enough seafood to feed thirty people, all the while insisting that lobster rolls wouldn't have been the sensible choice and that he'd clean the kitchen after lunch the way he always did. Always, as in almost never.

Seconds after I'd managed to break the news about Vicky and Al and Erica and Dave, our guests arrived for our lobster feast: Zara, Izzy, Rita, Quinn, Monty, MaryJo, and Uncle Oscar. Our next-door neighbor Kevin Dennehy and his obnoxious girlfriend got home from vacation in time to join us.

John Wilson wasn't there, of course. He'd vacated his room without bothering to strip the bed or to leave us so much as a hastily scrawled thank-you note. I didn't care.

I'd never liked him and hoped never to see him again. So far, I haven't.

Everyone was so busy talking to everyone else that no one, I think, noticed my preoccupation with my own thoughts and my effort to identify a confidant with whom to share them. Steve? Rita? Zara? Leah? Gabrielle? Kevin Dennehy would have been the obvious choice. As a law-enforcement professional, Kevin would understand my logic and my suspicions, but if my suspicions were confirmed, I wouldn't necessarily want to have the law enforced; and if I told Steve, he'd insist on telling Kevin, so Steve was out, too. It would be cruel and selfish to inflict my conclusions on Rita or Zara. Leah, Gabrielle, or the two together would listen to me, but I trusted neither to keep my confidences. Leah had an alarming habit of blurting things out; and it was easy to imagine Gabrielle swearing Buck to secrecy only to have him publicize the private in his moose-like bellow. Who was left?

Having resolved to confide in my dogs, I found it impossible to be alone with them. After lunch, our guests pitched in to tidy the yard and clean the kitchen, and before we'd even finished, it was time to leave. Rita had canceled her plan for our spa visit, but Rita, Zara, MaryJo, Leah, Gabrielle, and I were going to a fancy salon in the Square to get our hair and nails done. I'd initially resisted, but Rita had pointed out that a person who has spent as much time as I have doing the hair and nails of show dogs should be willing to receive the same treatment herself.

Although Izzy seemed fine, my father, who was crazy about Izzy, insisted that the outing would be stressful and that she had to stay with him. Zara indulged him. Buck is not sane on the subject of dogs. I felt a surge of love for him.

The trip to the human groomer surprised me: I had fun. In that public place, we had to avoid painful topics, and after the horrible events of the previous day, I enjoyed the escape into pampered frivolity. Gabrielle and Zara talked me into adding a few blonde streaks to my hair, and although I'd intended to insist on clear nail polish, I ended up with pink and liked it. My cousin Leah's red-gold curls drew oohs and aahs from the stylists and the colorists. MaryJo confessed herself to be nervous about the prospect of having a man do her hair, but she liked the smooth blunt-cut result and twittered, "Oh, I feel so sophisticated!" Rita and Zara entered the salon with perfect hair and left looking as sleek as ever. Gabrielle went an extra shade of blonde and made friends with the stylist, the colorist, and the manicurist, all of whom said to me, "Isn't your stepmother wonderful! You are so lucky!" I am, too.

When we got home, Buck and Steve had already fed and exercised the dogs. Because I had to get dressed for the rehearsal and the dinner, I had no time to consult with my malamutes before we left. Although Monty, MaryJo, Buck, and Gabrielle weren't members of the wedding, they tagged along for the rehearsal at Appleton Chapel, a sort of annex to Harvard's Memorial Church. The exterior was nothing special, but the interior had lacy-looking white wood on the upper half and lovely dark wood below; the small sanctuary took the form of an elegant woman dressed in a white silk tunic above a floor-length mahogany velvet skirt.

The service was so simple that there was little to rehearse: we learned who went down the aisle when and who stood where. Uncle Oscar walked Rita down the aisle. His morning on the golf course had been a bit too much for him, I thought. He was shaky and, beneath his sunburn, oddly pale; he begged off going to dinner, and my father drove him home.

In the absence of Rita's and Zara's parents and Uncle Oscar, there were only nine of us at the rehearsal dinner at Rialto, which is Steve's and my favorite Cambridge restaurant. Although Rialto is in the fancy-schmancy Charles Hotel and is always winning well-deserved awards for its fabulous food, it's unpretentious. Still, the menu is sophisticated, as proved to be ideal since translations and explanations of *sformato, salumi, gremolata,* and *straciatella* filled what might otherwise have been the empty conversational space. My father arrived in time to inform Monty and MaryJo that *andouille* meant a garlic hot dog. As Buck had intended, Quinn cringed.

Gabrielle rescued the dinner by expressing such genuine interest in the honeymoon that she had Rita and Quinn talking about the three days they'd spend in London before going to Southampton to board the cruise ship that would take them to the fjords of Norway. Buck encouraged Monty and MaryJo to talk about the route they'd take on their drive back to Montana and nobly refrained from putting forth his usual argument that the gigantic heads of Washington, Jefferson, Lincoln, and Teddy Roosevelt represented sculptural pollution and that Mount Rushmore should be cleansed of its three-dimensional graffiti and returned to its natural state.

The food was distractingly wonderful. Rita, Gabrielle, Zara, and I had butter-poached lobster—yes, lobster twice in one day. That's celebration. Steve and my father had venison. I forget what others had, but in spite of our lobster-feast lunch, everyone ate well.

Because we were concerned about Uncle Oscar, we almost hurried through dessert. Back at Rita and Quinn's, we gathered on the patio for coffee. Quinn served brandy and liqueurs. When Uncle Oscar joined us, he drank grappa, and we persuaded him to lead us in singing. My father, as he is wont to do, took possession of the dogs, in this case, Willie and Izzy, and sang along with "On Top of Old Smoky," the Scottie on his left, the Lab on his right.

Rita tapped my arm and whispered, "Let's not let Uncle Oscar overdo it. I don't like the way he looks, and his voice is a little weak."

"He's having fun," I said. "He enjoys being a star."

"He does, doesn't he. That's his role in the family, really. Uncle Oscar is the center of the family. He's our family star."

I felt heartsick.

chapter forty-one

I had no opportunity for a private talk with my dogs when we got home that evening and no chance the next morning, either, because Steve, Leah, Buck, Gabrielle, and all of the dogs were everywhere. The chaos that I'd once thought of as our family madness now felt like the epitome of sanity, with everyone too occupied and preoccupied with dogs to tell lies, put on airs, spouse-swap, accidentally discharge firearms, or whack anyone over the head with a poker.

At ten o'clock, I ran down the street to join Rita and Zara to do our makeup and to dress in our wedding finery. The master bedroom of Rita and Quinn's new house was done in fresh white and pale yellow, and sunshine flooded the room. Rita, having recovered from what she swore was a trivial bout of morning sickness, looked beautiful just as she was, but Zara insisted on applying serum, moisturizer, toner, foundation, tint, blush, eyeliner, mascara, lip liner, and lip tint to Rita's face, mine, and her own. In between painting us, she took photo after photo with her phones and cameras, and, over Rita's objections, splashed our pictures all over cyberspace.

So there I was at ten thirty on the morning of Rita's wedding day, my face plastered with twenty kinds of goop, my hair stiff with spray, my body swathed in deep-peach silk, my legs encased in honest-to-God stockings, my feet suffering in high heels, and to lessen Rita's anxiety, I said, "All this is against the laws of Cambridge, Rita! Any minute, a squad from city hall is going to arrive and give us a choice: either we can go to jail and lose our Cambridge citizenship, or we can shampoo our hair, scrub our faces, remove our nail polish, change into artisanal handwoven unbleached tunics, embroidered peasant skirts, and Birkenstock sandals with socks, and keep living here and voting here happily ever after. Which is it going to be?"

Rita stood up and, at the risk of wrecking her makeup and mine, gave me a big hug and said, "If you want to jump in the shower and wash your hair and scrub your face and put on kennel clothes and show up at my wedding with your half-wild malamutes, go right ahead. From now on, I choose my family, and I choose you and Steve and your dog-obsessed relatives."

"Love us, love our—"

"—dogs," Zara finished. "But you're keeping me, aren't you, Rita?"

"Of course. You and Izzy and Uncle Oscar."

"Don't cry!" Zara ordered. "Your makeup! You'll spoil it. Don't cry!"

Rita blew her nose. "Besides everything else, I'm upset about my diamond earrings. The police are going to return them, but how can I wear them? I can't. Not after—"

"Of course not," Zara said. "That would be disgusting. We'll clean them up and sell them on eBay."

Rita looked shocked. "Without disclosing their history?"

"Their history," said Zara, "is that Quinn bought them at Tiffany. We can provide the sales slip. That's the only provenance anyone needs. And their history doesn't matter. What counts is their beautiful future in some lucky woman's ears."

chapter forty-two

Rita had extracted from me the ridiculous and unnecessary promise to refrain from comparing her wedding to a dog show. Consequently, as she, Zara, Izzy, and I rode in the white limo that transported us to Harvard Yard, I kept to myself the realization that I finally knew how it had felt to be one of Geraldine R. Dodge's dogs. If you've read any of my articles, blogs, or Facebook posts about Mrs. Dodge, neé Rockefeller, my idol, you'll know that she was the ultimate grande dame of dogdom, the benefactor and guiding spirit of the original old Morris and Essex shows, and—

I seem to be drifting from the topic of Rita's wedding. Where was I? The limo, the limo that reminded me of the mile-long specially equipped limo that Mrs. Dodge commissioned Cadillac to build for her dogs so that they could travel to and from shows in comfort and style.

As to the wedding itself, the venue, Appleton Chapel, was too magnificent, too small, and too cluttered with pews to be suitable for a dog show, but as a site for the exchange of human vows, it was lovely and reminded me of the real thing, so to speak, in one principal respect: just as the American Kennel Club was fond of issuing detailed rules and regulations applying to dog shows, so Harvard set forth detailed rules and regulations applying to weddings at Appleton Chapel.

Specifically, whereas Rita and Quinn had wanted to plight their troths amidst a veritable indoor garden of greenery and blooms, Harvard restricted the floral decorations to one arrangement at the altar and smaller ones at the ends of pews. Rita and Quinn had chosen a lavish display of lilies for the altar and smaller versions for the pews.

To make sure of abiding by Harvard's rules about music on show grounds, Rita and Quinn had hired university musicians, including a gifted organist who played some stately but joyful piece as I processed down the aisle clutching a bouquet of peach-colored blossoms and baby's breath. Because of the supposed informality of the wedding, Quinn and Steve, who stood to the right of the mammoth lily display, wore dark three-piece suits. Trying to cultivate a positive attitude, I concentrated on feeling happy that Steve was the best-looking man at the wedding as well as the best man; and I struggled to suppress the thought that standing there next to Steve, Quinn looked old enough to be his father.

To the left of the lilies stood Zara, also in ghastly peach, and sitting proudly at her left side, Izzy, who wore a white lace service-dog vest that Zara had commissioned and a decorative collar of white ribbons that was a gift from Steve and me. Among the guests in the pews were psychotherapist friends of Rita's whom I knew or had met, together with three or four dozen strangers, friends of Rita's or Quinn's. My father, handsome in a summer suit, was holding Gabrielle's hand and beaming; in a flowing pale-blue dress, my stepmother was as radiant as a bride.

On my way to the altar, I saw no sign of Rita's or Zara's parents, and when I took my place next to Zara, I looked carefully and confirmed the impression that all four were absent. Escorting Rita down the aisle, Uncle Oscar had a broad smile and kept looking right and left in a way that reminded me of royalty.

In her palest-peach silk gown, holding a bouquet of white blossoms in steady hands, eyes on Quinn, Rita was impossibly lovely and, I was relieved to see, unmistakably happy. She wanted to be married and to have a child. She had decided—even contrived—to marry Quinn and have his baby. Steve's and my doubts about him didn't matter. I felt confident that Rita was getting exactly what she wanted. My principal memory of the service itself is of the music: the organ, a mezzosoprano soloist, and a brass quintet playing a song of celebration. I never cry at weddings. I might have made an exception for Rita's, but a sense of responsibility distracted me and weighed me down.

The absence of Rita's parents did not pass entirely unremarked at the reception, a luncheon in an elegant upstairs room at the Harvard Faculty Club.

The explanatory phrase I copied from Rita worked perfectly: *family crisis*. I uttered it in a confiding tone. The third time I did so, I realized that I was holding a finger to my mouth as if say, "My lips are sealed." With a shrug and a smile, Zara, too, kept saying, "Family crisis." MaryJo whispered it. Steve sounded as if he were diagnosing a serious but curable disease: "Family crisis."

In other respects, the reception was just as Rita and Quinn wanted it to be. The setting was all Harvardian crimson and white. We nibbled on little crab cakes, tiny dumplings, and spinach tarts before taking our seats for baby greens, beef tenderloin, poached salmon, fancy vegetables, and French wines. The same photographer who'd taken hundreds of shots during the ceremony took candids, the best of which is, I think, a close-up of the beribboned Izzy licking my father's craggy face. The champagne for the toasts was Dom Pérignon. Zara, Mary Jo, and Monty took only token sips, but Uncle Oscar consumed enough for four people before singing a Beatles toast that combined "All You Need Is Love" with "All My Loving." Speaking of love, Rita loves the photo of my cousin Leah giving Uncle Oscar a hug as he raises his glass. The pictures of the cake-cutting turned out well, too, in part because the cake was highly photogenic—dark chocolate with elaborate white icing—and in part because the clever photographer managed to show the joy on Rita's face while blurring the age visible on Quinn's.

All in all, the wedding was a tremendous success. By the time we returned to Appleton Street, the combination of champagne and emotional fatigue was making my head swirl, and I felt happy to be home to stay. Rita and Quinn still had a long day and night ahead of them. Zara was driving them to the airport for their flight to London, and although Uncle Oscar's eyes were unnaturally bright and his skin strangely whitish and purple, he insisted on going along for the ride.

Steve, Leah, Monty, MaryJo, Buck, Gabrielle, and I all saw them off and tossed confetti at Zara's car as they drove away. The next morning, Monty and MaryJo were leaving for Montana, Buck and Gabrielle were returning to Maine, and Steve was driving Leah back to vet school. Zara and Uncle Oscar would stay at Quinn and Rita's with Willie. Steve and I would be alone with our dogs. I'd find time to consult with my malamutes.

Then I'd decide how to do what had to be done.

chapter forty-three

Kimi is the most intellectually gifted of my three malamutes, and although she knows how to have fun, she's a fundamentally serious individual who forgets nothing and analyzes everything. Happy-go-lucky Sammy, in contrast, is so lighthearted that he can fool you into thinking that he's brainless, as he is not; when he needs to think, he does, but most of the time, his buoyant optimism wafts him from one cloud nine to the next with pauses in between when he rolls onto his back, waves his legs in the air, leaps up, and sings *woo-woo-woo*.

When Rowdy puts his mind to it, he's almost as brilliant as Kimi. Like Sammy, he's sure that the future will be sunny, but Rowdy bases his conviction not on faith in externals but on his happy belief that if he and the world get into a tussle, he will win, the world will lose, and all will thus be well. He is a dog of strong character.

On the morning after Rita and Quinn's wedding, I finally had the chance to summon all three malamutes for a private meeting. My father and stepmother had left for Maine; Steve was returning Leah to school, with Lady and India for company; and I'd already dashed down the street to say goodbye to Monty and MaryJo as they set out for Montana.

Although the day was bright and almost autumnally cool, the dogs and I convened in the privacy of the kitchen rather than in the yard, where I might have been overheard.

In effect, the four of us were an informal grand jury meeting in secret to decide what to do about someone whom I, in the role of prosecutor, suspected of having committed a serious crime. In presenting evidence, I offered only one document: Steve's timeline of the evening we'd gone to Vertex, the evening when Frankie Sorensen had been killed, the timeline I'd ridiculed as a waste-of-timeline but had just pulled from Steve's computer.

Mainly, I talked, and the dogs listened. I read their eyes.

I was seated on a chair with the dogs sitting neatly in front of me: Sammy on the left, Kimi on the right, and Rowdy in the middle. Sammy's expression was joyful, even frivolous, and in his beautiful almond-shaped eyes I saw nothing but levity. *What happened once*, he seemed to say, *won't happen again. The circumstances were extreme. Let it go! Forget it! It's a lovely day for a hike. Let's get out and have fun!* Shifting my gaze to Kimi, I found a severe condemnation of Sammy's attitude: *That mindless puppy is as illogical as he is irresponsible. Since it happened once, it clearly can happen again. And very well may! Consider the consequences of inaction! Go for a hike, indeed. Do what you need to do!*

Rowdy caught my eye, rose to his feet, and trotted to the door, hanging on which were leather leads in a variety of lengths and widths. We've never taught the dogs to retrieve their own leashes when it's time for a walk, and Rowdy hadn't figured out the trick on his own. He waited as I selected a six-foot leather leash, snapped it onto his collar, and said, "Yes, I get it. Enough thinking. Time for direct confrontation. Thank you for your good counsel, buddy."

A few minutes later, we arrived at Rita and Quinn's to find Zara's car in the driveway. When I'd said my goodbyes to Quinn's parents, Zara had told me that she and Uncle Oscar were going to have a quiet day at home.

He needed time to recover from the excitement of the wedding, she'd said; he'd overextended himself at the rehearsal and then again at the wedding. She needed to catch up on editing she'd promised to do for clients.

I had no intention of speaking to the two of them together but hadn't worked out a plan to arrange a one-to-one conversation. Maybe Zara would be indoors working while Uncle Oscar sat outside; maybe he'd be indoors while she sat on the patio with her laptop.

I rapped my knuckles on the gate to the yard, and when no one responded, I opened the latch and stepped into the yard with Rowdy at my side. Zara was nowhere to be seen, but Uncle Oscar was stretched out on a recliner in the shade near the glass doors to the kitchen, his eyes closed, his head lolling, his mouth slightly open. On his lap was a sheet of paper torn from a yellow legal pad. Stepping closer, I saw that Zara had left Uncle Oscar a note in big block capitals: GONE FOR A WALK. BACK SOON. XXXOOO, Z. AND I.

Lacking Rowdy's self-confidence, I hesitated. My heart was racing, and my mouth felt dry. Uncle Oscar was motionless—entirely at peace. It felt mean to rouse him. If I touched him, I'd startle him, wouldn't I? Procrastination tempted me: I'd awaken Uncle Oscar only after I'd made him a cup of coffee. I could make coffee for myself, too. Or get a drink of water. *Sure, Holly. While you're at it, make lunch. Check your phone for messages. Call someone. Send a text. Go for a walk. Put it off.*

I looked to Rowdy for courage, took a deep breath, silently carried a wrought-iron chair to Uncle Oscar's side, took a seat, and closed my eyes.

"Uncle Oscar," I whispered, "we need to talk." Almost inaudibly, I added, "I want you to know that I love you. Everyone loves you. You know that? We love your warmth. Your singing! I love your gift for uniting your family. Rita says that you're the family star. The center of the family. She needs that center. So does Zara. That's why

I didn't want it to be you, Uncle Oscar. I wanted it to be anyone else. Even Zara." I paused. "Even Zara. And for a while, I thought it was. I thought she'd gone back to the house for her Nikon and found the burglar and hit him with the poker. The silver, the wedding presents, must've felt like hers, or that's what I told myself. Zara was keeping track of them.

"So it made sense that she'd want to stop him from stealing them. But I was wrong. Steve made a timeline, you know, and it shows who left the restaurant, Vertex, and who could've been here at the house. Quinn was alone here for a while before he left for Vertex, but that was before the burglary. Monty went out, but now I know why: he was outside smoking. Vicky was gone for a long time, but except when she was checking on you, she was on her phone talking to Al. My neighbor Elizabeth overheard her."

My voice was softer than ever, all but inaudible.

"And what the timeline shows, Uncle Oscar, is that the one person who was here all the time, the only person with the perfect opportunity, was you."

Only after murmuring under my breath what I'd dreaded saying aloud did I open my eyes and notice Rowdy, whose behavior was more than peculiar. Quick to respond to anyone who habitually handed out treats, Rowdy was sprawled on the patio, his tail end toward Uncle Oscar, his chin resting on his paws. My alarm was immediate and intense. Rowdy, not nudging Uncle Oscar? Failing to turn on the charm of those big brown eyes? Not wagging and *woo-woo-woo*-ing for goodies? Rowdy? My Rowdy? He must be sick. In no time, he must have fallen horribly, terribly ill.

All concern for Uncle Oscar forgotten, I shouted, "Rowdy! Rowdy, what's wrong? Rowdy!"

The handsome boy lifted his head. His eyes were clear and alert. With his usual strength and vigor, he rose to his feet and shook himself. Ignoring Uncle Oscar, he came to my outstretched hands.

Slow to catch on to what Rowdy had grasped immediately, I turned to Uncle Oscar, who had remained entirely motionless. His eyes were still closed. His head still drooped. He hadn't shifted position since we'd arrived. His chest moved not at all. I listened for the sound of breathing and heard nothing. Overcoming a weird and irrational squeamishness, I reached out, placed my fingertips on his neck, and searched for a carotid pulse.

At liberty to speak aloud, I said, "I wondered about Zara. No, I suspected her. But once Elizabeth McNamara told me about hearing the voices of two men, I assumed that there'd been a falling out between the brothers, between thieves. And I thought that was a reasonable hypothesis until two days ago, Uncle Oscar, when I heard Gil say that he hadn't killed Frankie. He said, 'I swear to God, Cathy, I keep telling you, I found Frankie that way.' And I believed him. I'm a dog trainer, you know. I pay attention to tones of voice. And Gil had no reason to lie."

Still squeamish, still hesitant, I rested one hand on Uncle Oscar's shoulder. To give myself strength, I put my other hand on Rowdy's neck and dug my fingers into his thick ruff.

"At first, I thought you didn't have the strength. I was wrong. Bocce. Golf. And visits to the weight room. Frankie Sorensen must've made the same assumption I did. He must've seen you as no threat at all. And then there's the matter of your strength of character, to use an old-fashioned phrase. Yes, I'm thinking about your little foible, as your family calls it. Zara's camera. The sensor for our weather station. Even coffee pods! I watched you slip those in your pocket. Not to mention Quinn's drug samples. And for all I know, Uncle Oscar, your family knows what you did to Frankie, too. And makes excuses for you. Forgives you. I'll never know. And now I don't need to. I can stop worrying about my responsibility.

"I've been worried, you know. What if one of your neighbors at home had done something you just didn't like? One of your bocce buddies. A golfing friend. Someone in the weight room. Or even before you got home. Here. While you were staying with Zara? What if Zara had challenged you? Taken you up on something? What—?"

Zara interrupted me. "I'd never have challenged Uncle Oscar." With Izzy at her side, she entered the yard. After closing the gate, she unsnapped Izzy's leash. Rowdy's eyes lit up. I kept a hand on him and gave Zara a questioning look.

"She's fine," Zara said.

The beautiful dogs chased each other, ran giant figure eights, bounded, zoomed, and leaped.

"Zara," I said, "Uncle Oscar is—"

"Gone. Yes. When Izzy and I left, I thought maybe he was. I wasn't sure."

"You left a note."

She shrugged. "For him or for you. Uncle Oscar and I talked last night. He had a health-care proxy that named me as his agent. He drew it up quite a while ago. Last night, we went over what he wanted and didn't want. He made me promise that I'd never call an ambulance unless he was in pain. He wanted to sleep away."

"That's what he did, I guess."

The dogs had taken a little break to gulp water from the big dish by the kitchen door. Now they resumed their dashing and zipping and carousing.

Smiling at them, Zara said, "In the midst of death, we are in life."

Made in the USA
Thornton, CO
05/26/23 14:48:07

104af939-dd27-4d89-982c-c0506701b8acR01